D is for Daisy

Also by Shelley Shepard Gray

The Amish ABCs series

A Is for Amish

B Is for Bonnet

C Is for Courting

D Is for Daisy

The Amish of Apple Creek series

An Amish Cinderella

Once Upon a Buggy

Happily Ever Amish

D is for Daisy

Shelley Shepard Gray

kensingtonbooks.com

KENSINGTON BOOKS are published by

Kensington Publishing Corp.
900 Third Ave.
New York, NY 10022

All Kensington titles, imprints, and distributed lines are available at special quantity discounts for bulk purchases for sales promotion, premiums, fund-raising, educational, or institutional use. Special book excerpts or customized printings can also be created to fit specific needs. For details, write or phone the office of the Kensington Special Sales Manager: Attn. Special Sales Department, Kensington Publishing Corp., 900 Third Avenue, New York, NY 10022. Phone: 1-800-221-2647.

Library of Congress Card Catalogue Number: 2026935100

KENSINGTON and the K with book logo Reg. US Pat & TM Off.

ISBN: 978-1-4967-5882-8
First Kensington Hardcover Edition: July 2026

ISBN: 978-1-4967-5883-5 (trade)

ISBN: 978-1-4967-5884-2 (ebook)

10 9 8 7 6 5 4 3 2 1

Printed in the United States of America

The authorized representative in the EU for product safety and compliance
is eucomply OU, Parnu mnt 139b-14, Apt 123
Tallinn, Berlin 11317, hello@eucompliancepartner.com

For the members of the "Bunch" who dropped everything to share stories about owning dairy cows—most especially Jessica, who shared a story about a calf named Velvet that stole my heart.

I am certain that God, who began the good work within you, will continue his work until it is finally finished on the day when Christ Jesus returns.

Philippians 1:6

Old minds are like old horses; you must exercise them if you wish to keep them in working order.

Amish proverb

D is for Daisy

PROLOGUE

Walden, Ohio January 1

It was cold out and the forecasters predicted a batch of snow on the way. Though she was as cozy as could be in the rocking chair in front of the fireplace, Ruthie Miller glared out the window.

The snow and colder weather would mean shoveling a path from the front door to the barn's door, breaking any ice that had formed on the horses' and the milk cows' water troughs overnight, and even more days of being stranded in their house.

"*Nee*, not stranded," she corrected herself. "You just won't be able to go anywhere. You'll have to stay put until the roads clear."

Her words made perfect sense. A year ago, when she'd still been working at the fabric store, the idea of not having to get dressed, trudge down the sidewalk in her snow boots, or worry about falling on ice sounded heavenly.

Now, she wasn't so sure. Even though she could go back

to sleep after helping Mervin with the animals, she never did. There was always so much to do. She and Mervin had to take care of their front steps and the path to the barn. Ruthie hadn't ever thought about that, since all their neighbors had been salting their front steps and walkway for the last five years. Well, ever since they'd turned fifty-seven and Mervin had broken his wrist while he'd been taking out the trash.

They were alone now, and it was quiet, a bit lonely, and a whole lot of work.

Living on twenty acres was a lot harder than she'd ever imagined. Not that she'd actually admit that to any of their friends who had advised them not to move.

The whole plan had sounded so easy on paper. Mervin was finally going to take a step back from work and they were going to have fun together. For the past year, Ruthie had been counting the days until Mervin retired and she stopped working at Sew and So, a bustling fabric store in Millersburg.

At last, they were going to embrace the "simple" life. Instead of their big, beautiful five-bedroom home with the giant "farmhouse" kitchen on the same street where they'd lived for thirty years, they were going to relocate. Instead of wandering around in all that extra space, they were going to live in a cute little two-bedroom farmhouse with a tiny *dawdi haus* just a few steps away. Sure, the *dawdi haus* was worn down and their farmhouse seriously lacked storage space, but they'd make do. Why, they were Amish. They weren't supposed to have tons of stuff.

Instead of running to the store to get fresh milk and eggs, they were going to have their own cow and flock of chickens. She'd learn to milk Velvet and become friends with the hens. She'd heard some folks did that.

But most importantly, she and Mervin were going to have lots of time together while they puttered around their twenty-acre farm. Mervin was going to take up gardening! And when she wasn't collecting eggs and learning how to churn butter, she was finally going to learn to knit and make precious, darling blankets and hats for future grandchildren.

It was going to be so great.

Ruthie really hoped that it would be "great" one day, too. Because today was not that day.

Today, she had a bit of a cold, was nursing a small wound from one of the hens, and had just dropped another two stitches.

"I really hate knitting," she blurted to Lizzie, their spoiled four-year-old basset hound.

Lizzie, who'd been half asleep in front of the fireplace, lifted up her head, seemed to take in the mess of bright purple yarn on her lap, and then gave her a doleful look.

Ruthie didn't blame her. "I know. Picking purple was a mistake." There was nothing soothing about the hue. Unfortunately, the bold choice seemed to accentuate every tiny mistake she made. There were a lot of mistakes, too.

Frustrated with the fruits of her morning, Ruthie stood up and forced herself to wind back up the yarn ball and carefully place the needles and her project in the basket by the chair. It was so much better to do that instead of what she really wanted to do—which was toss the whole thing in the bag for charity and never think about knitting ever again.

Boy, Mervin had better know what was good for him and not tease her about the fact that he still didn't have the afghan that she'd promised she'd make for him for Christmas. If he wasn't careful, she was going to throw those stupid needles across the room in frustration.

She had just finished hiding the purple yarn in her basket and was petting Lizzie—a much more enjoyable task—when the kitchen door opened. She smiled when she heard Bethany and Aaron's voices float down the hall. She hadn't known their children were going to stop by.

"Mamm?" Aaron called out. "Hey, Mamm?"

Suddenly, her day was much brighter. "I'm right here!" she called out as she got to her feet. "In the living room."

Bethany came into view just as Ruthie was shaking out the skirt of her gray dress.

"Mamm, what were you . . . oh! I know. Hiya, Lizzie."

Lizzie, who'd been happily sprawled out on her side so Ruthie could pet her belly easier, stood up and padded to one of her favorite people on earth.

Bethany knelt down and kissed the top of her head. "Hi, you sweet, lazy lady. I've missed you."

Lizzie wagged her tail and gave Bethany a little head shake before padding over to Aaron.

Her son was just as fond of Lizzie as her daughter was. Aaron also bent down and greeted the hound. "You're looking a bit more svelte, Lizzie-loo. Farm life must be agreeing with you."

The hound yawned and returned to the fireplace as Ruthie hugged each of her children.

"What a nice surprise!" Ruthie said. "I didn't know you two were stopping by today. And where's Hanna?"

"With the weather the way it is, Hanna decided to stay home with her parents," Aaron explained.

"I hope she is feeling okay?" Aaron and Hanna had shared on Christmas Day that they were expecting their first baby.

"I think so. She feels queasy all the time but her mother said she'd felt that way, too."

"I had plenty of queasy days when I was pregnant with both of you," Ruthie said. "I hope it will pass soon."

"Me too."

"What would you two like to do? Are you hungry? I'd be happy to make you something."

"We're *gut*, Mamm."

"Okay . . . so, you two just decided to stop by?"

"Kind of." Looking at her brother, Bethany said, "When Aaron and I were talking last night, we decided to come see you." Bethany smiled, just as if that made perfect sense.

Ruthie didn't think it did. She narrowed her eyes. "Hmm."

"*Jah*," Aaron added. "Early this morning, Bethy stopped by the *haus*, said hi to Hanna and now . . . here we are."

Ruthie was now very sure that her kids didn't just "happen" to decide to visit. There was something on their minds. "I see." She was going to need some help. "Where is your father? Did you see him when you drove up?"

"*Jah*," said Aaron. "He was in the barn."

"I'm not sure what he was doing though," Bethany added. "He didn't seem to be doing a whole lot."

"He likes to be in there with the horses. And Velvet."

"Really?" Aaron asked. "I didn't think Daed liked hanging out in barns. He used to always sneeze and complain about the dust. Come to think of it, I didn't think he liked milking either."

"Oh, he's over that now," she said with more confidence than she felt. "Velvet was one of the reasons we were so excited about the farm. She's supposed to be a *gut* dairy cow." Though, the cow hadn't been producing much milk of late.

"Every time I've been around Velvet, she's seemed kind of grumpy. Or, maybe sad?" Bethany shrugged. "I didn't think cows could feel happy or sad, but then again, I don't know much about them. I should do some research, I think."

Ruthie was starting to think the same thing, not that she was going to admit it to her grown children. "That's because you two aren't friends yet. It takes Velvet a while to warm up to people." She cleared her throat. "Did Daed say when he was coming inside to visit with us?"

Aaron nodded. "*Jah*. He said he'd join us pretty soon."

"Perfect. Let's go in the kitchen. We'll have some *kaffi* while we wait."

"Is it fresh, Mamm?" Bethany asked.

"It will be, child. I'm going to make a fresh pot for us."

"Oh. Good."

Ruthie mentally rolled her eyes. Ever since Bethany fell in love with an Englischer and moved to the suburbs with her doctor-husband, she'd become something of a coffee snob. She liked fancy, five-dollar coffees from the drive-thru or freshly ground beans at her home.

She kept those thoughts to herself as she rinsed out the percolator and put in fresh water and coffee grounds. She was far more concerned about whatever was on the children's minds than teasing her daughter about becoming so fancy.

Just as she'd poured four cups of coffee and Bethany had placed four slices of chocolate-pecan pie onto plates, Mervin joined them at the table.

He smelled like the soap he'd just washed his hands with, fresh cotton, and horse. "Let us give thanks for the food we are about to receive," he said quietly.

When each of them raised their heads, Aaron stabbed a good bit of pie off his slice.

"Mamm, you make the best pies, but I love this one the most."

"I know you do, son."

"Did you have a feeling we were coming over?"

"*Nee*, but I've made it on New Years Eve for almost as long as I can remember. It's tradition." She winked. "Is that why you two are here? To have some chocolate pie?"

The kids exchanged glances. "Not exactly."

"What is the reason then?" Mervin asked. "Exactly."

Bethany clasped her hands together. "Well, Daed. See, the three of us have been talking."

"Bethy, me, and Hanna," Aaron explained.

"About what?" Ruthie asked.

"About the two of you living on this farm."

Mervin frowned. "What about it?"

When he paused again, Ruthie blurted, "Snow's coming, child. It's supposed to be a good one, too. The roads will get bad and Aaron's going to need to get home to Hanna. Tell us what's on your mind."

"Okay, fine. Here's the deal. We think you two are in over your heads with this farm. You don't know what you are doing."

"I don't think that's the truth, or very fair of you to say," Mervin said.

"It might be hard to hear, but that don't mean it's not the truth," Aaron replied.

"Well, we can't move. This is our home now."

"And, we'll get the hang of things," Ruthie added. "I think you are making too much of our small mistakes. I haven't killed a chicken yet."

"Well, you see, that's one of the things that we've been talking about. I don't think you're ever going to be able to eat one of those chickens, Mamm," Bethany said. "And I know you like eggs, but you've got a lot of them. Like *a lot*. And while we're at it, Velvet isn't a happy cow."

Even though she agreed, Ruthie felt defensive. "She is fine. She's just not sure how to handle her new owners."

"And you are not sure how to handle her," Bethany said.

"I don't know if that's the case," she protested.

Aaron cleared his throat. "Also, Daed . . ."

"Yes?"

"I was thinking that those fields you've set aside for planting are big. Plowing them with a team of four horses is going to be difficult for ya."

"It might be a challenge, but I'm going to learn."

But Ruthie noticed that her dear husband wasn't looking at any of them in the eye. She knew why, too. Mervin was becoming embarrassed, which broke her heart. She was getting mighty irritated with their children. Why in the world they thought that they had a right to come over unannounced and criticize their farming efforts, she had no idea. "Aaron, Bethy, what is the point of all this? Did you two decide to come over just to list off all the things we're struggling with?"

"*Nee*. Not at all." Aaron took a sip of coffee. "Guys, do you remember Kyle Hostetler?"

It took Ruthie a second to recall the name from the past. "Kyle from down the street in Millersburg?"

"*Jah*." Mervin nodded. "He was a nice boy."

"Well, he's been going through some things," Aaron said. "His girlfriend broke up with him, and his parents sold off most of their farm. They said they couldn't keep up with it any longer."

Ruthie was sorry to hear that. "That is very sad."

"It is, Mamm, because Kyle had always planned to farm that land when he got older. Now he's out of a job."

"Does he want to work at Kinsingers'?" Mervin asked. "I can put in a good word for him."

"*Nee,* Daed. He's always wanted to farm. He's been helping out on a couple of farms in his area. They call on him when they need an extra hand," Bethany said.

"But it's not what he wants or needs," Aaron added. "Kyle needs a place to stay and a steady job. Plus, his sister Sarah has some medical issues with her hearing. He needs to help pay those bills." Folding his arms across his chest, Aaron added, "He's willing to live in the *dawdi haus* and work for you two."

Mervin folded his arms across his chest. "You invited this boy to live with us?"

"I did. Come on. He ain't a boy and he ain't a stranger. It's Kyle. And he's great. He's been farming all his life. He could help you both a lot. Plus, he really is in a tough bind."

"Still. How much does he expect me to pay him?"

"We mentioned some numbers, but it's not a ton, Daed. He really just needs a year to figure things out and get over the breakup."

"I wonder what happened between him and his girl. Do you know?"

Looking miserable, Aaron nodded. "She cheated on him." After a pause, he added, "Kyle discovered her with one of his friends."

"What? Well, that's . . . that's terrible."

"Yeah, it is," Bethany said. "I can't believe a nice Amish girl would treat her boyfriend so shabbily."

"I canna believe any girl would do that," she corrected. "Amish or otherwise."

"Exactly. So, what do you think? Instead of getting someone to come over for a morning, Kyle can help you plow the fields."

Everything Aaron was saying made Ruthie want cry tears of relief and joy. Kyle sounded like a godsend. "I suppose we could feed him. I always make plenty for food. More than enough for two."

"I thought maybe you could have him over a couple of times a week. At least until he gets that ugly *dawdi haus* kitchen cleaned up and working."

It was an awful kitchen. "I could help him clean it. I should've already done that." And she would've . . . if everything else hadn't been so overwhelming.

Aaron looked at them both. "Mamm, Daed, the weather in January is going to be tough, and February will likely be worse. It's going to be cold and miserable here. You two are used to having lots of people in walking distance in case you need help. All you two have are the Lapps next door."

"They are very nice," Mervin blurted. "They've said more than once we could ask them for help."

"Have you asked them, though?" Bethany asked.

"Of course not. But we could start," Mervin said. "Why I even heard that their daughter knows a lot about farming." He looked at Ruthie. "What was her name again?"

"Daisy. Daisy Lapp."

"I'll ask Daisy for help."

"Will you, really?" Ruthie asked. "Last time I suggested we call her, you said you didn't want to ask a woman to do a man's job."

"I won't worry about that anymore. If I really need her, I'll reach out."

"That's not a *gut* plan Daed," Aaron said. "Daisy might help you, but she might not. People in the area are saying that she's in a snit because she was saving to buy this farm."

"I am sorry that our retirement burst her bubble, but that ain't our fault," Ruthie said. "It was up for sale and we bought it."

"I agree. I guess Mr. Burkholder told her a bunch of lies and promises over the last year when he needed her help. When he sold the farm right out from under her, she took it hard."

Mervin frowned. "That's a shame, to be sure, but maybe it's all for the best."

"Why would you say that?" Bethany asked.

"No Amish woman in her mid-twenties is capable of running a big farm like this," Mervin said. "She might be able to milk a cow and take care of chickens, but probably nothing more than that." He laughed. "I mean, have you ever heard of something so ridiculous?"

To Ruthie's chagrin, her children exchanged meaningful glances.

After the slightest of pauses, Bethany murmured, "As a matter of fact, yes. I have."

Feeling her cheeks heat, Ruthie speared another bite of pie. She'd never say it out loud, but her dear daughter had a point.

CHAPTER 1

April

There was no doubt about it. Her expensive, beautiful, metallic-blue electric bike was something of a mistake. Daisy had known that from practically the moment that she'd taken her first test drive in the back parking lot of Jonny Schrock's bicycle shop.

It wasn't Jonny's fault either. He was as laid-back, no-pressure a salesman as one could ever hope to interact with.

Unfortunately, the problem was all hers. She'd gone shopping in a snit because the beautiful, gorgeous, perfect farm that she'd been saving up to buy forever had been snapped up from under her. And by an aging, yet engaging couple who she couldn't even dislike.

Mervin and Ruthie Miller were excited about farming in their "second season." They were looking forward to new experiences and fulfilling their dreams.

Daisy was happy for them. She really was. She just wished

they'd picked a different parcel of land on which to follow their dreams. That piece was supposed to have been hers. She'd chatted with the owners, Samuel and Rachel Burkholder about it for years.

She'd cut out pictures of improvements she'd wanted to make. She'd worked at Melissa's bulk store for years in order to get the down payment. It was hard to forget about the many, many hours she'd carried around heavy cartons, dealt with Saturday sales, and haggled with customers who didn't even want to pay the discounted prices Melissa charged. She'd had to do all of that for forty hours a week.

Plus, Melissa wasn't even nice.

To make matters worse, she'd been so close to being able to buy the Burkholders' property. Well, Daisy had been just two years away—if she didn't up and quit working for Melissa like she privately threatened to do every month—when suddenly her goal was gone. Out of her grasp.

Like a really pleasant, swoony dream when she was a princess and a really handsome guy was her prince because he had a secret herd of fancy sheep. Yeah. It was like she'd been having a dream that was so good. So good! Until she woke up.

Samuel Burkholder hadn't even seemed all that guilty when she cornered him, either. He pretended he didn't remember his promises to her. And then, when that didn't work, he pretended he couldn't hear her protesting.

When all that happened—and yes, it was a lot—she'd walked down to Landon Bike Shop. She'd decided that the only reason she was still working for Melissa was because she could walk to work. But if she had a bike, she could work somewhere else and learn to be happy there.

Once inside, she test drove three models, and then bought the best one. For cash. Handsome Jonny Schrock was so pleased with the sale he'd thrown in a free bike helmet.

It was simply too bad that she was now experiencing buyer's remorse. Big-time.

It wasn't that she didn't enjoy the Aventon Aventure 3 step-through e-bike. It rode like a dream and the nifty solar-powered converter that Jonny sold her worked like a charm. She could ride anywhere she wanted with ease.

It was just that she couldn't seem to get the hang of the thing.

And, perhaps, that she had a terrible habit of gazing at pastures instead of the road while she rode. Which was why cars often honked at her and more than one person had forced her to listen to their well-intentioned advice.

It was also why just two minutes ago she'd been riding along, spied a pair of newborn lambs, braked too hard, and lost control of her new bicycle. She went flying into the fence, and her bicycle went sliding into the ditch.

"Oh my word! Are you okay?"

She blinked. Tried to discover the identity of the speaker, but everything was fuzzy.

"Huh?"

The speaker knelt beside her. "Hey, it's going to be okay," he said softly. "You're not alone. Can you move?"

At last, Daisy focused. The speaker was a man. A blond, tan, gorgeous, prince-like man. He was Amish, had a smooth, caring voice and a slight Southern accent.

Though that didn't make sense. Usually her dream-prince had dark hair and was riding a horse. Was she not dreaming after all?

"Mmmm," she said.

His brown eyes widened just before he stood up and yelled something to a car that had just stopped.

"*Jah*. We need an ambulance. She fell. I don't know. I just saw her go down and came running over. My name? Kyle. Kyle Hostetler. What? Oh. Okay. Yes. That makes sense. Thanks."

Kneeling back down beside her, he said, "That was an Englischer. He's on his phone and calling for help. An ambulance should be here shortly."

An ambulance? Those were expensive. "*Nee*. Don't do that."

"Sorry, but it's already done. And you're bleeding. I'm not exactly sure where you're bleeding from, but I don't think we're supposed to worry about that yet."

Daisy thought she was starting to feel better. "I need to get up. And get my helmet off."

He touched her hand lightly. "Settle. Sorry, but the 911 operator said to not move."

"I really need this helmet off. Can you unbuckle it?"

"I could but I won't. You might have a neck injury."

"I don't think I do."

"Sweetheart, what's your name? Do you remember your name?"

Sweetheart? That sounded rather prince-like. "I do." She smiled at him.

"My name is Kyle. What's yours?"

"Daisy."

He blinked. Grew concerned. "Yes, you're right. You landed in a field of wildflowers, and those are daisies . . ."

This man was an idiot and so was she for ever thinking that he was her dream Prince Charming. "I know I'm lying in a field of flowers. My name is Daisy."

"Oh."

"Yeah. Oh. So please, let me stand up."

He pressed a hand on her shoulder. As if he was pinning her down in some kind of awful wrestling move. "No. No way do I want to be responsible for you suffering a permanent injury. Don't move."

"Kyle, please. I'm mighty uncomfortable."

"Well, I'd be surprised if you weren't," he said. "I saw your accident. One minute you were flying down the road, and the next, your brakes screeched, you ran into that tire tread and then fell down here."

She would've rolled her eyes if her head didn't hurt so much. "Thanks so much for that recap."

Indignation, followed by a small grin, filled his expression. "Boy, you're a live wire, aren't you?"

"I'm not sure what that means," she lied.

"Oh. Well—" He took a deep breath.

No way did she want to hear anything more about something she didn't care about in the first place. "Kyle, if you are thinking that I want an education about phrases right now, you're mistaken. I do not."

"I reckon you are right. Sorry about that." He looked sheepish. "My only explanation is that seeing you like this has shaken me up something awful."

Daisy just stared at him. Was he expecting an apology?

While she was debating the pros and cons of what to do, he tilted his head to the side. "Ah, here we go."

"What?"

"Do you hear that?" He beamed. "The sirens are close. Things are going to be better for ya soon."

Her brain felt fuzzy, but Daisy was pretty sure she heard the sirens, too. *Jah*, sure. They would make her feel better.

But was her life about to get better?

That was doubtful. None of her dreams were about to come true. None of the things she used to talk about doing, back when she was still in school, had happened.

Remembering Winter Walker, her beautiful, slim, perfect archenemy, made her wince. Growing up, Winter had teased her all the time about being a tomboy. About wanting things that only boys should want.

And because Winter had been the most popular girl in their Amish school, everyone else had sided against Daisy.

She'd put up with so much because she knew she was going to prove everyone wrong one day. She was going to make everyone see that just because she had different dreams, it didn't mean that they weren't good ones.

But maybe she'd been wrong.

Because here she was, sitting on the side of the road next to a broken bike. She was hurting something awful. At the moment, there wasn't a whole lot that she felt good about.

Even though it was weak, Daisy decided this accident was the final piece of a life that suddenly felt like far too much to handle. The pain, the conversation, the knowledge that Melissa was going to be more concerned about being shorthanded than she was going to be worried about her. She closed her eyes. Shutting her eyes away from the world.

Until a gentle fingertip brushed a line across her cheek. "Daisy, don't go to sleep, okay? The EMTs are going to need to check you out."

"Mmmm, okay," she murmured.

"Daisy, what's your last name?"

"Lapp."

"Do you live nearby?"

"*Jah*. Ridge Road."

"Wait, do you live on the Lapp property? Is that your family's farm?"

"*Jah*," she said tiredly. "We've been there forever."

"Don't you worry. I'll make sure someone at your house knows what's going on."

She was prevented from replying by another man's voice. "Daisy, Daisy, can you hear me?"

"Yes."

"Daisy, my name is Camp," the voice said as he picked up

her wrist. "I'm an EMT and I'm going to take care of you, okay?"

"Okay," she said for what had to be the tenth or twelfth time. She wasn't sure. But as Camp started poking, prodding, and calling out numbers to someone nearby, Daisy decided she didn't much care anymore.

She needed to take a break.

CHAPTER 2

It had been hard to simply stand there while he watched the ambulance speed away with its lights flashing and the sirens blaring.

Kyle wasn't sure why. He didn't know Daisy Lapp and he wasn't responsible for her. All that had happened was that the Lord had put him in the right place at the right time.

He was glad of that.

The fact was, he had a lot of faults, but he also had a strength, and that was that he was the type of person to take care of things. He always had been. From the time his little sister, Sarah, had been born, he'd looked out for her. When the doctors had determined that a terrible year of constant ear infections had damaged her hearing so badly in one ear that she was never going to be able to hear in it, he'd been her greatest protector.

He'd been the same way in school, too. If someone needed help, he'd offer to try. If someone had been teased or bullied, he'd try to put a stop to it.

So he was thankful that he'd been able to help Daisy this

morning. But that didn't mean he should care about her. They were strangers.

Plus, she hadn't been all that sweet. She was nothing like his sister, Sarah. Or Mary, his ex-girlfriend. Well, Mary had been sweet until she'd cheated on him.

That was beside the point. What was important was that he'd already done everything that he should for Daisy. He'd fulfilled his responsibilities.

But even though that was the case, Kyle had still promised that he'd take her bicycle to her farm and let her family know about the accident.

He couldn't believe she lived on the farm right next to the Millers. It was just about the only farm he knew besides the one he was working on.

A truck slowed down beside him. "Do you need a ride, son? Looks like your bike is a little worse for wear."

"Thanks, but I'm almost there. The woman riding it was in an accident."

"She gonna be okay?"

"I hope so. Thanks for asking."

"All righty then. Good luck."

Kyle nodded his thanks as he continued his journey.

Thirty minutes later, when he was about halfway up the Lapps' driveway, the front door opened. It was a guy about his age with dark hair, blue eyes like Daisy's, and a dark expression. "Where did you get that bicycle? Also, what happened to it?"

Taken aback by his tone, Kyle held up a hand. "Hey, I'm only trying to help. This is Daisy's. I'm returning it for her."

"Why? What happened?"

Briefly, Kyle relayed the story about her accident and that the EMTs had thought she needed to get checked out at the hospital.

By the time he finished, a couple in their late forties and what looked like another brother had stepped outside. All of them looked crushed. "We just got a call from the police. We need to go to County Hospital."

"Are you sure she was conscious?" the first guy asked.

"I'm sure. Though I'm no doctor, I don't think her life was in danger. She's just injured."

"*Jah*. Okay." The guy's expression eased but he still looked like he was at a loss for words.

"I knew she shouldn't have gotten that bike," the woman said. "I couldn't tell her no, though. She was so broken-hearted."

The guy with the glower placed a hand on her shoulder. "Hey, Mamm, it wouldn't have mattered if you had given her ten reasons not to get the bicycle. No one can tell Daisy no when she's determined to do something, and she wanted that electric bike bad."

"That's true."

Feeling like an interloper, Kyle cleared his throat. "If you all would tell me where you'd like this, I'll wheel it over and then get out of your way."

"*Nee*, wait."

Kyle stopped mid-step.

"Listen, please forgive us. I'm sorry," the daed said. "Where are my manners? I'm Jed Lapp, this is my *frau*, Esther. Obviously, we're Daisy's parents. And these two are her brothers, Lukas and Ben."

Both men had Daisy's blue eyes. Beyond that, it looked as if both men resembled their father while Daisy was a younger version of their mother. Kyle could see their resemblance to each other, but it wasn't readily apparent, mainly because one was obviously Amish and one was dressed in jeans and a T-shirt, and sneakers. He was definitely English.

"I'm Kyle Hostetler. Pleased to meet you."

"Good to meet you, too," Ben, the English brother said. "I haven't seen you around here before. Are you visiting?"

"*Nee*, I just moved here a couple of weeks ago."

"What part of town?"

"This part." He grinned. "I got a job with Ruthie and Mervin Miller. I'm helping them with their farm."

Within a few seconds, a new tension appeared.

Lukas was the first to speak. "Do you mean the Millers next door?"

"*Jah*." Kyle was still feeling as if something was wrong. Well, wrong besides the fact that Daisy had just been taken to the hospital. "Do you know Mervin and Ruthie?"

"Only slightly," Esther said. "As you know, they've only recently moved here."

"*Jah*. From Millersburg."

"Is that where you're from, too?" Ben asked.

"It was at one time. I was friends with the Millers' son Aaron, growing up. My family moved to Kentucky when I was twelve and I've lived there since."

"Whereabouts in Kentucky?"

"Northern. Around Elizabethtown."

"Ah," said Jed.

Esther clapped her hands together. "Here you've been so kind to bring Daisy's bicycle and we've been keeping you out in this heat. Where are my manners? It's warm outside and you not only took care of our girl but walked her bicycle all the way here. Would you like some water?"

"*Danke*, but I'm good. I'll get out of your way so you can get to the hospital."

"Oh. Okay, *gut*." Just as he was about to leave, he added, "For what it's worth, she spoke to me for a few minutes before the ambulance arrived." He grinned. "She didn't like the fact that I wouldn't unfasten her helmet. No matter that

I explained we needed to be careful of her head and her neck, and that I was only following the 911 operator's advice."

Lukas shook his head. "That don't surprise me one bit. She's a bit stubborn."

Ben chuckled. "She wouldn't be Daisy if she didn't try to argue about something."

Kyle didn't know what to say about that so he raised a hand. "I'll be praying for her. I hope she recovers quickly."

"Thank you," Jed said. "I hope so, too. We're beholden to you for doing so much for a stranger."

"Well, we're not strangers anymore. Even though I was rattled and she was hurt, I thought she was nice." And pretty.

"Daisy is nice," Esther murmured. "Sometimes to a fault, I fear. I'll be sure to let her know how much you did for her."

"No need for that. But, if you wouldn't mind, maybe you could let her know that I'll try to stop by in a few days. Just to say hello. Granted, of course, that she is up to seeing visitors."

"We would like that very much. Thank you again for helping my daughter, and also for bringing us the news and the bicycle," Esther added.

"Of course."

Ben strode forward to take the bike. "Hey, let me have a phone number. I'll give you a call as soon as we get some news at the hospital."

"*Danke.*" After giving him a number, Kyle added, "That's the Millers' kitchen phone. They're New Order."

"Gotcha. Thanks again."

After waving his goodbye again, Kyle turned around and headed back to the Millers'.

He'd been planning to go out to breakfast and maybe stop at the library or something. Now, though, his mind was on Daisy, her accident and the strange vibe that had been emanating from the Lapp family. For some reason, he thought they weren't too thrilled about the Millers, but that sure didn't make sense. Mervin and Ruthie were two of the nicest people he'd ever met.

Making an impulsive decision, he decided to ask them about the Lapps as soon as he got back.

That is, if they hadn't messed up something else around the farm.

CHAPTER 3

Lying in a hospital bed for almost two hours gave a person a lot of time to examine one's surroundings, Daisy decided.

The hospital walls had been painted what she supposed was a soothing apricot. There was a rather large window in the room, too. The midday sun was shining through the pane, making the orange walls shine brighter.

In the corner of the room was a chair that could be reclined, if one pushed hard enough on the back of it. It was a muted green. Beside her bed was a pale yellow plastic chair, which completed the majority of the room's décor. Altogether, Daisy thought it looked like she'd been deposited into the middle of a bowl of rainbow sherbet.

Most people would probably think there were far worse-looking rooms in which one could recover from an accident.

Unfortunately, Daisy didn't seem to be one of them. Maybe it was her recent trauma, but all she could think about was that this place was yet another place where she didn't want to be.

She'd really believed that she would be much further along in life when she'd reached twenty-four years of age.

Feeling depressed all over again, she closed her eyes. If she slept, she wouldn't have to stare at the walls. Or, most important, continually remember how it had felt to get tossed off her bicycle and into a ditch.

Barely a minute later, the sound of footsteps ruined her escape. She opened her eyes. Expecting to see Jamie, her nurse.

Instead it was her eldest brother, Lukas.

"Hey, little *shveshtah*. How're you doing?" Lukas asked as he plopped down on the lemon-yellow chair at her bedside.

"I'm fine. I decided to take the day off from work and relax in an air-conditioned room for a spell," Daisy joked. "This fancy bed is a bonus." Picking up the remote, she added, "I discovered that if I push the arrow buttons on both the top and bottom sections, it will practically make me into a sandwich."

He didn't smile. Instead, his gaze remained worried.

She reckoned Lukas had reason.

Looking down at herself in the hospital bed, she winced. Her "little" bike accident had caused a lot of pain and discomfort. She had a minor concussion, two bruised ribs, and a broken leg, which was the main reason she was still stuck in her hospital bed. An orthopedic surgeon was supposed to stop by after he had time to examine the CT scan results on her leg. There was a chance that she could have also torn a ligament and might even get to have surgery, too. "How are Mamm and Daed?"

"Oh, you know. They are currently outside in the waiting room chatting with two other families." The dimple in his cheek popped. "I'm pretty sure Mamm decided that she needed to counsel a family whose ninety-year-old grandmother was in poor shape."

"That sounds like Mamm." Her mother was a born caretaker. She excelled at helping people in need—whether they wanted her help or advice or not.

Luckily, their mother was also blessed with a pleasing disposition. Everyone in their church district knew that her offers to help were always given with the best of intentions.

"Between you and me, I think she scared the nurses a little bit," he added. "One of them suggested that we all don't come in here at once."

"Oh no."

"I told everyone that I thought it was a good idea." His expression still gentle, he added, "That way I was able to see you first."

Lukas was the quietest of them all, which everyone in her family considered to be a blessing. He was a farmer, handsome, steady, and stalwart. Each of them depended on him in one way or another.

"I'm grateful for that. Thanks for coming."

"Of course I was going to be here." He unfolded his legs out in front of her. They stretched out far enough for him to put the toe of his boot on one of the bottom rungs of her bed.

All in all, he looked much like he did at home, when he was lounging on their farmhouse's famously large front porch. "Ben was here, too, but he had to go into work. He said to tell you that he loves you." Grinning, he added, "Also, you aren't to worry about your chores tonight. He'd take care of them."

That was Ben. Emotional, always sweet to her, and always afraid to let anything in his type A personality falter. He also loved to tease her. "Gee. Thanks. I was just wondering how I was going to be able to clean the stalls tonight."

Lukas chuckled. "He was just teasing ya. Besides, we both

know that it's gonna be me who will be picking up the slack around the farm. Ben don't do squat."

"True. At least he's doing well at the factory."

He grunted. "He is at that."

Thinking about their Englischer brother, Ben, being so good at working at the factory but forever trying to get out of farmwork, she thought of Melissa. "I guess I should call my boss. Melissa's probably wondering what's going on with me."

Lukas shifted. "Um, about that."

"What about it?"

"I went ahead and called Walden Bulk Foods for ya."

"Did anyone answer the phone?"

"*Jah*. Someone did. After I told them who I was and that you had an accident, the man who answered put me right through to Melissa."

Noticing that Lukas was looking even more uncomfortable, Daisy decided to make his life easier. "Let me guess how she reacted. She wasn't happy when you told her that I was probably not going to be able to work for two days."

Lukas shifted again. Now he was sitting up straight and facing her directly. His expression was as solemn as she'd ever seen it. "Daisy, you and I both know that you're gonna have to stay off your feet for a lot longer than two days. Especially if your leg is broken. Especially if you have to have surgery."

"I doubt I'll get surgery. That's only going to happen if the doctors think the break is real bad or a tendon is torn." She hoped she sounded more hopeful than she was. The truth was that her leg hurt very bad. It was in a temporary plastic brace and seemed to be doubling in size every hour.

She hadn't been able to put any weight on it at all. The nurse had to help her walk to the bathroom.

"Even if it's just a sprain, it's a bad one. You're going to have to take it easy."

"I suppose." She took a breath. "Come on, *bruder*. Tell me what Melissa said."

Lukas sighed. "There ain't no good way to tell you about this, Daisy."

"Just spit it out."

"All right. It's like this. Melissa don't want you working there anymore."

"What? She fired me because I had an accident when I was on my way to work?" Daisy was stunned, and she'd been pretty sure that she could no longer be shocked by anything Melissa did.

Looking like he'd just bit into a sour lemon, Lukas nodded slowly. "I questioned that, too. At first she hemmed and hawed, saying about how business was a little slow right now."

"She was lying. It's been busier than ever."

"*Jah*, I kind of told her that you'd said that." He rubbed the back of his neck. "She didn't care for me correcting her. I'm sorry to say that the conversation quickly went south after that."

"I'm not surprised." Melissa didn't like to be contradicted.

"Yeah. Well, the gist of it is that if you canna work, she's going to find someone who can."

"Great." Tears pricked her eyes.

"Oh, come now. I am sorry I didn't handle the call better, but the job wasn't worth it."

"Lukas, you can say that because you don't have to work for anyone else."

"True, but you canna be upset about losing this job. You hated it. Please don't cry."

"I can't help it. It's not just the job that I lost. It's *everything*."

"Everything?"

It wasn't fair, but she hated that he couldn't read her mind. "It's that the Millers bought my farm. It's that I spent all that money on that stupid bike, and all it got me was a hospital visit, a lost job, and probably a bunch of hospital bills." Meeting his gaze, she finished her sad little sob story. "All of my dreams are gone, Lukas."

"Don't say that."

"It's true." She swiped her cheek with the side of her hand. "And, *jah*. I know I shouldn't be so negative, but it feels like I don't have much to be happy about right now."

Lukas reached for her hand again. "Listen, all that's happening is you're in a slump. We've all been in them. I sure have."

"Not like this."

"Don't you remember how disappointed I was when Elizabeth moved away? She'd been my girl since I was fifteen."

"I remember." They'd all thought Lukas and Elizabeth went together like peas and carrots. She was sweet and calm. In some ways she'd been the feminine version of Lukas.

Lukas had been upset about their breakup, though he could have married her, moved, and worked on her family's farm with her father and brothers. If he had wanted that. He hadn't.

Of course, Daisy also remembered that he'd only been sad for a couple of months. Mamm had whispered to her that was a sure sign that Elizabeth hadn't been the one the Lord had intended for Lukas.

"You know what?" he asked as he stood up. "I'm going to tell Mamm and Daed that you're awake. They're going to want to see you."

"All right. Thanks. And Lukas?"

He paused at the door. "*Jah*?"

"Thanks for being here. And for calling Melissa for me."

"I'm glad I was the one to speak to her instead of you. She was rude. And as far as visiting you here? Don't ever thank me for that. You're my little sister. Of course I'm always going to do my best to help you, no matter what."

"I love you."

"I love you back." His expression softened before his usual gruff mask appeared again. "Now . . . you go take a sip of water or something, because our parents are going to come in here hot."

She laughed at his phrase and when he was out of sight, she carefully picked up her cup and sipped a good amount of ice-cold water.

When she heard footsteps approaching, she reached for the remote control switch the nurse had shown her how to use. Figuring facing both of her parents' questions while sitting up would make answering them a little easier, she tapped the top button a couple of times.

Her body protested the new position but settled in.

"Here she is!" her father boomed. "Daisy, darling, are you decent?" he called out.

She groaned. No doubt every other patient in the hall heard him. "*Jah*, Daed."

No sooner had she answered when her mother followed him in with a big smile.

"You'll never guess who I met in the waiting room, Daisy!"

Her mother was right about that. Daisy had no idea, because it could've been an Amish couple, an Englischer lady on vacation . . . even a policeman or a plumber who'd gotten called in by the hospital staff. Anyone and everyone was fair game for Esther Lapp.

"Who?" she asked.

"Kyle!"

"Who?" She had just looked over at her father when a man walked through the door. A handsome, blond man holding a bouquet of multicolored daisies.

"Hey," he said.

She pulled her sheet and blanket up more securely over her body. "Who are you?"

His tentative smile faded into obvious embarrassment. "Ah . . . I'm Kyle Hostetler. Do you remember me? I'm the guy who found you after your accident."

Staring at him, it all came back.

Kyle had knelt down in the ditch. No doubt getting muddy when he'd inspected her for broken bones. When he'd checked her pulse.

When they'd talked and she argued with him about her helmet.

When he'd ignored her protests that she was all right and instead flagged down an Englischer driver who called 911.

When he'd stayed with her until the ambulance came.

Through it all, he'd been wonderful. Incredible. He'd gone above and beyond in order to help her.

And now, here he was, taking time out of his day to see her again. He even bought her a bouquet of flowers.

This Kyle Hostetler had to be one of the nicest people she'd ever met.

He was also the man who was working for the Millers. Doing her dream job.

And even though he was probably a great farmer, his presence in her hospital room wasn't welcome. In fact, he was currently the symbol of everything she was not.

He was handsome, healthy, friendly, and had a good job.

She was on the plain side, injured, had a fierce headache, and had started to carry around a chip on her shoulder right around the time Winter encouraged half their school to call her boys' names under their breaths.

Last but not least, she was currently unemployed. So not only was she not a farmer, she wasn't much of anything. Especially now that she was sitting in a hospital bed.

All she was at the moment was a burden.

"*Jah*, Kyle Hostetler, I remember you," she said without enthusiasm. "I remember you well."

CHAPTER 4

Kyle's parents would call this the day that kept on giving. They'd always say that phrase tongue in cheek, and usually when either he or his sister would complain that everything in the day seemed to go wrong.

"It's days like that when you know that the Lord is looking out for ya," his father would say. "Otherwise, you'd be wondering how you were able to take it."

Truthfully, Kyle's day hadn't been all that bad. Not like Daisy Lapp's was. But it had definitely entered the weird category when he'd impulsively decided to pick up a bouquet of flowers for Daisy and bring them to her room at the hospital.

Things had taken a strange turn when the receptionist informed him that the nurse was limiting Daisy's visitors. She'd told him this news as she walked into the waiting room and stopped directly next to Daisy's parents.

He'd had no choice but to sit down and wait, though he would've been perfectly fine if he'd been able to leave the bouquet for her.

Then, because Mrs. Lapp was a chatty sort—and because his bouquet of daisies must have appeared to be a conversation starter—Mrs. Lapp asked him many questions.

When they realized that he was currently living in the *dawdi haus* on the Millers' farm—which Mr. Lapp insisted on calling the Burkholder property—they were shocked.

Daisy's *daed* had seemed very taken aback. "I've seen the *dawdi haus*. Is it in better condition than it used to be?"

Kyle knew what he meant. It had been in rough shape when he'd first arrived. But loyalty to Mervin and Ruthie inspired him to shrug. "I'm not sure how it used to be, but it is fine now."

"That's *gut*."

As for Daisy's mother? A new light had entered her eyes and she'd started asking him far more personal questions. He'd begun to feel as if he was being grilled, and kept looking for the door. Unfortunately, Lukas Lapp, Daisy's eldest brother, didn't seem to be in any hurry to leave his sister's room.

Kyle had been pretty curious about that. After all, his sister, Sarah, hardly got through the day without either stopping by their *haus* or calling the mother on the phone. Mamm had told him more than once that daughters and mothers were always close.

In any case, by the time they'd finally walked into Daisy's room, Kyle was more than ready to leave. His twenty-minute, impulsive visit had now been stretched to an hour.

Then things just got worse when Daisy stared at him like she wasn't sure if she wanted to know him or not.

After a few minutes of awkward conversation, he edged toward the door. "I hope you feel better, Daisy. I'm going to be on my way now."

But just as he was turning to leave, a doctor and a nurse walked inside.

"Oh, good. Everyone's in here," he said. "I'm Dr. Alvarez. I'm an orthopedic surgeon and took a look at the scans that were done on Daisy's tibia downstairs."

"What did you see?" Daisy asked in a soft, hesitant voice.

"It's fractured, dear," the doctor said, looking as if he hated sharing the news. He sighed. "To make matters worse, it wasn't a clean break. A chip broke off, which if untreated could be life threatening. I'm afraid this means that you're going to need surgery."

"Are you sure?" She looked completely heartbroken.

He nodded. "Luckily, it shouldn't be a long surgery and there are rarely complications."

"I see."

Kyle thought Daisy looked slightly green.

"Afterward, you'll wear a cast for several weeks. Your leg won't heal without surgery and careful attention to our orders."

"My life is falling apart," she whispered to herself.

"Pardon me?" the doctor said.

"Sorry. That was nothing," she said far more loudly. "It's just that . . . well, I don't know what I'm going to do."

"I know this is a lot to take in, but I'd like to schedule the operation for tomorrow morning."

"So soon?"

"It's best to take care of this now, Daisy." Glancing around the room, Dr. Alvarez gestured to the nurse who had been standing quietly next to him. "Everyone, this is Dana Green. She's my PA, otherwise known as physician's assistant. She's a pro and can answer any questions you might have about the surgery. When you are ready, she'll walk you through what will happen, the probable recovery process, and get you started on everything we need to do for your pre-op."

"Thank you, Doctor," Mr. Lapp said as they shook hands.

After he exited, there was a new tension in the room. Kyle knew he had to get out of there. There was nothing he could do for her. Besides, he was a relative stranger. Just as he was about to excuse himself, Dana spoke.

"What are your questions?" Dana asked.

"I need a moment," Daisy blurted.

Her mother gasped. "Daisy, what in the world is going on with you?"

"A lot, Mamm." Looking even more upset, she added, "Dana, thank you. I know you are busy, but if I could have just ten minutes by myself, I would appreciate it."

"That isn't how they do things here, daughter," her father said under his voice.

"No, no. I understand," Dana said. "And you know what? I think Daisy has a good point. All of us here at the hospital sometimes forget that the things we talk about—and ask our patients to do—are completely out of their comfort zones. I think it's an excellent idea to take a moment to let everything sink in."

To Kyle's relief, Dana stood by the door, obviously making sure that Mr. and Mrs. Lapp didn't ignore their daughter's wishes.

Knowing that it was past time that he got out of there, too, Kyle turned to Daisy. "Goodbye, Daisy. I'll be praying for your recovery," he said.

"*Nee*. Wait."

He turned around. "Yes?"

"Please stay a moment." Looking frustrated with herself, she added, "That is, would you please stay a moment after everyone leaves?"

"Of course. I mean, if that's what you want."

She nodded.

Her mother frowned. "Daisy?"

"Please, Mamm." Raising her eyes to Dana, she said, "Thank you. I promise I only need ten minutes."

The PA winked. "You know what? I think I can even give you fifteen. I'm going to check on another patient and have a sip of coffee. I'll be back in fifteen minutes."

"Thank you." She looked meaningfully at her parents.

They sighed but did as she asked. When Dana closed the door and they were alone, Kyle stepped closer. "How may I help you?"

"First, could you sit down? It's hard to look up at you from here."

"Sure." He sat down on the edge of the chair. He was willing to do whatever she needed, but he was kind of ready to get out of there, too. This is what he got for imagining one thing when the reality had shown him something else altogether.

"Kyle, I wanted you to stay because I wanted to apologize for how rude I was when you came in. The flowers are beautiful and thoughtful. Plus, you helped me so much when I fell. I don't know what I would've done if you hadn't been there. Thank you for everything."

And just like that, all the confusion and irritation he'd been feeling faded. "Don't worry about it." He held out his arm. He was wearing a short-sleeved green shirt that his mother had given him on his birthday. His bare arm was tan. His hands were full of callouses and there were freckles and two scars on his forearm—the product of an accident when he was fourteen. "Obviously I have tough skin," he teased.

Daisy stared at his bare skin. "*Jah*, I guess you do." Meeting his eyes again, she whispered, "Everyone has difficulties, don't they?"

"I reckon so." He swallowed, "I don't know if this will help, but someone once told me that life isn't a windy road. It's more of a long journey through jungles and prairies and sometimes even river crossings."

Daisy raised her eyebrows. "That's a lot."

"I've always liked that comparison because it felt apt. Like a river crossing. Sometimes, the river is shallow. Or calm. Or it's just a little thing, something that wasn't hard to swim across without even getting winded. But other times, it's a perilous thing. The water is deep, the current is strong. Or there are water moccasins in it."

"Or maybe it's not too terrible, but the traveler never learned to swim," she said softly.

He nodded, liking her example a lot. "Exactly. That river crossing might not be difficult for an Olympic swimmer. But for someone who never learned to do much besides dog paddle? It's a scary, dangerous thing indeed." Leaning back, he shrugged. "But who is to say that one person is better than the other?" It's just where they are in life, ain't so?"

"The Olympian might have no experience trudging through the prairie."

Glad she understood what he'd been trying to convey, Kyle smiled at her again. "This moment in your life might be your treacherous river crossing, Daisy Lapp. And what that means to me is that I don't care if you need to take double the amount of time as other people, or that you need a life preserver, or even if you have to walk down a mile and cross where it feels safer. All I think you should care about is getting across."

She blinked slowly, like she was trying his suggestion on for size. "I need to stop worrying about the 'how' or how clumsy I might look when I do it. All I have to do is just cross. That's what counts."

"*Jah*, Daisy. The worst thing to happen isn't that you might end up with some nicks and scratches or be a little embarrassed because you canna swim all that good. The worst thing isn't even that you might get hurt or even get off course and a little lost." He lowered his voice. "The worst thing that could happen is that you don't try to cross at all. Because then . . ."

"Then I will be in the same exact place that I was in the first place," she finished.

"*Jah*. And if you didn't want to be there in the first place, what would it matter if you stayed there, safe and sound?"

"I need to do that surgery, don't I?"

He nodded. "It's your leg, and ultimately your decision, but it seems so."

"I know I don't deserve it, but, um, would you mind visiting me after the surgery? If you have the time?"

He'd already been planning on it. "I wouldn't mind visiting you, and even if I hadn't planned to come over, I'd make the time."

"I . . . I've never met anyone like you."

"I could say the same about you." He winked. "And I mean that in a good way, so remember that before you decide to take offense."

"Okay," she whispered.

Giving in to impulse, he bent down and pressed his lips to the top of her forehead. "Safe travels, Daisy. I'll be looking for ya on the other side."

"I'll call out your name when I get close."

Then she smiled. A real, full smile, showing off beautiful teeth and brightening her eyes.

It was a bit dazzling. So much so that he felt slightly dazed when he stepped out of the room.

"Is she all right?" Mr. Lapp asked.

"What did she want?" Mrs. Lapp asked.

"She's good . . . and I'm afraid that's between the two of us." He tipped his hat. "*Gut* day."

Just as he reached the elevator, Kyle saw Dana leaning against the side of the nurse's station, the aforementioned cup of coffee in her hands. Her eyes flickered toward him. "She doing okay?"

"Yes. I think she's doing just fine."

"That's what I wanted to hear." She smiled as she glanced at the clock again.

His last view of the busy hospital floor was of Dana sipping coffee, several nurses and orderlies walking around with carts and poles and electronic notebooks. And farther down the hall, Mr. and Mrs. Lapp standing outside their daughter's door with their heads down. Quietly praying.

Kyle was no expert, but he was pretty sure that everything was going to be just fine.

CHAPTER 5

Five days later

"You know, I could use a little bit of help with this, D," Ben said as he walked into her bedroom. In his hand was a spiral notebook of crossword puzzles. Just the sight of it made her cringe.

She raised her eyebrows. "With a crossword puzzle? Please."

"What is that supposed to mean?"

"What I think we both know what it means, Ben. I'm terrible at crosswords." Not only did she not enjoy them, she was a rather poor speller. Every time Ben told her that a word had five letters, she felt a minor panic attack. Years of poor spelling grades in school came back to haunt her with a vengeance.

"Sometimes you're helpful."

"Sometimes you make me feel as if I am, though both of us know that the only time you do that is when it's a special occasion, like my birthday."

"That's not true." When she directed a knowing look at him, he said, "You helped me solve that giant crossword a couple of Christmases ago."

It was a wonder she didn't have nightmares from that experience. Ben, with his big brain and years of schooling, loved big words and puzzles of all kinds. He never wanted to believe that she hated word games. "No offense, but I think you're going to let me get a right answer today, too."

He looked away. "If you did just happen to get a right answer on this crossword, that doesn't mean I'm letting you do anything."

"I love you, Ben, but maybe you could just sit with me instead of making me name rivers in Oklahoma or attempt to think of the names of various world leaders in 1972? It would be less stressful and I'd be much better company."

"Fine." He carefully sat down on the bed next to her and put the notebook on her side table. "Is this okay?"

She had a queen-sized bed. It was another purchase she'd made after realizing that she wasn't going to be owning a farm anytime in the near future. Every one of her family members had been against it. She'd not understood why until Lukas had told her that most people only got a queen-sized bed after marriage.

When she'd pointed out that no one had said a word about Ben buying a bigger bed, he'd rolled his eyes and reminded her that he was several inches over six foot. No way was he going to sleep in a small bed. Then he'd pointed out that while she might be what a lot of people called "big boned," she wasn't so big that a twin wouldn't do.

Her mother had even gone so far as to refuse to sit on the side of it for two days after the deliverymen came to the house, put together the metal bedframe and put her lovely new mattress and boxspring on it.

Daisy hadn't regretted the purchase for one moment. Not only had she gotten a good price on it, but it was comfortable, roomy, and now there was room for her leg and its very large cast.

And, it seemed, her brother Ben.

"*Jah*," she said at last. "It's fine. You ain't bothering my leg at all."

"Want to tell me how you're doing now that you've been home for three days?"

She'd had surgery the following morning, had been released the next day, and now she'd been home for the three he mentioned. Nothing about her recuperation had been easy or all that pleasant.

She wasn't going to tell him that though. "I'm okay."

"Daisy."

"What, Ben?"

With exaggerated patience, he lowered his voice. "Daed told me that you haven't complained about your pain once."

"You're acting as if that's a bad thing. I'm supposed to be all right."

"You not only had to get your tibia fixed, but you had anesthesia. I also heard from the nurses that you had a lot of bruises and a minor concussion. And a pair of bruised ribs."

"My concussion is better. I barely have a headache."

"I know, D. But you seem to be intent on staying silent about the pain after your surgery. Mamm and Daed are worried and so am I."

"You shouldn't worry so much."

"No, you should tell me what is going on in that head of yours. Why are you so determined to keep all your discomfort to yourself?"

She knew why, but she was fairly sure that her reason wouldn't do either her or Ben any good. At best, Ben would tease, and at worst, he'd get upset with her. So . . . she shrugged.

He tucked his chin so their eyes could meet. "Come on, D. Talk to me."

"Ben, I know you mean well, but I'd rather not."

"And I know you are thinking that keeping whatever is in your head inside is for the best, but it isn't." He shifted.

The movement caused her mattress to adjust.

Which sent a few uncomfortable twinges through her sore body. And yep, she winced.

Ben almost appeared pleased. "Come on, Daisy. It's time to be honest. Tell me what is going on inside your head. Are you keeping silent because you're worried about the medical bills? If that is the case, don't give it another thought. Not only are Lukas and I going to help you pay the bills, but Daed spoke to the administrator at the hospital. They're going to reduce some of the costs and put the rest on a payment plan. Everything is gonna be fine."

No, it wasn't. Everyone around her was going to have to foot the bill for her stupid bicycle accident.

Worse, she hadn't even started worrying about how to pay for the accident. But now that she realized the strain her hospitalization and surgery was going to put on everyone she loved, she felt even worse.

She took a deep breath in a futile effort to not sound like she was about to cry. "Ben, I know you are thinking that you're being helpful, but you aren't."

"Are you worried about taking your medicine?"

"*Nee.*"

"The nurses said that the extra-strength pain reliever will help but we should expect you to still be pretty sore for several days. She said if the pain gets really bad, the doctor will call in a prescription for a few real strong pain relievers. She said that sometimes a patient needs one or two of those to take the edge off the pain."

"I don't need any prescribed pain pills, Ben." She didn't know how to get that through his head.

"Fine. If it's not the bills, and you're not in pain, then what is wrong? Talk to me, Daisy."

"Fine." She sighed. "I feel like I've wasted my life."

"At twenty-four?"

And . . . there was his grin, which looked more like a smirk. Seeing that hurt.

She felt like pushing him off her bed. "I can't believe you're smirking. Ben, this is why I didn't want to talk to you."

Immediately his amused expression faded. "Hey, are you being serious?"

She waved a hand. "Of course I am."

Frustrated with their conversation—and the fact that she hadn't wanted to have it in the first place—Daisy glared at him. "Not only do I not have a family, I'm not married. I'm not even seeing anyone." Too afraid to utter the complete truth, which was that she'd *never* been courted, not even once, Daisy blurted, "I don't have a job, I've spent money on things that I shouldn't have bought, and now I'm reaping the rewards."

"Are you comparing yourself to Grace?"

"*Nee.*"

"Are you sure?"

"I can't believe you brought up her name." Grace and she had once been best friends. Grace was beautiful, she was popular, and she aced every spelling test. Daisy had known that she was none of those things.

They'd still been close, though. Even when Winter Walker had started making fun of Daisy.

By the time they'd graduated the eighth grade, things between them had changed. Jacob Beachy, Grace's longtime not-so-secret crush, had started paying attention to her. Not too long after, he'd become her boyfriend. When she was seventeen, he'd begun paying formal calls on her at her house.

Grace had been engaged at eighteen and gotten married a week after she'd turned nineteen. Now she had four *kinner*, and lived in a lovely house that Jacob's parents had given to them as a wedding present. She had also retained her figure and did all kinds of volunteer work.

Though they were still friendly with each other, they were no longer close. They didn't have much in common with each other anymore. And sometimes, if her mother got really frustrated with her, she'd bring up Grace and how happy she was.

Which hurt. A lot.

And now, here was Ben bringing her up!

"Grace has nothing to do with what I'm feeling, Ben."

"I hope not, because she has nothing on you, Daisy."

He was so wrong. The truth was that Grace had *everything* on her. "If you thought that comparing me to Grace was going to put me in a better mood, you were very mistaken. Go away."

"Daisy, I know you think that she has had a charmed life, but no one likes her much."

"Don't say that."

"It's true. What did Grace do every time that she got the award for winning the year's spelling bee?"

"She went out of her way to tell everyone that I always refused her help to study."

"Uh-huh. And she might have gotten Jacob to marry her, but she never looks very happy with him." He lowered his voice. "Or he with her . . . because she nags him. They aren't happy together."

"Don't put her down, Ben. Grace's life has nothing to do with mine."

"All I'm trying to say is that you've worked hard for as long as I've known you and put up with Melissa's bossy ways for years."

"I don't know what to do now. My goal was always to get a piece of land and farm it."

"Lukas would let you help around here. I'm sure he would."

"That's not the point. I mean, I'll be glad to help Lukas

around here. I have helped him, and I will again. No matter what I'm doing, I'll always be glad to help him and our parents." She took a deep breath. "But, don't you see the difference? Helping my older brother around our farm is always going to be that. I'm going to feel like I'm not making a difference."

"You know that every job on the farm is important. Don't forget the chicks, right?"

She groaned. When they were all much younger, their father used to point out how even a small job like taking care of baby chickens helped the farm. She could hear his low, caring voice in her ear now. *Your care makes a big difference in their lives, Daisy. Don't you ever forget that.*

Sure, it was true, but she wanted to do more than take care of small things.

"What I'm trying to say is that I want to do something on my own. I want to accomplish something on my own. I want to do something that I can be proud about."

"I understand."

"Do you?" She studied his expression. "Do you really?"

He nodded. "There's a reason I decided to work at the trailer factory. I didn't want to have to compete with Lukas here." Looking sheepish, he added, "Plus, I don't enjoy farm life all that much."

"You really do understand."

"I do. But you must take your pain relievers and take care of yourself, Daisy. This time in bed isn't forever. It's just a temporary blip in a long life."

"I suppose you're right."

"In a couple of weeks, your cast will be off, you'll be mobile again, and you will have another job. Maybe one that you like better." Ben paused, then added, "Also, if you have your heart set on farming, I'll help you look for the right place."

Before she could interrupt, he added, "There are other farms, Daisy. If land is what you want, you could always move."

"Move?"

"*Jah*. Sure. You could move to Kentucky or Missouri or someplace where land isn't as expensive."

"I hadn't thought of that." But was she willing to leave her whole family for her dream?

Now she was even more confused than ever.

"Don't start twisting things and act like I'm trying to push you away. But I am saying that you have options. You are a smart woman, a hard worker, and a good farmer. Use this time to start making plans."

"Okay."

"Okay?"

"*Jah*. You're right, Ben. Do you like hearing that?"

"Of course I do. Why, it's music to my ears." He grinned. "Want to say it again?"

She giggled. "*Nee*. I don't want your head to get any bigger."

"So . . . if you don't want to do crossword puzzles, want to play cards?"

"Sure." To her amusement, Ben pulled out a deck of cards. "You just happened to have that with you?"

"Yep." He winked. "Before we get started, tell me the truth. On a scale of one to ten, how much are you hurting?"

"A seven," she finally admitted.

He stood up, filled a glass from the water pitcher on her dresser, and then got out two pain relievers. "Take these."

"*Danke*." She took them dutifully.

"The nurse said every four hours. It's two o'clock now, you may have two more at six. When you are eating your supper."

"Okay."

Looking pleased, he moved to the chair by the bed, rearranged the table in between them, and then started shuffling cards. "Chin up, girl. I promise, the Lord has a plan. Trust in Him."

"I'll try."

"That's all you can do. So . . . gin?"

"Yes, but we have to keep score. And you can't let me win."

Ben looked appalled. "Have I ever done that?"

"*Nee.*"

"You are right. I have not, and I'm not about to start now." He retrieved the notepad and a pencil off her desk. "You set it up, I'll shuffle the cards a couple more times."

"*Danke*, Ben."

Looking completely serious, he nodded. "Anytime, D. Anytime at all."

CHAPTER 6

Kyle was a sweaty mess and he'd been that way for most of the day. For the last four hours, he'd been plowing the Millers' largest field with a team of four horses.

The horses, all of them Percherons, were beautiful and lived up to their breed. Docile and strong, the team worked in perfect unison. Kyle reckoned a team of men would have difficulty working as well together as they did. But the ground hadn't been as soft as he'd hoped and the temperatures had risen a bit higher than he would've liked.

The only saving grace was that he'd been able to get Mervin out of the way.

For the first hour, his boss had attempted to help but had done more harm than good. He was always a little too slow and didn't keep his balance behind the horses as well as he needed to.

When Mervin had tripped and the horses had needed to stop abruptly, Kyle's heart had felt as if it was lodged in his throat. The Percherons were strong and steady, but they were also expensive animals who could get hurt.

Then, too, was Mr. Miller. Mervin might be a spry fifty-eight-year-old, but he was still a lot older than Kyle. He also had little to no experience leading a plow team through a large field.

Kyle had been so afraid Mervin was going to hurt himself, the horses, or the plow, he'd asked Mervin to help Ruthie plant potatoes and carrots in her garden.

The way Mervin had hardly protested about his help had been a good indication that the man had been as ready to walk off that field as Kyle had been ready for him to leave. After he'd gone, even the horses had settled down.

"Y'all could sense his nervousness, didn't ya?" Kyle asked when the five of them took a brief water break.

One of the geldings, a gorgeous seven-year-old named Bandit, gave him a side-eye in response. Probably to let him know that he not only agreed but thought it was an understatement.

After allowing each horse to partake a bit of water from the portable trough attached to the plow, he hooked them up again.

George and Wilma blew out wet bursts of air but stood complacently while Kyle hooked them up. The last member of the team, a four-year-old mare named Mint, attempted to prance a bit.

"Settle on down now, Minty. We have less than two hours to go. That ain't too long, all things considered."

Mint pawed at the dirt and blew out a burst of air. It was obvious that she wasn't buying his optimistic reassurance one bit.

"You make me laugh, girl," he teased good-naturedly as he snapped the reins, signaling them to move forward.

And move forward, they did. The four were powerful together and Kyle couldn't help but give thanks that he had the opportunity to work with them. The horses were a fine team and he felt that it was a blessing to lead such good stock. He was especially grateful that they had gotten used to him quickly.

Mervin had even teased him, saying that the horses enjoyed listening to his Kentucky accent while they worked.

Since he exaggerated it because they seemed to enjoy the lilt, Kyle thought there might be something to that, though he also thought it was his constant praise and encouragement that enabled the horses to give their workday an extra push.

After drinking one more cup of water, he got back on the plow and spent one more hour finishing tilling the soil. In two days, he and Mervin would plant the corn. It would be a far easier task, given the fact that they would be walking down the rows and not involving the horses.

After he brought the horses in, watered and rubbed them down, he cleaned the plow and straightened the equipment in the barn.

By the time he felt good about leaving to take a shower, it was nearing four o'clock. Though he'd brought a couple of Ruthie's surprisingly good homemade granola bars for sustenance, he was ready to have a meal. Preferably a huge one at the Millers' table.

Almost every evening, he went to the Millers' dinner table for supper. It was part of his pay and work agreement. He worked five and a half days a week. Usually, he had Sundays and Wednesday afternoons off. In addition to his pay, the Millers provided him with basic necessities like milk, eggs, and a loaf of bread a week, along with two loads of laundry.

Ruthie had even offered to feed him every evening—telling him that she was cooking no matter what—but Kyle had been the one to refuse.

The Millers were wonderful people, but he was used to a far quieter life. His parents were on the quiet side and his younger sister, Sarah, had a hearing disability. She could only hear out of one ear, and not all that well.

He'd gotten used to eating without much conversation so as not to create more stress for Sarah.

Though, now that he thought about it, she might have preferred to listen to chatter while she ate.

He enjoyed the food and the conversation, but also appreciated the silence in the evening as well. Three suppers a week seemed like a good compromise.

By the time he finally walked into the *dawdi haus*, everything in the barn was in good order and the horses were happily munching their supper.

Of course, taking so much care of them meant that he'd barely had time to shower and change before rushing through the door from the living room into the main house.

"Kyle, you're here on time. I'm so glad," Ruthie said. "I hope you're hungry."

"I am. What is for supper this evening?"

She smiled happily. "Roast, mashed potatoes, canned green beans, and gravy."

"Ruthie made blondies, too," Mervin said as he joined them in the kitchen.

His mouth was watering. "It smells so good. Thank you."

"You're welcome. I know it's a warm day, but plowing looks like a mighty exhausting job. I figured you needed something to stick to your ribs," Ruthie added as she handed him the serving bowl of potatoes to take to the table.

"Ruthie was going to fry up some fish, but then noticed how long you were out there with the team," Mervin said as he carried the gravy boat.

"I was worried that fried walleye might not fill you up enough," Ruthie explained as she brought over a plate of sliced roast.

"Anything you make is wonderful, but I'd be lying if I

didn't admit to being grateful for this hearty meal. I'm grateful and it smells delicious."

Ruthie's cheeks pinkened. "You're a pleasure to cook for, son. I tell that to Aaron every time he calls."

After each of them trotted back and forth to get the last of the serving dishes, they took their places at the table. In many ways, it reminded Kyle of the way he grew up. Ruthie sat at one end and Mervin sat at the other. Kyle was on the side, just as he and Sarah had been with his own parents.

After they prayed and gave thanks, Ruthie began passing the dishes.

The routine was different than the way he'd grown up. His mother hadn't enjoyed washing dishes and therefore hadn't seen any reason to wash serving dishes when one could serve themselves from the pots and pans and then carry their own plates to the table.

Kyle had at first worried that Ruthie and Mervin were treating him like company instead of their worker, but Aaron had confided that was how his mother liked to do things. She enjoyed doing everything "just so," and that included how she liked to serve meals in the evening.

Now that he'd gotten used to it, Kyle couldn't deny that it was rather nice to have all the serving bowls right in front of him. Ruthie's cooking was so good, it was nearly impossible for him to not have second helpings.

As he'd expected, his first bite of roast beef was as good as it had looked. So were all the sides. Especially the mashed potatoes, since Ruthie added cream cheese to them.

They also had lemonade and ice water.

He was happy to quietly enjoy the meal as Ruthie and Mervin discussed the weather and a visit from two of Ruthie's friends from the quilt shop where she'd worked.

"By the time I showed them around the house and we took our cups of coffee to the parlor, it had seemed as if we hadn't seen each other in two days instead of two months," she said.

"You were the glue at Sew and So," Mervin pointed out. "You were organized and caring." Turning to Kyle, he explained. "Ruthie talked to them about work, but also about their families and interests. That's rare to have in a manager."

"You give me too much credit, Mervin."

"I disagree," he replied with a sweet look her way. "All I'm saying is that I'm sure they miss you. Your replacement had big shoes to fill."

"I suppose they miss me at work, but we were friends, too. It's hard to go from seeing *gut* friends nearly every day to just a few times a year."

There was a wistful note to her voice that was new. Resting his fork on his plate, Kyle felt compelled to give her some encouragement. "Maybe you should set a date and time to see them once a month, then you wouldn't miss them so much."

Longing filled her eyes before she promptly shut it down. "Oh, they probably wouldn't have time."

"You're busy here but you would make the time," Mervin said. "That's a *gut* idea, Kyle."

"Thank you, but my parents used to do the same thing. They'd have standing supper dates with friends once a month. Daed used to tell me that farming was a lonely life for a guy like him."

"A guy like him?"

"He liked conversation. My mother was the type to be happy enough to see her friends at church twice a month and maybe for a coffee break every now and then. But Daed was the social one."

Mervin seemed taken aback by the idea. "I thought he liked farming."

"He did. But one can like to farm and still need to do other things, too. Like you, Mervin, Daed hadn't grown up as a farmer. His father was a blacksmith."

Mervin nodded in understanding. "Ah. Well, that there is a social job, for sure."

"For sure." Kyle grinned. "My *dawdi* knew everyone in our community. He was as strong as an ox, too."

Mervin nodded. "Blacksmiths usually are."

"All right. You've talked me into it, Kyle. I think I will ask Jenni and Sylvia if there's a day and time every month when we could see each other."

"There you go."

She sighed. "Farming is different than I thought. I hope I'll get the hang of things, but maybe I won't. When I was chatting with Esther Lapp over the fence, she was telling me that one of her sons disliked farming from the get-go."

"*Jah*. Ben Lapp works at the teardrop trailer factory. He told me about it when we talked at the hospital."

"Probably just as well that the younger son has an interest working someplace different," Mervin said. "Lukas will be running the farm. It would be difficult for Ben to do the same."

Ruthie nodded. "It's good the Lord gave them different strengths. It worked out for all of them."

"You two are forgetting about Daisy," Kyle said.

"What about her? She's their youngest, yes?"

"*Jah*. But she likes farming, too."

"Well, it's not a woman's job. It's a man's job." Mervin chuckled. "Why, I could hardly handle that plow and I was only out there for two hours."

Kyle knew that the problem hadn't been Mervin's strength, it was his ability. Plain and simply, Mervin was nervous and had only read about plowing a field. His book sense didn't help him manage either the horses or the plow any more easily.

Kyle sure couldn't tell him that, though.

"Have you seen Daisy since she came home from the hospital?" Ruthie asked.

"*Nee*. But she's probably resting." It had only been a week.

"Her leg is in a cast, isn't it?"

"*Jah*." Thinking of how restless she'd seemed, even in the hospital bed, he grinned. "I think she's going to be a little bored very quickly."

"I thought she had a job."

"She was let go when they realized that she wasn't going to be able to be of much use at the store where she worked."

"That wasn't very nice."

"I didn't think so either, Ruthie."

"We should visit her soon."

Wait, we? "You mean you and Mervin?"

"*Nee*, Kyle. I mean that you and me should both pay her a call." Glancing at him over the top of her silver-rimmed eyeglasses, she added, "You're the one who saved her, after all."

"I didn't save her, I just saw her accident." And asked the person who stopped to call 911. Then stayed with her until she was in the ambulance. All before he visited her in the hospital with a bouquet of flowers in his hands.

She shrugged. "Same difference."

Early the next morning, after speaking with Mervin and checking on the team of horses, Kyle decided to wait another day before plowing another field.

There was a chance of rain that afternoon, which would help the plow the next day. He also didn't want to chance injuring any of the horses, in case one of them was feeling more sore than they let on.

Personally, he was glad to have the day off, too. It was Saturday. He decided to do a little bit of cleaning in the *dawdi haus* and even put a fresh coat of paint in one of the spare bedrooms. One day in the future, his parents and Sarah were going to visit. If that happened, he wanted to be sure to give them a nice place to rest in the evening.

He'd just been thinking about how nice and relaxing his day was going to be when he entered the kitchen for breakfast.

Ruthie had made biscuits, gravy, fried ham, and eggs.

After giving his thanks in prayer, he dug in happily.

They didn't usually eat breakfast together. Instead, it was understood that he would eat sometime between a quarter to seven and seven thirty every morning. On his day off, he ate cereal or something easy in his own house.

After helping himself to a second cup of coffee, he was surprised to see Ruthie sit down beside him.

"Kyle, Mervin just told me that you weren't planning on plowing today."

"That's right. We want to give the horses a break."

"I think that's a good idea. Especially since I think there's something to do."

He was slightly disappointed but what could he do? It was a work day and he worked for them.

"Of course, what did you have in mind?"

"It has to do with Daisy Lapp. You know, she's been on my mind all morning . . . especially since you brought her up in conversation last night."

Hating that she was right, he hedged. "I was only making conversation."

"Perhaps."

Kyle narrowed his eyes at Ruthie. Did she know something more than she was letting on? If that was the case, it wouldn't be the first time. He'd already observed that she was very good at discovering details about her children's lives that they'd never intended her to know.

It seemed she was just as talented as getting him to bend to her will.

Knowing that it was better to not argue, especially since he wouldn't hate to see Daisy again, he nodded. "Whenever you want to go see her, I'll be happy to take you."

"I was hoping you would say that." Looking pleased, she stood up. "I think now is a very good time to pay her a call. I just happened to have made two apple pies early this morning, and while you do eat quite a bit, I think it would be a good idea if we gave Daisy and her family one, too."

"Really?" He'd just been played by a spry retiree. Played like a deck of cards.

"Like I said, Daisy was on my mind." She beamed at him. "I know apple pie can't help a leg heal, but I do think it might make someone feel better, don't you think?"

"*Jah*. Sure. I suppose now is as good a time as any."

"Wonderful. Let me put one of these pies in a basket and then we can go as soon as you wash up."

"Wash up?"

"Your shirt looks a bit damp and sweaty, Kyle. You don't want Daisy to think you smell, do you?"

"*Nee*."

"Well, then? Come on, now. We've got things to do."

He looked at Mervin, who had somehow snuck in the room but was still suspiciously silent. "Will you be joining us?"

"*Nee*," he said quickly. As if he knew he was sounding too eager to stay behind, Mervin added, 'I mean, I think it would be best if I let the two of you go without me."

Feeling a bit panicked, Kyle blurted, "Ruthie. Let's rethink this. Just because I was concerned about her, it doesn't mean that I wanted to pay her a visit." Again.

"I'm sorry, but I think you did. You just said that you would be willing to go whenever I was ready." She smiled sweetly. "I'm ready now."

His boss had just played him like a piano in a church choir. Expertly and with verve.

In spite of himself, he was impressed. "You're right. Let's go get this over with." The sooner he got the visit over with, the better.

CHAPTER 7

"Hey, lazy bones," Lukas called out from the other side of her door. "Are you decent?"

"You know I am," Daisy said from the cozy chair in the corner of her room. Two days ago her brothers had brought it—and the matching ottoman—to the house. It was covered in a plush, soft pale blue fabric. Somehow they'd found a chair that fit her frame perfectly. It had become her favorite place to sit, since she could rest her cast on the ottoman. "Come on in."

"Ah, there you are." Even though she was still sitting with her leg perched up, Lukas studied her intently. "Hey, I think you've got some color in your cheeks. You look like you feel a lot better."

Relief filled his gaze. That made her happy. She hated to worry him. "I do," she replied in as cheery a voice as she was able. "Today's been a good day." Lifting her chin, she added, "I haven't had to take any pain reliever."

Crossing the room, he leaned on the side of her bed and faced her. "Are you sure that is wise? I thought you were supposed to keep ahead of the pain."

"I am. Don't worry." Motioning to her yellow dress and the *kapp* on her head, she smiled. "I was feeling so good I put on my new dress."

"I like the yellow on you."

She chuckled at his attempt to sound gallant. Her brother farmed all day and was usually more inclined to notice when one of the horses needed a good brushing or when the crops were looking good than any sort of detail on a woman. "*Danke*. Now, is there a reason you came to check on me? Was there something that Mamm needed?"

"Hmm? As a matter of fact, yes." He stood up straight. "I came up to let you know that you have a visitor. Two, in fact."

"Really? Who is here?"

"Kyle Hostetler and Ruthie Miller."

"Oh, no." Immediately she felt ashamed of her reaction. "Sorry. I mean, that's kind of them to stop by. But, um, any chance you could tell them that I'm busy right now?"

"Busy sitting in your chair? *Nee*. I'm not going to tell them that."

"I figured."

Lukas stepped forward and held out a hand to help her to her feet. "I know neither are your favorite people, but they're concerned about ya."

"I don't dislike them. You're right. They're nice folks."

"Kyle has been nothing but kind to you, Daisy. And Ruthie and her husband have done nothing except buy their dream farm. Sorry, but you need to get over your disappointment and move on."

"I know I do." What she didn't want to share was that she was starting to realize that Kyle wasn't making her feel angry and disappointed. He was making her feel the opposite things. Sometimes, when he looked at her, she felt a little tremor of anticipation. A nervous, excited jitter.

Which she'd never felt in her life.

It was embarrassing.

Oblivious to the direction of her thoughts, Lukas said, "Ruthie even brought over an apple pie." He smiled. "It looks tasty."

Yep. There was longing in his voice. "I suppose that no one is going to eat a slice unless I am there?" she joked.

"You supposed right." He bent down and handed her the crutches.

She slowly got to her feet, pleased that she was no longer huffing and puffing as she attempted to get her bearings. "Let's get this over with, then." She held out a hand to grip his arm before grasping her crutches

Lukas stayed steady but all of the tender sympathy that he'd been showing her the last few days was long gone. "I meant it, Daisy. Don't embarrass Mamm by being rude. These folks are our neighbors."

A lump formed in her throat. "You are right. I'll stop all this feeling sorry for myself."

"I hope so. You have so many blessings that you have elected to be blind to. That feels like a shame, don't it?"

"*Jah*. It, ah, does indeed."

She felt near tears as Lukas helped her descend the steps. She hated making him feel ashamed, and he obviously had been feeling that way, since he'd felt the need to remind her not to embarrass their mother.

Daisy promised herself right then and there that she would finally stop focusing on herself and concentrate on the needs of other people. Lukas was right. She had started to take all her blessings for granted. That was a shameful way to live.

"At last," her mother said when Daisy and Lukas stepped into the living room. "I was beginning to wonder if your brother had to wake you up, Daisy."

Across the room, Kyle's eyes widened.

"I wasn't asleep. But, um, I, ah, had to fix my hair," she fibbed. "Please forgive me for making all of you wait."

Standing up, Ruthie shook her head. "No need for apologies. I'm glad you are feeling up for visitors."

"I was just telling Lukas that I feel sure that I am feeling much better every day. Thank you for your concern."

"Come sit down. Do you like apple pie? I hope so. It's fresh. I made it this morning."

"I don't know anyone who doesn't like apple pie," Lukas said after he helped Daisy sit back down. Reaching out a hand, he shook Kyle's. "Good to see you again."

"Same to you." Turning to Daisy, Kyle added, "You are looking very well, Daisy."

"*Danke*."

"I think yellow must be your color," Ruthie added.

"With a name like Daisy, I hope it is," she joked.

Looking pleased with Daisy's good manners and smile, her mother started slicing the pie. "I was just telling Ruthie and Kyle that I hope they'll attend the county fair that's coming up."

"Do you think your cast will be off by then?" Kyle asked.

"It's supposed to. Do you enjoy going to fairs?"

"I do. We went to the Holmes County when I was young. It was easy because it was in Millersburg. The one in our county in Kentucky wasn't near as easy to get to."

"I like them, too. Ours is far smaller than the Holmes County fair, but it's still a lot of fun." She grinned at her mother. "When I was younger, I used to whine and say that I wanted to enter all the contests. I didn't understand that it wasn't our way to not do such things."

"I imagine you aren't the only Amish girl to yearn to enter a pie or pickles."

Lukas laughed. "Our Daisy wasn't interested in baking pies. She always wanted to enter a calf in the fair."

Her mother's lips twitched. "Or a chicken. Or a goat . . . even though we don't keep goats."

"I fear they are right." Though she tried not to be embarrassed about her interests, she'd been poked fun about by more than one girl, growing up. "I fear I've always enjoyed spending time in the barn. I like animals and enjoy raising them."

"There's nothing wrong with that, dear." Ruthie looked from Kyle to her. "Since Kyle doesn't know too many people around here yet, perhaps the two of you could go together."

Alarmed, Daisy caught Kyle's eye.

He looked just as alarmed as she felt. *I'm sorry,* he mouthed.

Which made her feel amused all over again.

"Daisy, what do you think about that idea?" her mother prompted.

"I think that I'd like that very much." She pointed to her leg in its bright pink cast. "I mean, as long as I can get around okay."

"That will be something to look forward to, ain't so?" Ruthie asked.

"Indeed."

"Almost as much as this first bite of pie," Lukas murmured, reminding them all that a mouthwatering slice was resting in front of each of them.

Bending their heads, they silently gave thanks for the food.

Daisy also took the time to give thanks for her brother's not-so-gentle reminder to look for the many blessings in life.

She hadn't had to look far at all.

All she'd had to do was open her eyes.

CHAPTER 8

"Well now, that was a nice visit, wasn't it?" Mamm asked Daisy after they said goodbye to their visitors and walked into the kitchen.

"It was," she replied. "It was kind of them to pay us a call."

While her mother helped her get settled at the kitchen table, Lukas helped bring in the dishes from the dining room and then headed back outside.

"You smiled more than once," she said as she began hand-washing the dishes. "That was good to see."

"*Danke*, Mamm. But it wasn't hard to be pleasant. Both Kyle and Ruthie are friendly and easy to talk to."

"Are you upset with me for mentioning the county fair?" she asked as she placed several wet plates on the towel next to Daisy.

From her seat, as she picked one up and began to dry it, she tried her best not to burst into laughter. "Mamm, you're going to ask me that now? It's a little late, don't you think?"

"Possibly."

Putting down the dish she'd been drying, Daisy craned her head to get a better look at her mother. She was glad to see that she looked slightly guilty. "You know there was no other way for me to respond than to say that I'd be happy to go to the fair with Kyle."

"I suppose I did put you on the spot."

Daisy felt it had been a bit more than that. "It felt a little bit like a trap."

"It wasn't. But I do think you two could be friends. I mean, one canna have too many friends, ain't so?"

"*Jah.*" Privately, Daisy thought that in another time and in another life, there might have been the chance for her and Kyle to be something more than just friends. She found him attractive and he was nice. She'd always hoped that her future husband would be a kind person.

Even better, she and Kyle liked a lot of the same things. She'd loved being a farmer's daughter and she'd always hoped to be a farmer's wife. And sure, she wanted to work on the land and help her husband create something wonderful with the Lord's help. But she'd also wanted to have a good, solid relationship with a man who she loved.

That didn't seem to be too much to ask at all.

But no matter how much she might wish that she and he could be a couple, it wasn't possible. She didn't have a lot to offer a man at the moment . . . and he was only staying for a year.

"I can't help but wonder why he hasn't already been snapped up."

"There's no telling." It also wasn't any of their business.

Her mother waggled her eyebrows as she brought over the pitcher she'd put out for cream. "Maybe Kyle has a tragic past."

"Mamm, you've been reading too many novels."

"It's a common thread in stories, though." She took a seat

at the table next to her. "In stories and in life. Everyone has been through something, and those experiences shape us all. Sometimes for the worse, and sometimes for the better."

"I can't argue with that."

"I'm pleased to hear you say that, Daisy."

"And, uh. Let's not forget that Ben is about Kyle's age and Lukas is three years older than him, and they aren't married."

"I suppose." Mamm frowned for a second before smiling at her again. "Daisy, dear, it might be too soon for you to see it but I think one day you're going to be glad that you weren't able to buy that land."

Boy, that stung. She knew her mother meant well . . . but yes, it was too soon to put this new spin on her disappointment.

She also kind of hated that her mother was choosing to ignore all the sacrifices Daisy had made in order to save the money that she had. She'd not only worked at the bulk food store, but she'd done all sorts of odd jobs here and there to make an extra hundred bucks. She'd even cleaned houses and babysat children.

"Mother, please don't tell me that this broken leg of mine is going to be something that I'll be grateful for one day, too."

"All right. I won't." She reached for Daisy's hand and put it between her own.

Like always, her mother's strong, slightly rough hands felt as comforting as a soft quilt on a winter's day. Her mother had three children, had been a good wife to their *daed*, and somehow made a warm, meaningful life for them all. Through it all, Daisy could never recall her mother ever being negative or admitting that she wished she'd been able to do more things.

Mamm had certainly never complained when the weather had been bad and their crops weren't as successful as in other years.

"I sure have a lot to learn from you, Mamm."

"Oh? What about?"

"Life."

"Is that all?" she teased.

"I was just thinking that you seem to take everything in stride. Both the good and the bad. I need to be more like you."

"May I tell you a secret?"

"Of course."

"I've had plenty of moments when I've been frustrated or disappointed. Sometimes, when a cow was sick or a horse fell lame or when you or your brothers were sick, I spent many an evening wishing things were different." She took a deep breath. "But that is what prayer is for."

CHAPTER 9

Lila was a good friend. She had a sunny disposition, was thoughtful, and only one year older than Daisy. From the moment Lila's family moved into their church district when she was in the fifth grade, they'd become close friends.

Every other Sunday, Daisy would look forward to sitting next to her at church. They'd catch up on each other's lives, joke about some of the same people they found amusing, and even trade recipes or names of books that they'd checked out at the library.

Daisy was grateful for Lila's presence in her life, especially since she'd drifted away from so many of her other girlfriends.

It had started when she was in the seventh and eighth grade. Even at that young age, some of the girls were already flirting with the boys in their school. After their eighth grade graduation, most would enter into rumspringa, and some of the girls wanted to be dating during it.

Daisy hadn't wanted anything to do with that.

By the time they were all in their late teens, many of the

girls were either being courted or were getting engaged. When Daisy was still spending most of her extra time in barns, some of the girls started making fun of her.

As the years passed and Daisy still wasn't interested in courting, marriage, and babies as much as farming her own piece of land, her former friends had fallen by the wayside.

Now when they ran into each other at the store or at a restaurant in town, the conversations were cordial but felt a bit empty.

At first, Daisy had been upset by the changes. Then her mother had gently taken her aside and explained that such things were only natural. Those girls were now married women. Their lives were filled with tales about their husbands and managing their own homes. As the years passed, pregnancies and babies consumed their lives. There was only so much one could talk about to a woman like Daisy, who was still living at home and didn't seem to have any interest in the things that consumed them.

She could absolutely see their point of view.

The distance that had grown between them had still hurt though, especially when she'd worked for Melissa, had hated her job, and was dreaming about improvements she'd make to the farm next door.

Lila didn't seem to care about their differences, though. She often whispered to Daisy that they were kindred spirits, which was a reference to Anne of Green Gables.

Daisy wasn't certain if they were that or not. All she did know was that Lila was the type of good friend to come over as soon as she'd heard about the accident.

Lila's auburn hair, blue eyes, and pretty smile were a sight for sore eyes.

"I'm so glad to see you."

"I feel the same way!" Lila exclaimed as she crossed the room to take a seat by her side. "I've been so worried about you. I can't believe you hurt yourself so badly on an electric bicycle."

"I wish I hadn't."

She squeezed Daisy's hand. "We prayed for you the whole time you were in the hospital."

"*Danke*."

"No thanks is needed. I was concerned about you. Truly, I couldn't believe it when Brandt told me about your accident."

"Your husband told you?"

"Oh, *jah*. He was at the feed store and crossed paths with your brother Lukas. He filled my Brandt in. I must say, we were so shocked about what happened to you." Reaching out, she clasped Daisy's hand. "It's a blessing that you weren't hurt worse than you were."

"I agree. I am grateful."

Scanning her from head to toe, she added, "How are you feeling, really?"

Daisy chuckled. "Really? Did you think I would lie to you?"

"I think you are going to put a good face on a scary experience. So come now, be honest."

"To be honest, I'm still sore."

"That's too bad. I thought that maybe your leg would be feeling better since it was encased in that cast."

"It doesn't hurt too badly, but my body has a lot of bruises still. And my ribs are paining me something awful."

Her blue eyes widened. "You hurt your ribs, too?"

"*Jah*. I have two fractured ribs."

"And a concussion, *jah*?"

"*Jah*. My concussion was minor, though. It is much better." Honestly, a lot of her aches and pains were from the way her body was attempting to adjust to her injuries. Sometimes she wasn't sure if she would ever stand straight and tall ever again. Though, of course she would. She just needed time.

Hating that their conversation was centered around her injuries, Daisy said, "Let's not talk about me anymore. Tell me about you."

A shadow filled Lila's eyes before her smile returned. "Nothing with me is of consequence."

"Are you sure? My leg might be broken but the rest of me is in pretty good working order. I'm happy to listen."

Lila peeked toward the door. After obviously checking to make sure that they were alone, she said, "Both my mother and my mother-in-law want me to go to the *doktah* because I'm still not pregnant after two years of marriage."

Daisy blinked. And for maybe the first time, she realized that there was a reason that she didn't have a lot to say to her old girlfriends. She had no idea about the topic.

But that didn't mean she couldn't commiserate on feeling pressured by family members. "I'm sorry they are getting involved in your business."

Relief shined bright in Lila's eyes. "This is why I knew that we were going to be lifelong friends, Daisy. Even though you haven't had to think about such things, that is what it has boiled down to. Our parents are sticking their noses into something that isn't their business."

"What does Brandt think?"

"Oh, Brandt thinks the same as I do. He hates that something so personal is talked about at the supper table."

"I am sorry for that. But at least you have your husband's complete support."

Lila nodded, but she still looked troubled.

Making Daisy realize that there was still more to their story. "Lila, is there something more?"

"Oh, Daisy." Lila's bottom lip trembled before she visibly pulled herself together. "The truth is that I'm not sure what to do anymore." After glancing around her again, she whispered, "Sometimes I think Brandt agrees that there must be something wrong with me."

She was shocked. Of course she wanted to defend Lila and tell her that she was perfect. But there was some truth to the statement. The newspapers were filled with stories of people discovering diseases and tumors and such that they'd had no idea they had.

"Forgive me if this is too personal, but why don't you want to see a doctor?"

"Because I don't want to know the answer." She looked away. "If they do find something is wrong, I'm going to be devastated. I mean, what if I can't have a baby?"

"Lila, there are a great many things in between 'you are perfectly fine' and 'you can't have a baby.' There's a good chance that you won't get a diagnosis like that. Don't you think? I mean, shouldn't one always try to look on the bright side of things?"

Lila shrugged. "I don't know. At this point, I'm confused about a lot of things. I'm also worried that there might be nothing wrong with me."

"But that would be wonderful-*gut*, *jah*?"

"Not if the problem lies with Brandt." She looked away.

"I know you don't want anything to be wrong with him either. But doesn't that mean he should be excited to get checked?"

"One would think so." She sighed. "I can tell you right now that my husband is not going to want to do that visit."

"I see." Well, she didn't, but what could she say? She felt as if she and Lila were going around in circles and that maybe her girlfriend would rather do that instead of reach a resolution.

"If you do, then you must see why I don't want to do anything. Besides, it's only been two years. And it wasn't like we were really trying at first," she said in a rush. "I think it would be best for the Lord to tell us what to do."

Daisy privately thought that the Lord was telling them to go to the doctor, but she sure wasn't going to say that. "I hope things get better soon."

"*Jah*. Me too." She slumped.

Daisy's heart went out to her. It was obvious that she'd come over for answers and was disappointed not to receive any. "What a pair we are!" Daisy teased. "We're sure a lot different than the two women we used to know back at the Amish school."

"You're right. Back then all we had to worry about were passing quizzes, spelling tests, and getting the boys to notice us."

"You might have been worried about the boys. I was just trying to pass those spelling tests."

"You always were such a bad speller. Are you any better now?"

"I don't know. Probably not." Realizing that she'd long ago accepted the fact that she was never going to suddenly easily spell most countries in the world, or even simple words like "niece" or "people," Daisy shrugged. "It doesn't matter too much to me anymore. I learned to keep a dictionary by my side if I have the need to write a letter to someone."

"Good point. With hardship comes adaptation."

"*Jah*. It's all right, though. My mother has been reminding me that it's better to focus on one's blessings than one's disappointments."

"That's a good point." A sparkle lit Lila's expression. "You are very right. After all, I did get Brandt, and he is wonderful almost all of the time. Plus, we have our own *haus*. It's cozy and cute."

"Yeah, you could be me. I not only am still living in my

childhood bedroom, I have no job, no man, and a cast on my leg." She'd meant for Lila to laugh at her joke.

But Lila wasn't giggling.

Actually, she looked rather happy that she wasn't Daisy Lapp. "You're right," Lila whispered as she leaned over and clasped Daisy's hand. "My situation could be worse. Much, much worse. Thanks for the reminder."

"Anytime." She smiled slightly, hoping the smile eased some of the sarcasm in her tone.

Lila didn't seem to notice, though. She'd simply smiled, too, and began to talk about a vacation to Niagara Falls that she and Brandt had just booked.

Long after Lila left, Daisy realized that her momentary reprieve from her blue mood had ended.

Once again she was re-examining her life, and what she saw gave her no peace of mind. Something needed to change.

CHAPTER 10

The most unexpected thing had happened just when Kyle had thought nothing else could take him by surprise. He'd met Winter Walker. He'd been walking through downtown Walden, trying to think of something to do on his afternoon off, when he'd practically run into her.

He'd been looking in the window of the hardware store, fascinated by the fancy egg-shaped grills that cost a small fortune but seemed to be mighty popular, when he knocked into the beautiful brunette.

Of course he'd immediately apologized. "I'm so sorry. Are you all right?"

"*Jah*. I mean, I think so." She stared up at him with a pair of luminescent eyes the color of Lake Erie in the winter. A stormy, pale blue. They were the perfect contrast to her raven-black hair and ethereal temperament. She looked like a perfect angel.

Then her words registered. "You think so?" Had he knocked into her that hard? Before he realized what he was doing, he'd taken her elbow and guided her to a wooden bench that had recently been painted a deep forest green. "Here. Take a moment and get your bearings."

"Only if you sit with me while I do it."

He would've thought she was flirting if she didn't look so innocent and fragile. He sat down, of course. "Since I practically ran over you, I should probably tell you my name. I'm Kyle."

"I'm Winter."

"That's a pretty name." It was most unusual, too. Though, as he gazed at her, he had to admit that the name suited her. Her dark hair, pale skin, and icy-blue eyes did make him think of chilly, snowy mornings in January.

Her eyelashes fluttered. "Do you really think so? Sometimes I wish I had a more traditional, common name."

"If you had that, then your name wouldn't suit you as much." He meant it, too. She was unusually pretty. It was on the tip of his tongue to share that he thought she was the opposite of most other women he'd met, but he stopped himself just in time. She was so sweet, such earnest words would likely scare her away.

Winter blinked, then smiled softly. "*Danke.*"

"You're welcome, but I'm only speaking the truth."

"Are you new here or just visiting?"

"I recently moved here from Kentucky. I live in Hart County, where Mammoth Cave is. Have you heard of that?"

"I have." Her eyebrows lifted. "That's so far away."

"It is, but not as far as other places." The moment the words left his mouth, he wished he could snatch them back. Could he have uttered anything more inane? Kyle darted a glance her way, but to his relief, nothing showed in her expression but interest.

"This area isn't completely foreign to me, though. I was born in Millersburg. I lived there until it was time to start school."

"What brought you here? A job?"

"*Jah*. I had kept in touch with a guy from here. Long story, but his parents recently bought a farm in the area and needed a helping hand. I offered to move here and help them for a while."

"That's so generous of you."

He'd never thought of it that way, especially since they were paying him a good salary. He shrugged off the comment. "They are good people. I'm glad to help."

"What is the name of the family?" She blushed. "I mean, if you don't mind sharing."

Had he ever met a sweeter woman? He couldn't remember if he had. "They're the Millers. Mervin and Ruthie Miller. They recently bought the Burkholders' old property."

The faintest of lines appeared in-between her eyebrows. "I haven't met the Millers yet."

"They are nice folks. Good people."

"I hope you are finding our community to be welcoming?"

"To be sure. I met the Lapp family. They live next door."

"Oh, *jah*. I suppose you would be living next to the Lapps."

"Do you know them? Daisy Lapp is just about your age."

"*Jah*, I know Daisy. Didn't she just break her leg or something?"

Winter's new expression took him slightly off guard. If she wasn't so sweet and innocent, Kyle would have sworn it was a smirk.

"*Jah*," he said. "She hurt herself on a bicycle."

"Oh, yes." She nodded. "I remember now. She was riding one of those newfangled electric bikes."

"You don't sound as if you are a fan of them."

"I'm not, but then again, I'm not Daisy."

Kyle was beginning to suspect that Winter was going out of her way to make him think less of Daisy. "I don't know what you mean."

"Well, I'm sure you haven't gotten to know her yet, but she's something of a tomboy." She wrinkled her nose. "A little rough around the edges."

"I didn't find her to be like that." Sure, Daisy had a bit of fire and snap to her personality, but he wouldn't describe her as a tomboy.

She pressed three fingers to his forearm. "Please forgive me if you thought I sounded unkind. There's nothing wrong with being . . . different, is there?"

"I never thought so."

Winter's expression eased. It was as if she'd been so disturbed that he might have taken what she said as hurtful that it had truly worried her.

Once again Kyle felt drawn to her. She was so shy and good, he realized that he needed to only act proper around her. His mother would be embarrassed if he didn't give a woman like Winter the respect she deserved. "Winter, I should let you go. That is, if you are feeling better now?"

"Oh yes. I am feeling much better. Thank you so much for sitting with me. I hope I didn't ruin your day?"

"Not at all." Taking a chance, he lowered his voice. "Forgive me if this is presumptuous, but do you have a beau?"

"*Nee.*"

"I'm shocked. I would've thought a woman as lovely as you would've been snatched up."

"Oh. Well, I was in a relationship, but we broke up."

"I'm sorry."

"Me too, but I suppose it's best that I found out his true colors before we got engaged."

That was what had happened to him and Mary. "Something similar happened to me," he said quietly.

"Then you understand how I'm feeling." Her bottom lip trembled.

His heart went out to her. Winter had been heartbroken, too. No wonder she was so shy and fragile. "Winter, would you be opposed to me calling on you one evening soon? Or perhaps we could take a walk together?"

"I wouldn't be opposed at all, but we'll need to be at my house. My parents like me to be chaperoned."

He was a bit surprised by that. Usually, most women ceased needing a chaperone by the time they were twenty-one. But of course, most women were not her. "I would expect nothing less," he said. He hoped he sounded reassuring and not corny. If his sister, Sarah, could hear him, she'd be giggling up a storm.

"I hope to see you again soon. Maybe even on Wednesday night?"

"*Jah*. Sure," he replied, a bit taken aback by her setting the date. But it was obvious that she didn't have a lot of experience with men. "Wednesday is fine."

She exhaled.

It was adorable. Just like she'd been holding her breath on the off chance that he would tell her that Wednesday night wasn't acceptable for him.

He stood up. "I'll look forward to calling on you soon, Winter."

Instead of rising as well, she held out her hand. Obviously she needed help getting to her feet. As he carefully gripped her slim, pale hand, he noticed that the faint scent of rose shimmered around her and her palm was smooth and soft.

It was as if it had never done a day's hard work. Which was ridiculous, since she was Amish. He didn't know of any Amish man or woman who hadn't been taught the value of a full day's work from the time they could walk.

"*Danke*," she whispered.

He tipped the brim of his hat. "I wish you a good day."

"Ah, Kyle?"

"Yes?"

"Aren't you forgetting something?"

"I'm sorry, what?"

"You didn't ask me my last name or my address."

She was right. It was a wonder that she still was giving him the time of day. First, he'd run into her and now he hadn't even taken the time to ask her for the most basic of information. "Forgive me, I assumed that everyone around here would know you."

She blushed again. Her chin lifted slightly. "I imagine they might. I mean, because I've lived here for so long. But if you are still interested, my last name is Walker, and we live on Cherry Hollow Lane."

"Winter Walker, of Cherry Hollow Lane. I won't forget that."

She smiled at him, then. A perfectly lovely smile. So much so, that he gaped at her for a split second. Startled by her beauty.

Then she turned away and headed down the street. Walking much more quickly than he'd anticipated.

Not wanting her to catch him staring at her retreating form, he walked into the hardware store to take another look at the green egg grill.

"May I help you, young man?" the owner asked.

"*Nee*. I'm just looking."

"If you change your mind, please let me know."

"I will, *danke*."

As he stared at the grills, he realized that he could've been staring at a wasp nest and it wouldn't matter. All he could seem to think about was Winter Walker.

And how very different she was from any woman he'd ever met.

Especially Daisy Lapp.

CHAPTER 11

"You've been quiet all supper, Kyle," Mervin said when Ruthie stood up to bring them slices of chocolate cake for dessert. "Did you not have a good afternoon off?"

"No, I did." Unable to help himself, he smiled. "It was a very good afternoon."

"Oh? What did you do? Did ya end up going over to the hardware store to check out the grills like you mentioned you might?"

Kyle couldn't believe that Mervin had zeroed in on the one place that he couldn't seem to stop thinking about. "I did go there. As a matter of fact, it was my visit there that I can't stop thinking about."

"It must have been some set of grills," Ruthie teased as she placed a thick slice of cake in front of him.

He laughed. "Oh *nee*. It wasn't the grills that caught my fancy, but something else. Or, rather someone else."

"That sounds mighty cryptic," Mervin said as he took his plate from Ruthie before she sat down with her own. "Well, don't keep us in suspense. Who did you see?"

"A woman. We ran into each other. Or, rather, I guess I ran into her, though I'm still not quite sure how that happened."

"Who is it?"

"I don't know if you know her. Her name is Winter. Winter Walker."

Mervin frowned. "Is she Amish?"

"*Jah*. I guess that means you don't know her?"

"I don't, but I haven't met too many folks outside of our church district. Have you heard of her, Ruthie?"

"That name does sound familiar, but I can't place her. What was she like?"

"She's beautiful. She's got dark hair, pale, creamy skin, and the most unusual eyes I've ever seen. They're a cross between silver and blue."

"Her looks sound as if they're as unusual as her name," Ruthie said.

"But she's so much more than that. She's as sweet and innocent as any woman I've ever met." He chuckled softly, remembering how she'd held out her hand for him to help her stand up. "After I ran into her, she needed to sit down and recover."

Mervin frowned. "What did you do to her, son?"

"Nothing. I think she was just extremely shaken up. Or maybe she's just more tender than most women? Anyway, I sat down on the bench next to her and we started talking. She was so sweet."

"*Jah*, you mentioned that," Ruthie murmured. "It's a shame I don't know her."

"She knows Daisy, though. I think they attended the same Amish school."

"Oh, so you can learn more about her from Daisy."

Remembering how Winter's expression pinched slightly when he brought up Daisy's name, Kyle figured that their neighbor might not be the best source of information. "I suppose I could ask Daisy, but they're nothing alike. She might not have much to tell me about someone like Winter."

Ruthie put down her fork. "What do you mean? Daisy is a nice young woman. I'm sure she has a lot of friends. She's pretty, too."

Kyle smiled at Ruthie. As usual, the woman was determined to champion their new neighbor, just as she'd always been happy to champion him when he and Aaron had been teenagers.

Not wanting to hurt her feelings but still be completely honest, he weighed each word carefully. "*Jah*, Daisy is nice. But like I said, she's very different than Winter. Plus, Winter didn't sound as if she got along with Daisy very well. I don't think they're close."

Mervin sipped his coffee as he leaned back and crossed his legs. "It sounds as if you discovered a lot about this young woman in a short amount of time."

"I did learn a lot about Winter, but it's more than that." He waved a hand. "All I'm saying is that Daisy is strong. Strong willed and hardy."

Ruthie's eyebrows lifted. "Hardy?"

"*Jah*. Sure. I mean, she can practically plow a field. I mean, she could if she were a little bit stronger." Chuckling softly, he added, "I can't even imagine Winter being able to walk across a large field, let alone do any work in it."

"If she's that tender, she must be sickly," Ruthie murmured.

"Or special." He flushed. He sounded as moony as a teenager.

Ruthie speared a bite of cake. "She sure seems special to you."

There was no mistaking the thin veil of sarcasm in her voice. Kyle didn't take offense to it as he took a bite of cake.

"I know that I'm making her sound perfect. I'm sure she isn't. I can't help myself, though. She made an impression on me."

"You sound smitten," Mervin said.

"Perhaps I am."

"In that case, I hope you run into her again," he joked.

"It's better than that. She gave me permission to call on her."

Ruthie blinked. "Really?"

"Why does that surprise you?"

"I don't know Winter. Obviously, I do not. But most young ladies who seem to be as uh . . . innocent and frail as this young woman is, usually have to wait for their parents to agree to a man calling at her *haus*. That means they would have to know him, have a conversation . . ."

Mervin nodded. "She's right. Our Aaron had to go through quite a few hoops with Hanna's family before they allowed them to sit together after church. We supported their decision, too. I must have told Aaron five times that if Hanna was worth it, then he wouldn't mind doing whatever her family wanted, to make sure she felt happy and secure."

Kyle was surprised. "Aaron never told me that."

Ruthie shared a smile with Mervin. "That's likely because Aaron was completely focused on Hanna. All he ever said when Mervin told him to honor her parents was that he was glad she was so protected. Aaron figured if he couldn't call on Hanna without a chaperone, then no one else could either."

"Well, maybe things are different in the Walker household. She said that her parents would chaperone my visit when I go on Wednesday."

"Wednesday's not too far away."

"I know. I'm excited."

"I hope it goes well."

Mervin was acting like his fascination with Winter was wrong, which made Kyle uncomfortable. "I hope so, too. Well, I know our meeting seems odd, but I am glad that our meeting was unexpected. Honestly, I think the Lord meant for me and Winter to meet. She's all I can seem to think about."

Mervin's eyes widened. "She must be quite the beauty."

"She is beautiful, but she was more than that. She was sweet and innocent. All I've been thinking about is our conversation in front of the hardware store. Do you think tomorrow makes me seem too eager?"

"*Jah*," Mervin said.

"I agree," Ruthie said. "Also, I think it might be a good idea if you asked someone about Winter. You need to get more information."

"Why?"

"No reason," she said slowly. "Well, no reason other than the fact that I'd hate for you to fall head over heels for a woman who might not be everything she seems."

Kyle didn't agree. He felt so protective of Winter already, he even resented the idea that Ruthie and Mervin might not agree that she was perfect for him. But the Millers were his employers, not his parents. And, waiting a week would probably be the best idea anyway. Some of the women he'd called on in Kentucky had been very different sitting in their living rooms than when they were at a Sunday night singing with all their friends.

"Thanks for the advice. I appreciate it."

Looking relieved, Ruthie patted his arm. "I'm glad you aren't upset with us, Kyle. To be sure, we're not your parents, but I canna help but think if Anna Kate and Levi were sitting at this table, they'd tell you the same thing."

"*Mei mamm* is fond of saying that patience is a virtue."

Ruthie winked. "She's right. Give this conversation with

Winter a few days to percolate. Why, I bet her parents are saying the same thing to her!"

"*Jah*. I reckon you are right." Feeling better, he picked up his fork again while Mervin and Ruthie stood up.

Sitting in the silence, he imagined Winter telling her parents all about him. He was sure she'd felt the same connection he had.

No doubt they were also advising her to be patient. After all, future happiness was always worth it.

CHAPTER 12

Church was at Lila's parents' *haus* on Sunday. As usual, they hosted the service in their barn. Because there was no chance of rain in the forecast, they'd elected to serve lunch on the driveway.

Tables were set up on the grass near the drive, in the barn, and on the Troyers' back patio. Like most everyone did, Jenna and Burke had taken special care with their lawn. The grass was lush and green, every flower bed was freshly mulched, and a wide variety of tulips, daffodils, and pansies were blooming.

The yard looked as beautiful as Daisy had ever seen it, and she made sure to tell Lila's parents that.

"*Danke*," Jenna said. "Our weekend snuck up on us, but now we are going to be able to enjoy the fruits of our labor."

"I'm sorry I wasn't able to help you."

"Please don't worry about that. Lila told us about your accident." Frowning, Jenna added, "It's a miracle you weren't injured worse."

"My parents said the same thing."

"We're on our way over to sit with them," Mr. Troyer said. "Would you like to join us?"

"Thanks, but I'm going to say hello to some other people first."

Jenna smiled. "Enjoy your day, dear. Come over one day soon when you are feeling better. With or without Lila."

"*Danke*. I will."

When the couple turned away, Daisy worked her way over to where Ruthie and Mervin Miller were sitting with Kyle.

She felt a happy little adrenaline rush at the thought of spending more time with him. He was so handsome and kind.

Once again, Kyle was wearing a blue long-sleeved shirt and gray pants. Today, though, he'd switched to a straw hat instead of his usual black felt one. She thought the straw hat looked nice with his tan and blond hair.

Kyle stood up when she approached. "You are sure getting around pretty good on your crutches now."

"They're getting easier, that's for sure and for certain," she said with a laugh. "May I join you?"

"Of course, dear," Ruthie said. "Kyle, help Daisy with her chair."

He dutifully pulled out the fold-up chair and held it steady as she lowered herself onto the seat. Then, he even went so far as to take her crutches from her and lean them against his chair.

"There's no need to do that," she protested. "They can go on the ground."

"I was about to get going before you got here." He folded his hands behind his back. "I hope you are feeling much better?"

He sounded so formal. She wasn't sure if it was because he

was with the Millers, at church . . . or if it was for another reason?

Realizing that she was thinking too hard, she said, “I am. Almost all of my bruises and cuts have faded and the doctor says my leg is healing nicely.”

“Are you following his directions?” He stared at her intently.

“Of course.” Curious, she tilted her head to one side. “Why would you think I wouldn’t?”

“No reason.”

“Well, how are you? I haven’t seen you in over a week.”

“I’ve been good. Busy.” Kyle’s voice sounded distant. Not unkind, but so different than how he’d sounded when she’d first gotten home from the hospital.

Hoping to get him out of his shell, she said, “How is your plowing going?”

“It’s *gut*. Hot, but that is to be expected.” Before Daisy could comment on that, he turned to Ruthie. “I’ll be back at the farm by supper.”

“This is your day of rest. Enjoy it. I’ll leave a plate for you in the refrigerator if you aren’t home when we eat.”

“*Danke*.”

“Have a good afternoon, Kyle,” Daisy called out quickly.

“*Danke*. You too.”

Kyle had been acting like he couldn’t wait to get away from her. But surely that wasn’t the case? She turned to the Millers. “Where is he going off to in such a hurry?”

“Any number of places, I’m guessin’,” Mervin joked. “Ruthie, let me know when you’re ready to go. I’m gonna go sit with Henry Troyer for a spell.”

“Sounds *gut*.”

As she watched Mervin head over to the men on the back patio, Daisy felt embarrassed. “Gosh, I feel like I just ran off your men.”

"Not at all. Mervin enjoys fellowship with the other men, and a day off work for Kyle is a rarity right now. The fields have kept him plenty busy."

"I guess so."

"To be honest, I'm rather pleased that they left. I was hoping I could speak with you about something." She looked around the area. "Or are you getting ready to leave as well?"

"Not yet. Sometimes I leave early with Ben or Lukas, but both of them had plans today. I'm all yours," she joked. Unbidden, Daisy thought about Kyle again. Maybe Ruthie knew something special about him that she wanted to share?

"I'm glad about that. Daisy, more than one person has told me that you're good with animals."

"I do like animals. That's true."

"As you might imagine, I've been discovering that life with farm animals is much different than only seeing them at other people's farms from time to time."

"Indeed it is."

"I am comfortable with Lizzie. She's our basset hound, you know. But there's another animal that has kept me up worrying quite a bit. I need some advice."

"Of course. What's going on?"

"It's Velvet. Our dairy cow." Ruthie frowned. "Do you have much experience working with cows?"

"No more than most other girls who've had to milk in the morning. But I'll be glad to talk to you about her. What's going on?"

"I think Velvet is having a difficult adjustment after the Burkholders left."

"What do you mean?"

"She seems listless. Plus, she won't hardly look at me." Ruthie leaned forward. "I know, I know, she's a cow. But . . . I saw how she was with Rachel Burkholder. That cow practically glowed when she spied Rachel. It was obvious that she liked Rachel very much."

"Let me guess. Velvet isn't glowing whenever you walk in the barn?"

"Nope. She's not glowing even a little bit."

Glad to be concentrating on something that she could help with, Daisy asked, "What about her milk? Is she producing much?"

"Some, but not as much as she did when we first arrived." Looking more worried, Ruthie added, "At first I thought I was imagining things, but when I asked Kyle what he thought, he agreed."

"Anything else?"

"*Jah*." Looking completely serious, Ruthie whispered, "Velvet has also been kind of mooing. What do you think that means?"

Daisy couldn't help but chuckle. "Cows are supposed to moo, ain't so?"

"Of course they are, but this is different. Daisy, this isn't a happy moo. It's a mournful-sounding one. I'm beginning to be very worried about Velvet."

"Maybe she's sick? Is Mervin worried, too? And what has Kyle said? What did he suggest when he agreed about Velvet's milk production?"

"Well, you see, that's where I'm stuck. Neither of the men want to call a veterinarian yet. Vet calls can be very expensive, you know." She shrugged. "I do think Kyle wishes he could help, but he's been busy with the fields and planting." She bit her lip before lowering her voice. "And supervising Mervin, I'm afraid."

Daisy covered her mouth so Ruthie wouldn't see that she almost smiled. "Why does Mervin need to be supervised?"

The frown lines around Ruthie's eyes seemed to deepen.

"Here's the thing, Daisy. I fear that Mervin isn't enjoying farm life as much as he thought."

"I'm sorry."

"*Jah*, me too." Lowering her voice, she added, "Sometimes I am afraid that neither of us are enjoying farm life as much as we thought."

"Farming is hard work. Very hard."

"It's more than that. It's that there are no days off. It's expensive. Plus, we're both nervous nellies around here. We don't want to do the wrong thing so sometimes we wait too long and then don't do anything."

"I'm sorry."

"Daisy, does hearing this make you angry?"

"What? Not at all."

"Are ya sure?" She averted her eyes. "Of course, we had no idea, but since we've moved in, we've learned that it is well-known that you've been saving for a long time to buy the farm. That is true, isn't it?"

"It is. I had hoped to buy the Burkholders' place."

"And now here we are, having all sorts of trouble with it. Why, I wouldn't blame you if you were upset about Mervin and me not doing as well as we'd hoped we would."

"I'm not upset." When Ruthie still didn't look as if she believed her, Daisy confessed something of her own. "If I'm being honest, you are right. I was. But lately, I've been wondering if there might be something to that saying about unanswered prayers."

" 'More tears have been shed over answered prayers than unanswered ones,' " Ruthie murmured.

Feeling bad about Ruthie's dilemma, Daisy said, "I don't know if I can be of much help with Velvet, but I'll be happy to help. I could stop by whenever you'd like."

"Would it be too much trouble to ask you to come over this afternoon?"

"Well . . ."

"I know this is pushy, but Velvet does seem to be in a state, and we have our buggy. Mervin and I would be pleased to drive you to our house and then back to your home afterward. Please?" she asked again. "Mervin was joking about selling Velvet if she doesn't begin producing milk like we expected, and you know what happens to dairy cows who aren't good milkers."

They were butchered and used another way.

Tears pricked her eyes, not because she had a strong attachment to Velvet, she didn't at all. But because Ruthie cared so much. She didn't want to give up on an animal that might be simply going through a difficult time.

Like she was. Like Ruthie was. Like Lila.

Like maybe most everyone, from time to time.

Making the decision, she nodded. "I'll be happy to do that, Ruthie. Let me let my parents know what I'll be doing and then I'll meet you back here."

"You are a lifesaver, dear. *Danke*."

"Don't thank me yet. I'm not sure if I'll be able to do a thing to help her."

"If you're willing to try, then that is enough."

"I can certainly do that." She smiled as she stood up and adjusted the crutches underneath her arms.

An hour later, armed with a variety of fruits and vegetables from the Millers' kitchen and a cool glass of water for herself, Daisy sat down on a chair next to the stall.

Mervin had been first stunned then amused by his wife's concern for Velvet. He'd been agreeable enough about taking Daisy to their barn, however.

When they got there, he decided that it wouldn't do for Daisy to sit on a milking stool. She needed something with a back to help with her cast. Luckily, there was an old wooden chair in the tack room.

After he set her up and Ruthie brought out a variety of treats for Velvet, Daisy asked if they could leave her alone with the heifer for a while.

Velvet did not seem to be a fan of Ruthie. Her soft brown eyes kept glaring at Ruthie's crossed arms. Who could blame the cow, anyway? No one liked to be stared at.

Now that they were alone, Daisy reached for a banana. "Do you like fruit?" she asked as she peeled off a piece and held it toward Velvet's nose. "Want to give it a try?"

Velvet only gave her a side-eye before looking away.

"I don't blame ya," she murmured as she placed the piece back in the bucket. "I wouldn't take a snack from a stranger either."

Velvet seemed to snort in response.

"You know what? We should probably get better acquainted. Then neither of us will be so skittish around the other." Feeling silly but determined to forge ahead, Daisy folded her arms across her chest. "My name is Daisy. And *jah*. I know it's an unusual one, but I don't hate the name. What's more important is that I was once hoping that you would be my cow. What do you think about that?"

Velvet shifted but turned to look at her again.

"*Jah*. Long story there, but the fact of the matter is that I didn't have enough money to buy this farm and your new owners, Ruthie and Mervin, did. Plus, they have Kyle, who seems to know a lot about farming. I hate to tell you this, but you could do a lot worse than your current situation."

Warming into her one-sided conversation, Daisy continued. "I'm sorry to share that Ruthie is pretty worried about you. She thinks you might be depressed. To be honest, I didn't know cows could get depressed but then I started thinking that you might be lonely."

She cleared her throat. "Or maybe it was Ruthie who did. I'm here because I currently have too much time on my hands. You see, I bought myself one of those electric bikes and crashed when I'd only ridden it a few times."

Shifting a bit, she added, "Then, I lost my job because I wasn't going to be able to do the work I was hired to do." Realizing what she'd just said, Daisy smiled. "So, in a way, we have something in common, right? Each of us is acting a little bit off right now." She lifted her left leg. "So, here is my broken leg. What do you think of the cast? It's bright, right?"

Velvet blinked.

"*Jah*, I agree. I think it's too bright."

She took a breath. "Between you and me, if I ever have the opportunity to pick another color, I might choose white. I sure wish that's what I would've picked in the first place. I didn't because the nurse said that casts always get dirty, even when one is careful with them. I started thinking that the only thing worse than having a cast on my leg would be to have a big old gray cast. So, you see, Velvet, you might be missing Rachel Burkholder, but your life could be worse. I mean, at least you have four good legs to stand on, ain't so? I only have two and one of them is broken."

Velvet stepped closer.

She was closer!

Excited that her monologue might actually be working, she reached into the bucket again and this time pulled out half of an apple.

After steadying herself on the crutches, she stepped forward. "What do you think about apples?" She placed it in Velvet's feed trough.

Velvet watched her put the apple down, then bent her head and took a bite.

She took another bite, then slowly chewed, the way only a cow could seem to do.

Unable to help herself, Daisy reached through the slats of the stall and ran a hand along Velvet's neck.

The fur was coarse but not prickly. Velvet's muscles tensed under her hand, then appeared to relax as Daisy continued to pet her.

"What do you think, Velvet? Could we maybe be friends? For the record, I don't need anything from you. Not even your milk. It's like I told you. I like farms, I like cows, and I've got some time on my hands. I'd like to come over and visit you as much as I'm able. Would you like some company?"

Velvet turned back to look at her empty trough.

"*Jah*, okay. If I need to bribe you for your company, I can do that." Bending down, she carefully picked up both the piece of peeled banana and the other part, skin and all. "Want to give this another try?"

Velvet watched her, stepped back to the trough, and took a tentative bite of the banana peel.

Then she lifted her head. "Mooo!"

It was a mournful, maybe slightly irritated moo.

"All right. I get it. Banana peels aren't your thing. But good job for giving it a try, right? You know what everyone says, you have to try something in order to decide if you like it."

When she smiled at Velvet again, Daisy realized that this friendship thing with the cow was going to take a minute.

Because Velvet was currently pooping with her eyes closed. Then, she exhaled yet again.

"I'm not sure what you meant by that, but I suppose it's natural, huh? I've never walked through a field without having to dodge a cow patty or two." Or twenty.

"I think this is a good time for me to be on my way. See you soon, Velvet," she said as she set the bucket on the seat of the chair and then crutched her way out of the barn.

Mervin was sitting on the milking stool whittling. "All done, Daisy?"

"*Jah.*"

"What do you think? Have you made our cow happier?"

"Not yet. I'm sorry."

"Meh. I could be wrong, but I reckon cows are just like anything else . . . It takes them a bit to warm up."

Daisy decided not to give Mervin any details, especially the part when the milk cow seemed to let her know in no uncertain terms that she didn't care for either conversation or bananas.

"I told Velvet I'd come back soon. Is that okay with you?"

"*Jah*. Sure." He winked. "Ruthie is positive that I'm about to send that heifer to the butcher shop, but that ain't the case. I might not want to sit and chat with our cow, but I sure don't want to turn her into hamburger."

Even the idea of such a thing made Daisy cringe. "I'm relieved to hear that."

He smiled. "Let's get you on home. I reckon you're ready for a break."

"Thanks, Mervin."

He smiled as he walked by her side to the small buggy that was in their drive. Most folks would call it a courting buggy, but it was easy to maneuver and not near as heavy for a horse to pull. "This okay with you?"

"Of course."

He smiled. "I like you, Daisy Lapp. You're a good'un."

"*Danke*, Mervin. I try."

That was the last thing they said to each other as he drove her the rest of the way home.

Later, when she was supposedly reading a book on the back porch, Daisy realized that her visit with Velvet had relieved a bit of depression.

Maybe not for Velvet, but she felt a little bit lighter. She decided that she needed to have another heart-to-heart with the cow again.

CHAPTER 13

"Daisy, Kyle Hostetler is here to see you," her mother called from down the hall on Tuesday afternoon. "Do you need help with your crutches?"

"*Nee*, I've got it." Daisy rolled her eyes. She couldn't help but be amused that no one in her family was questioning if she wanted to see him. His welcome was now seen as an obvious choice.

Thankful that she was learning to get around pretty well on one foot and two crutches, she hefted herself off of her bed and maneuvered herself to the bathroom connected to the bedroom.

She was so grateful that Ben had moved upstairs while she was still in the hospital. He'd taken the majority of his things, too. And, somehow, he, Lukas, and her parents had moved her clothes and toiletries into his bedroom and bathroom.

She was so happy not to have to navigate her way up and down the stairs all day long. She was also getting a bit spoiled having her own private bathroom. Upstairs, she and Lukas shared the one in the hall.

It was going to be disappointing to not have a bathroom all to herself.

"Which just goes to show you that you are getting spoiled, girl," she told herself as she glanced at her reflection in the mirror. "You need to be feeling thankful more and mopey less."

After brushing her hair, pulling it up, and pinning on her *kapp*, Daisy figured that she looked presentable for a caller.

Which caught her off guard.

Was that what Kyle was?

Her brothers had been teasing her, saying that Kyle had not only been her savior on the side of the road, but he'd also become smitten. Although she'd strongly refuted that, protesting that the man was simply nice, she'd secretly wondered if he had developed some special feelings for her.

To her surprise, she didn't hate the idea. Kyle was strong and handsome and kind. Three things she figured any woman would find appealing. Even more special was the way he'd never acted as if she was foolish and boyish for wanting to spend her days working with animals and in the fields.

Oh, sure, he'd pointed out that she was too slight to handle a team of four horses in a field, but he'd been right. As much as Daisy would've liked to imagine that she could handle plowing a field by herself, she knew she wasn't strong enough. She certainly could've helped Mervin Miller, though.

But maybe, if Kyle did like her, one day she could live on their farm together. They could be true partners, and one day even raise a handful of *kinner* together. They'd teach them about God and grace and nature and cooperation.

"Daisy? What's keeping ya?" Ben called out.

"Nothing! I'm on my way," she replied as she pulled herself out of her daydream and back to reality.

Well, almost. She might be firmly in reality now, but that didn't mean that she wasn't happy to see Kyle again.

"I'm sorry it took me a moment," she said as she joined

Ben and her mother in the family room. "I had to pull up my hair and pin on my *kapp*."

"It's all right," Kyle said as he got to his feet. "Do you need help getting settled on the couch?"

Hearing Ben's chuckle, hidden by a very fake cough, she flushed. "*Danke*, but I'm getting better and better at maneuvering this cast."

"I'm glad." When she finally set her crutches on the ground and smiled up at him, he grinned right back at her.

Making her feel warm and special all over again. In spite of herself, she glanced at her mother. She was looking pleased and proud of her.

Maybe everything that had happened had been by the Lord's design. Before her accident, she'd been in a constant state of disappointment and worry, and that didn't even count how much she'd hated her job.

However, she had received some blessings. She no longer had to go to work, she had her own bathroom, and her mother was pleased with her. Most importantly, she'd somehow gained the regard of handsome Kyle Hostetler. And he was so wonderful that not even her protective older brothers could find fault with him.

"How are you this afternoon, Kyle?"

"I am well, thank you." Looking more at ease, he added, "I was just speaking with your mother and Ben about how nice the weather is."

"*Jah*. Yesterday, I spent much of the afternoon reading on the front porch. It's always a blessing when the spring weather turns warmer."

"I'm glad you enjoy reading."

"Do you like to read, too?"

"*Jah*. For sure. Not that I have much time for books. But I find it a *gut* way to spend my spare time. Especially in the winter."

She nodded, "*Jah*. The winter is the best time to appreciate long, quiet evenings."

Kyle smiled at her. "It looks as if we have something besides farming in common."

She felt like a wilted flower, basking in his sunny smile. Meeting his gaze, she murmured, "It would seem so."

Her mother cleared her throat. "You know, Ben . . . I could sure use your help in the kitchen."

He frowned. "With what?"

"I'll tell you about it when we get there."

Her brother's gaze darted to hers and then at Kyle before clearing his throat. "Oh. Sure. I remember now," he said as he stood up.

Daisy bit her lip so she wouldn't start laughing. Her mother and Ben weren't fooling anyone, but she did appreciate their willingness to allow her and Kyle to have a more private conversation.

"*Nee*, wait," Kyle said.

It was no lie to say that she, her mother, and her brother all stared at him in confusion.

"What's wrong?" Ben asked.

"Well, you see, I came over here to ask all of you a question."

Ben blinked. "All of us? Sorry, but don't you mean my parents and Daisy?"

"Well, sure. I mean, I guess your father might have some information, but you might be better." Kyle seemed to realize he wasn't making any sense. "Really, I'd like your help. It won't take long," he added in a rush. "Please stay, if you don't mind, that is."

A line formed between her mother's brows but she sat back in her chair. "Of course we don't mind, Kyle. Whatever you need, we're glad to help. Right, Ben?"

"*Jah*. Right."

Ben moved across the room and sat down next to her on the couch.

Daisy looked at him curiously. It wasn't like him to move around like that, but perhaps he just thought the couch looked more comfortable? Whatever the reason, Daisy supposed it didn't matter.

She leaned forward as well as she could and smiled at Kyle. "What is on your mind?" she prodded, when it seemed as if he was still trying to figure out where to start.

"This sounds strange, and I'm not all that sure it's a *gut* idea, but Mervin and Ruthie suggested I speak with you." He took a deep breath. "You see, a few days ago, when I was standing outside the hardware store, I nearly ran into someone."

This was very curious. And, if Daisy was being honest, rather deflating. Here she'd been sure he'd been going to ask her family if he could have permission to start calling on her.

Obviously, that hadn't been the case at all.

"What happened next?" Ben asked.

"Well, the girl I walked into, the woman, rather, she was rather sweet. We ended up sitting on a bench and talked for a spell. While she recovered, you see."

"While she recovered?" Mamm repeated. "Dear me. How hard did you hit her, Kyle?"

"I didn't hit her." His cheeks flushed. "To be honest, I only kind of stepped in her path. But I must have done more than that, because she was very flustered." He took a deep breath. "She said she knew you, Daisy."

"Oh? Who was it?"

"Her name is Winter. Winter Walker." He grinned. "Do you remember her? She said you were in school together."

Winter? Kyle was acting so happy and pleased about *Winter*?

No, it was worse than that. Kyle was acting as if he'd just

experienced Christmas morning and his birthday all at the same time. Maybe a carnival mixed in. He was glowing.

She felt as chilly as if the first harsh blast of January had flown into the house from the cracked window.

Beside her, she felt Ben tense up. And who could blame him? Her brothers knew how much she detested Winter. The girl had made her life miserable for the last two years of school.

Realizing that some kind of response was expected, Daisy said, "Yes. I do know Winter, and she was right. We did go to school together." Her voice had come out even. Flat. Void of emotion.

She was rather proud of herself about that. It was far better that she sounded monotone instead of near tears.

Kyle was staring at her. Obviously waiting for more information. But what could she say that wasn't mean? Feeling desperate, she looked at her mother.

Silently begging for help.

But unfortunately, Mamm looked just as taken aback as she was. Her mother was one of the nicest people in the world, but even she had thought that Winter had been especially unkind to her.

"Kyle, forgive me, but I'm still not sure what you'd like to know," her mother said at last.

"This is awkward, isn't it? I'm sorry. I . . . well, she invited me to call on her soon, but I thought I'd better be prepared in case I say the wrong thing."

"Are you saying that you want to call on Winter?" Ben asked. He sounded almost as incredulous as he looked.

And as Daisy felt.

But Kyle continued to be oblivious. "Well, *jah.* Why wouldn't I?"

"No reason, except that she is known to be rather . . ." Ben's voice drifted off. "Frail."

Daisy looked down at her lap. Winter was also known to be a liar, too. But of course, they couldn't share that with Kyle. It wouldn't be right.

But she sure wished it was.

"Daisy, I was hoping you could tell me something more about Winter so when I go calling on her I won't make a fool of myself."

"I doubt you will do that," her mother said quickly. "Kyle, all you have to do is be yourself."

"That's kind of you to say, but I think I need something more. Do you happen to know what she's interested in?"

"Interests?" Mamm looked completely taken aback. "*Nee*, I'm afraid not."

Kyle turned to face her. "Daisy, you must know what Winter likes and doesn't like."

The conversation was excruciating. "Well, um, she and I weren't all that close."

"Winter did tell me that," Kyle said.

"That girl," Ben grumbled. "She'd say that the sky was gray even if the sun was shining if she thought it meant she could get her way."

Their guest drew back. "Now I understand. You don't like her, do you?"

Ben crossed his arms across his chest. Gritted his teeth. It was obvious that he was about to tell Kyle exactly how he felt about Winter.

But that wasn't fair.

Sure, her family did not like Winter, but that didn't mean that Kyle shouldn't have the right to make up his own mind. No matter what, they shouldn't be talking badly about Winter behind her back.

"That's not what Ben is saying," she blurted. "I'm sure the two of you will find you have a lot of things in common."

Kyle didn't look convinced but did seem to be more at ease.

When he left ten minutes later, Daisy felt as if all of her dreams had just shattered. But that was her own fault.

She hadn't been able to compete with Winter when they were children, so there was no reason to think that she could compete with her now.

She should've known better than to get her hopes up.

CHAPTER 14

It hadn't been difficult to locate the Walkers' *haus*. It was located on the edge of Walden and surrounded by fields of apple trees. Her family ran an apple farm and cider business. When he'd asked around, not a lot of people had much to say about Winter, but had mentioned that their farm was beautiful in the spring when all the apple blossoms were on the trees.

The white and pink flowers were pretty and smelled wonderful, too. As Kyle rode Mervin's bike down the driveway, he realized that he'd likely misjudged Winter. She'd looked so delicate and slight, but she had to be much hardier than that. No doubt she picked her fair share of apples every fall.

After he parked the bicycle next to one of the hitching posts in front of the door, he tucked in his short-sleeve shirt a bit better and then slowly climbed the steps to the front porch.

Just as he reached the door, it opened. A woman was staring at him. She looked exactly like Winter. Well, no doubt what Winter would look like in twenty years.

"Hi. Mrs. Walker?"

"*Jah?*"

"My name is Kyle Hostetler. I met Winter the other day in down. She invited me to call on her."

"Did she now?"

"Is she available?"

"I reckon so." Looking a bit frazzled, she said, "You might as well take a seat here on the porch. The *haus* is warm today."

"It is a hot day, for sure."

"Hmm."

He thought her response was a bit strange, but who was to say how she should have reacted? Instead of dwelling on it, he took a seat on the rocking bench seat and rocked back and forth.

A white and gray cat sauntered up the walkway and stared at him. Then, the cat must have decided he was *gut* company, because he leapt up the steps, circled the area until he was pleased with the position of the sunny spot, and at last lay down. Seconds later, his eyes were closed and he looked completely content.

"You've got the right idea, cat."

The door opened and Winter walked out.

She had on a pale lavender dress that somehow made her skin look almost translucent and her eyes even more vibrant. She was holding a tray with a pitcher of water, two glasses, and a plate of lemon bars on it.

Kyle jumped to his feet to help her carry the tray.

"*Danke*," she whispered shyly.

"Of course. These trays can get heavy." He smiled. "I'm happy to help you."

After he deposited the tray on the table, Winter went to work, pouring them each a glass of water and then gave each of them a lemon bar, a napkin, and a fork. "I hope you enjoy lemon bars?"

"I do. I mean, I think I do. I don't know if I've had one in years."

"I made them this morning, just in case you decided to come over tonight."

"Winter, I told you I would."

"*Jah*, but sometimes people don't keep their promises."

He remembered what she'd said about having her heart broken in the past. "Did your ex-boyfriend not keep his promises?"

"Not always. It was difficult. I never knew when I could trust him."

"I'm sorry. If he was like that, then I'm glad you broke things off."

"He broke things off with me. I was willing to put up with his lies, but even that wasn't good enough."

"I'm sorry."

"Have you ever had a serious girlfriend?"

"I did. Back in Kentucky, I courted a woman named Mary. She, ah, wanted some different things out of life than I did. She's the one who broke things off with me, too."

"We are quite a pair, aren't we? Two people who've had their hearts broken by people we trusted."

His situation hadn't been quite like that. Mary had cheated on him with one of his friends. When he'd found out and confronted her, she'd been shocked. So shocked, she'd started crying and apologized several times.

Though his heart had softened and he forgave her, Kyle knew that he'd never take her back. Too much damage had been done. Aaron Miller couldn't have reached out about the job with his parents at a better time. He'd been sure that he would be torn up for months about Mary's betrayal. But it turned out that he'd barely thought about her since he'd moved.

But Winter sure didn't need to know all of that. "*Jah*," he said. He took a bite of the lemon bar. It was rather warm, dry, and slightly burnt. The taste was slightly bitter, too. As if she hadn't put in enough sugar.

"What do you think?" Winter leaned closer. "Do you love it?"

There was only one answer that was acceptable. He just wished that that answer wasn't going to mean that he was going to have to eat the entire treat.

"*Jah*," he said with a smile as he ate another bite. "It's delicious."

"I'm so glad." She pushed her plate toward him. "You may have mine, if you'd like."

"Ah, no thank you. One is enough." It was more than enough.

CHAPTER 15

It was the coolest day they'd had in a month. Ruthie had opened all the windows, done two loads of laundry, and then pinned everything on the clothesline. Then, in celebration, she and Lizzie pulled out a blanket and decided to have a little break, out on the field.

As usual, after Lizzie wandered around a bit and smelled everything she could find, the portly basset hound sat down in the middle of the quilt and promptly fell asleep.

Ruthie knew from experience that she could either attempt to move the silly dog, which was an exercise in frustration . . .

Or, she could simply sit on the edge and let Lizzie sprawl in comfort.

"You are lucky you have a home with me, you silly *hund*," she said as her bare ankles rested in a nest of grass. "Most owners would surely put you in your place."

Lizzie opened one eye but didn't budge an inch. Honestly, Ruthie was pretty certain that the dog had understood what she said and was pleased about it.

When she spied Kyle putting Velvet out to pasture nearby, she waved him over. "What's going on?"

"Oh, I needed a project to keep my mind off some things, so I decided to work with Velvet a bit."

"What do you intend to do?"

"*Jah*, I know, but I agree with you that she's been a bit off."

"That's why I asked Daisy to come over. Velvet did seem to be a little bit brighter after she spent some time with her. I haven't thought about her much at all, I'm afraid. Now that you do the milking every morning, all I think is that I'm happy I don't have to sit on that milking stool when it's cold and dark outside."

Kyle grinned. "I'd probably do the same thing."

"Do you think she's sick?" Guilt for taking the cow for granted hit her hard. But so did worry about vet bills. She and Mervin had talked more than once about how ignorant they'd been about veterinary expenses.

"*Nee*." Staring at the cow some more, he shrugged. "I guess it was more of a feeling. Like, maybe Velvet is lonely or something."

She shook her head. "Cows don't get lonely."

"How do you know that?"

"Because they're cows," she sputtered. "I think they only are concerned with eating and being milked."

"Umm, I think you might be wrong about that, Ruthie. I know that Velvet hates thunderstorms, enjoys being talked to when she's getting milked, and she watches me and Mervin whenever we visit the Percherons."

Now she just felt foolish and ungrateful. Here Velvet was a living, breathing animal who provided all their milk. "Would you like me to call the veterinarian?"

"*Nee*, not at all. Like I said, I wanted to see if all she needed was a change of scenery for a few hours today."

"Thank you for taking such good care of our animals."

"No need for thanks. It's my job."

Ruthie realized that Velvet wasn't the only creature on the farm who was acting a little under the weather. "Hey, are you all right?"

"Of course."

"I'm serious. Maybe you need a day off?" He had been working an awful lot. Maybe she and Mervin had been allowing him to overdo it. "A break from here might do you a world of good." She smiled so Kyle would know that she was being sincere.

"No, I am fine." Kyle's expression clouded for a moment before he blurted, "I've been thinking about Daisy."

"Is her recovery still going well??"

"*Jah*. But . . . well, did you know that she'd been saving to buy this farm? And that Samuel Burkholder had verbally promised that he'd wait to sell it until she had enough for the bank to go in with her for the loan?"

"I had heard something about that, but I didn't think anyone was serious about her wanting to run a farm."

"She was very serious."

"That's a pity, then. But, Kyle, as much as I feel sorry that she didn't get her wish, Samuel's choice to sell the farm to Mervin and me was his choice. When the broker reached out to Mervin about this farm being available, he never said that we were taking it from another prospective buyer."

"I understand. It's just . . . well, I know a little bit about being caught off guard."

"I do, too, but this isn't what it was. The truth is that Samuel was exhausted. This farm was too much for him to handle on his own. He was ready to go live with his daughter and her family and start sleeping past five in the morning. It's a shame he didn't take the time to tell Daisy that, but she surely didn't expect he would continue to live here on his own until she could buy an expensive piece of land."

"I don't know if she did or she didn't."

"If she did, then I feel sorry for her, because simply buying this land isn't enough. One has to pay for the grain, the water, the gas line . . . and vet bills. Plus, she would've had to get some help to plow the fields. It's a hard job for even a strong man like yourself."

Kyle seemed to consider what she was saying. Nodding slowly, he murmured, "*Jah*. You're right."

"I hope she hasn't made you feel guilty?" she asked, since she was starting to feel like Kyle was taking too much on his shoulders.

"I don't feel guilty."

She didn't believe him. "Kyle, all you've done is taken a job that your best friend asked you to do. You had nothing to do with the Burkholders selling their farm, Mervin and me buying the farm, or Daisy not having enough money to purchase it."

Kyle held up a hand. "Okay. I get it. I'm sorry I brought it up."

So much for her trying to have a gentle conversation with him! All she'd done so far was defend her and Mervin's purchase!

"*Nee*, I'm sorry if I've said too much. Listen, I know I don't sound sympathetic about Daisy's disappointment, but it's not because I don't care about her or wish that she'd been able to have worked something out." She chose her words with care. "But listen, life is filled with disappointments. Kids don't get picked on teams, vacations are cancelled, accidents happen, people get fired . . . the list goes on and on. It's unfair of her to hold on to a grudge about something that was never hers to begin with."

"I understand."

"I hope so."

"I think I'm going to pay her a visit and see how she's doing."

"I'll make another pie and you can take it over for me. Or, if you'd like, I'll go with you," she added eagerly. Anything to make him feel more at ease.

"If you don't mind, I'd like to go over on my own. But I'll take the pie, if you were serious."

"Oh, I was serious. I don't ever joke about pies," she teased.

CHAPTER 16

Kyle hadn't expected Daisy's older brother, Lukas, to open the door. He really hadn't expected him to act like Kyle was an interloper into their lives. Beyond working for the Millers, he wasn't sure what he'd done to garner such a dark look from him.

"Is there something you needed?" he asked.

"*Nee*. I mean, not beyond the reason I'm here. Is Daisy up for callers?"

Lukas frowned. "Are you calling on my sister? In the middle of the afternoon?"

"What? *Nee*!" Realizing that he sounded like calling on Daisy was a bad thing, he hastily attempted to smooth things over. "I mean, she and I are friends. I decided to come over to see how she was feeling."

Lukas's frown eased but he didn't move away from the door. "Her injuries are getting better, thank you."

"I'm glad to hear that." Of course, he knew that, too. What he was really hoping was that she'd be up to talking to him. "Is she free? I thought maybe the two of us could talk for a few moments."

"Lukas, let Kyle in," Mrs. Lapp called out. Rushing toward them, she looked frazzled. One of her hands was clutching a dish towel and the other was halfheartedly attempting to brush off a dusting of flour on the front of her dress. "So sorry about my eldest son's attitude. He's a bit overprotective of Daisy."

"I'm not overprotective, I'm doing what I'm supposed to do," Lukas grumbled as he stepped backward and motioned Kyle inside. "We can't let just anyone call on the girl."

"I'm not here for any romantic reason," he blurted. And, yes, he sounded stupid. Why had he thought this was a good idea?

"Don't mind him, Kyle," Mrs. Lapp said. "My goodness, what's that in your hands?"

He'd been so taken aback by Lukas's questioning he'd completely forgotten that he was holding a pie in his hands. "It's a cherry pie. Ruthie asked me to take it over."

For some reason that explanation seemed to set Lukas off again. "Why didn't you tell me you were only here to drop off a pie?"

"Because that isn't the only reason I'm here," he bit out.

Mrs. Lapp hurried forward with outstretched hands. "Thank you for the pie."

"It's still a bit warm. I'll be happy to carry it to the kitchen for you."

"*Danke*, Kyle." As she turned around, she glanced at her son. "Lukas, go tell Daisy that Kyle has come over. Help her with her crutches if she needs it."

"Will do." After closing the front door, he headed down the hall.

"I'm so sorry about his attitude," Mrs. Lapp said as she led the way down the hall. "I'm afraid Daisy's accident has taken a toll on all of us . . . but on Lukas most of all."

"Why?"

She turned back toward him. "Why? Well, um, it's all intertwined with my daughter's wish to be a farmer." She lowered her voice. "As you know, running a farm is exhausting, back-breaking work. Lukas has never wanted her to help him with any plowing or the livestock because he didn't want her to get hurt." She set the pie on the large butcher block island in the center of their kitchen. "Now because of everything that's happened—her impulsive bicycle purchase and then the accident—he feels guilty for not letting her be more involved around here."

"I see."

"Especially since she lost her job at the bulk food store . . . would you like *kaffi*?"

"*Nee. Danke.*" He cleared his throat. "I'm sorry, is Daisy available or not?"

"I suppose we'll find out soon, hmm? Why don't you have a seat. If you don't want coffee, would you like water?"

This was one of the most frustrating and confusing visits he could ever remember having with a woman's family. "If Daisy doesn't want to see me, I'm going to go ahead and leave."

"I'm here, Kyle," Daisy said.

Turning, he saw her balancing herself on her crutches. Some of the bruising that had been on her face had lessened. "Hi," he said. "You look like you're feeling better."

Her bright blue eyes lit up. "Do you really think so?"

He folded his hands behind his back. "I really do."

"I was just trying to convince Kyle here to sit down and have a glass of water. Or coffee." Her mother pulled out a chair. "Come sit down, you two."

"We're not going to sit at the kitchen table," Daisy said. "Kyle, want to sit in the living room?"

Before he could answer, Lukas blurted, "Why do you need to go there by yourselves?"

Daisy sighed. "Because we do, *bruder*."

"Do you want water or not, Kyle?" Mrs. Lapp asked.

Kyle felt as if he had walked into the middle of a three-ring circus. "It doesn't matter to me."

Mrs. Lapp held up a glass. "Are you sure? It's no trouble."

"He doesn't want any water right now," Daisy said. Tossing a look of sympathy his way, she added, "Come on, Kyle."

As he watched her carefully crutch her way to the living room, with both her mother's and her brother's eyes fastened on her, Kyle strode to her side.

From both her brother's attitude and her mother's thrown-out explanations, Kyle was realizing that there was a whole lot more going on with Daisy—and maybe even her family—than he'd realized. What that was, he had no idea.

He hoped by the time he left he would have some more information. He was starting to feel like Daisy Lapp was a woman who was surrounded by love and family . . . but just happened to be feeling as alone as he was.

CHAPTER 17

Daisy knew that she needed to say something and it needed to be good. She wasn't sure about how a few words could do that, unfortunately.

After Kyle helped her sit down—ignoring her protests the entire time—he said, "I'm sorry if my being here has caused a commotion."

She had to smile. "Don't worry about it. Practically everything that happens around here causes a commotion. We Lapps are an excitable bunch."

"I was starting to get that idea. But still, it does seem that my appearance here has taken everyone by surprise."

"Are you really that shocked?"

"Honestly? Yes. I thought everything was okay between us," he said.

"Everything between you and my family is great. Wonderful-*gut*."

Yes, sarcasm was thick in her voice, but what did he expect? He not only had helped her when she was injured, but had brought her flowers. He and his mother had stopped by, too. Ruthie kept making the pies.

Kyle was also one of the reasons her brothers felt justified in never wanting her to farm in the first place. He was obviously doing real well at the Millers' farm. He, Mervin, and Ruthie were all working together to make it a success. And since they were next door, Lukas had a good view of their work. So far, her brother hadn't found a thing to complain about.

If Daisy had gotten her wish, she knew that she wouldn't have done nearly as good a job. She would've been drowning in work, and likely too full of pride to ask for help.

"What is that supposed to mean?" he asked.

It took Daisy a second to remember what he was referring to. "I promise, everything between us is fine." She swallowed. "I told them that you are interested in Winter Walker and not me. They understand."

Kyle's blue eyes clouded before he recovered. "I've only gone calling on Winter a few times. That's all."

"I understand."

"I, ah, wanted to see if you had any idea about what you wanted to do next. Are you going to return to work at the bulk food store?"

"*Nee*. Even if Melissa took me back, I don't want to go back there. It wasn't a good fit for me."

"So . . . what will you do?"

"I'm not sure. Lukas said I could help him around here. I'll probably do that for a while."

"Ah."

Kyle didn't appear to be all that enthused about the idea either. She waved a hand. "I've been thinking that maybe I should look at some other jobs, too."

"Oh? Like what?"

"I don't know. I like to read. Maybe I could read to children at the library? Or perhaps volunteer my time in the school?"

"I can see you doing both of those things. I bet working in a library might be fun. If you don't mind the quiet and all."

She chuckled. "Since most of the animals around here stay pretty quiet, I don't think that will be a problem."

A sweet appreciation appeared in his eyes. Warming her spirit and making her want to share more about herself. "Everyone keeps telling me that I have lots of time to figure out my future. I need to remember that."

"Time really does heal wounds." His expression tightened. "You know, I've always loved farming, too. I had hoped to stay on our land in Kentucky, but that wasn't meant to be."

"Aaron told me that your parents sold off some of your land."

"They did. They got a good price for it." He took a deep breath. "I've been going through some growing pains as well. I had a longtime girlfriend back in Kentucky. We, ah, broke things off."

"I'm so sorry."

"*Jah*, me too." Taking a sip of water, Kyle added, "I didn't break my leg, but I have been feeling rather broken up lately. All my grand plans for Mary and me disintegrated within a matter of minutes."

"Ouch."

"*Jah*. Ouch." He smiled at her suddenly. "We have a lot in common, don't we, Daisy?"

"I think we do."

"Let's concentrate on being good friends, then. I could use a good friend here in Walden."

"I could use one, too." She winked. "Especially if Ruthie sends over pies with you."

He lowered his voice. "She's an amazing baker. I'm going to be lucky if I don't gain ten pounds this year."

"Does that mean that you wouldn't be opposed to sharing a slice of cherry pie with me?"

"I wouldn't be opposed to that at all." He gently squeezed her bicep. "I'll go ask your *mamm* for a slice and two forks. You stay here, okay?"

"Okay," she said.

When he was out of sight, she smiled.

And only had to remind herself that they were "just friends" four times.

CHAPTER 18

Ruthie would've never guessed it, but she was starting to look forward to spending an hour every morning with Velvet. After she straightened the kitchen, made the bed, and did most of her morning chores, she and Lizzie would walk out to the barn, put Velvet's new bridle on, and lead her out to the pasture to the left of the barn.

She was no expert, but Ruthie thought that field was the best part of the entire farm. The ground was slightly rolling, the grass was thick and vibrant green, and dandelions, daisies, and black-eyed Susans grew in clumps here and there. The Burkholders had confided that the field had once been set aside for their goats, but they'd ended up selling the herd when they realized that their goats were both smart and wily.

Needing to do something with the field, they'd planted an assortment of wildflowers, intending to let the field support flowers and bees for a year or two before it became useful again.

They'd never done so. Rachel had even confided that the

beauty had been too hard to give up. When they'd first moved in, Ruthie had considered growing corn and pumpkins in it, but that idea had evaporated when she realized that the vegetables were going to take a great amount of time that neither she nor Marvin had.

Now, inadvertently, it had become Velvet's morning happy place. The heifer seemed to truly enjoy being out in the morning sun. She'd wander around, nibble on fresh grass and would constantly look for her and Lizzie. If Ruthie ever had to go inside for a spell, Velvet would make a mournful noise.

Truly, it sounded as if she was crying.

Mervin, unfortunately, wasn't all that sympathetic to the milk cow's need for sun and companionship. He took every opportunity he could to fuss about her.

"Have you noticed all those cow patties, Ruthie?" he asked almost a week ago. "It's near impossible to walk in a straight line without running into one."

She was tired of his complaints, so she just shrugged. "I think that walking in a straight line is overrated."

He'd been so irritated with that retort, he'd barely talked to her for two days. Ruthie felt a little guilty for being snippy, but not really. After all, Velvet had become theirs when they bought the farm. She was theirs and it was their duty to make their milk cow happy.

Ruthie thought spending time together in the morning or midday was helping Velvet's disposition, too. Now when she approached Velvet's stall, the cow's pretty brown eyes seemed to light up. She stood still when Ruthie attached the bridle and line and walked without a bit of fuss to the field. She didn't even seem to mind when Lizzie barked at birds. Instead, the hound's antics seemed to amuse the cow to no end.

After eating some grass, watching a pair of cardinals with Lizzie, and wandering around a bit, Velvet lay down on a particularly fluffy-looking patch of grass and took a nap.

Ruthie, who'd begun taking the milking stool outside with her, sat down and stretched her legs out, too. Sure, it was a lazy way to spend the morning, but she reckoned that that was what retirement was for.

"It looks like Velvet's penchant for sunbathing has worn off on you," Kyle called out.

Startled, she looked up, then stood up when she realized he wasn't alone. He was walking with Daisy on the Lapps' land. Daisy was using a crutch but she seemed to be getting along okay, especially since it looked as if Kyle was staying close to her side.

Realizing they were probably waiting for a response, Ruthie joked, "*Jah*, this cow should've been born in Pinecraft. Sometimes I think she would enjoy lazing on the beach more than most folks there."

"Wouldn't that be a picture?" Daisy giggled. "I can see the postcards now: Come to Velvet's favorite beach."

Enjoying the silly conversation, Ruthie pretended to consider the idea for a second. "Eh, the sand might irritate her hooves, and there won't be a flower in sight. I think I'll keep her here."

"Probably a *gut* idea," Kyle murmured as they walked closer to the fence. "How is Velvet doing today?"

"I think she's happy as a duck in water. She sure seems more content."

"What helped?" Daisy asked.

"I'm not sure if it was just one thing. I think she was maybe longing for a change of scenery." Feeling the need to confess the whole truth, she added, "*Mei mann* is sure I've lost my mind."

"Because you care about your milk cow? Certainly not." Daisy let her crutches fall to the ground as she rested her arms on the top of the white fence. "Velvet has an important job in your family. You depend on her for your *millich*, *jah*?"

"We do. She provides all our milk and butter."

"Then there's nothing wrong with seeing to her needs from time to time."

Velvet, seeming to realize that she was the topic of conversation, boosted herself up and then ambled over to Daisy.

"Hiya, girl. Are you enjoying these flowers as much as the rest of us?" Daisy cooed.

To Ruthie's amusement, the cow seemed to nod her head right before she ambled closer to the fence. She stopped right where Daisy's outstretched hand was.

"Careful now," Kyle said.

"I'm all right," Daisy said as she began to gently rub the soft fur just next to one of the heifer's ears. "I'm glad that I'm getting to know Velvet better."

"You have a way with her."

"She probably realizes that I'm a farm girl," she said, then immediately looked ashamed.

The young woman was still sad about them buying the farm. "Daisy, dear, maybe we need to clear the air." She took a deep breath. "I know you feel as if we took your future right out from under you. I promise that we had no idea Samuel had verbally promised it to you already."

Her blue eyes looked stricken. "*Nee!* No, I don't blame you. I don't even blame Samuel for not wanting to wait until I could get the rest of the down payment. I'm just frustrated with my life right now."

"Is your leg feeling better?"

"I think so. I don't have to take near as many pain relievers. Sometimes only one at night."

"That's *gut*, *jah*?"

"*Jah*."

"Ruthie, Daisy and I got to talking, and I invited her to help out from time to time after she gets to feeling better."

"Why?" Ruthie knew she sounded rude, but she was taken aback, she wasn't going to lie. Kyle hadn't given her any indication that the farm was too much work for him.

"Not for a salary," Daisy said quickly. "It's just, well, until my leg is completely healed, I can't get another 'real' job. And when I'm home, my mother is encouraging me to do more feminine pursuits."

"I see. Like cooking and laundry?"

"*Nee*, I am more than happy to help her with those things. It's things like sewing or canning that I don't care to do." Daisy looked like she'd rather pick up some of those cow patties in the field than pick up a needle and thread.

"I used to manage a sewing shop in Millersburg. I could help you with that."

"*Danke*. But what I'm trying to say—"

"What she's trying to say is that she'd much rather keep company with a cow instead of make a shirt for one of her *bruders* or make jam," Kyle said.

"Hmm." Ruthie didn't mind Daisy wanting to help out on the farm, but most every chore she could think of needed two good arms and two good legs.

"It's okay if you don't want another person around," Daisy said quickly.

Looking into the younger woman's eyes, Ruthie saw something very familiar. A wish to be useful. She wanted to fulfill a dream, even if it didn't make a lot of sense to everyone around her.

She couldn't discourage that.

She also didn't think there was a need to be yet another person to tell Daisy what she should and shouldn't be doing with her life. Plus, if it wasn't going to cost her and Mervin any more money, what did it matter?

"I hesitated because I don't want you to get hurt. A broken leg is a big injury, ain't so? But I suppose it's all up to you. I don't mind if you'd like to help out around here."

"Really?"

"*Jah*."

"I'll look out for her, Ruthie."

"I know you will."

"I'm so excited," Daisy said.

Ruthie laughed as Velvet gazed at Daisy with love in her eyes. "You just made my cow a happy heifer. I shudder to imagine what would happen if she never saw you again."

"Thank you so much." Reaching out, Daisy petted the cow's neck. "Velvet, it looks like you and I are going to be seeing more of each other for a while."

"*Danke*, Ruthie," Kyle said.

Ruthie winked. She might say she was doing this for Daisy, but she had a feeling she was helping Kyle, too. The boy didn't realize it, but he seemed to have eyes for pretty Daisy Lapp, too.

Why, it was practically a match made in heaven.

CHAPTER 19

It had been a while since he'd chatted with his sister Sarah. As Kyle waited for the machine attached to the Millers' phone to connect with her, he realized that he was feeling a flutter of bees in his chest.

That wasn't unusual. Sarah was fourteen, so pretty with dark blond hair and eyes a shade that could only be described as silver. She had prominent cheekbones and a lithe figure. From the time she'd been born, everyone had said she was beautiful. He'd always thought so, too.

But she was also sweet . . . and had a significant hearing loss.

The doctors said that it all stemmed from a terrible cold she'd contracted during the winter she'd turned three. Her constant ear infection had gotten worse. So much so that she'd stopped crying from the pain and simply slept a lot. It had also been in the middle of an unexpected and unusually harsh snowstorm. The roads—even for emergency vehicles—had been unpassable for thirty-six hours.

When his parents had finally realized that Sarah had been

too sick to cry and been able to get to the hospital, the damage had been done. Sarah's hearing in one of her ears was essentially gone and next to nothing in the other.

She could hear loud noises, but conversation was difficult. They'd all learned some basic sign language, and the state had put in the special Clear Caption phone for her. Whenever he called, she could read the words on a screen. Sarah could then either type in words or speak into a microphone.

Their parents, being the way they were, felt terrible for Sarah but had eventually come to terms with her handicap and had encouraged her to do the same.

Kyle knew that was the right thing to do, but he also felt his sister needed a little bit extra care and patience. Sarah had a heavy burden on her shoulders. And while the Amish community was forgiving and kind toward her, not every child her age was all that understanding about it.

Some kids teased her, or took advantage of her hearing loss to talk about Sarah right in front of her. Others simply weren't sure how to relate to her so they ignored her completely. She said she'd gotten used to it, but he never would.

He missed her terribly.

When the phone rang, he eagerly picked it up. "Hey, silly. How are you?"

Dots appeared on the Clear Caption phone that the Millers had allowed him to install in his kitchen. Seconds later, her reply appeared. "Okay."

"Just okay? What's going on? Did something happen at school?"

After another brief wait, her answer appeared. "Kind of."

"What happened?"

"Nothing new. It's just John Beachy has been teasing me again."

Kyle gritted his teeth. That kid was a weasel. "Did you tell your teacher?"

"She knows."

"And?"

"And nothing, Kyle. Miss Addie doesn't do anything. You know that."

Miss Addie was Addie Kaufman. Addie was his age, a spinster, and timid. He wasn't sure why everyone thought that she would be a good teacher.

Immediately he felt bad. Addie wasn't a bad teacher. The problem was that she wasn't all that good for Sarah. Addie was the type to pretend she didn't see children passing notes or whispering when they were supposed to be doing packets. She'd hated any sort of confrontation when she'd been a teenager and hadn't seemed to have gotten any better with it as an adult.

"How can I help?"

"There's nothing you can do. You're in Ohio."

"I can visit. Would you like me to visit soon?"

She paused again. "*Nee.*"

Feeling more frustrated with his helplessness, he asked, "Sarah, have you told any of this to Mamm and Daed?"

"Not really."

"Why not?"

"They've got a lot going on, Kyle."

Sarah was right about that. Their father was a diabetic and was happily ignoring all of his doctor's advice. That meant that he was often feeling poorly or missing work. Money was tight.

Once again, Kyle wished that he'd taken more time to think things through before agreeing to work at the Millers' for one year. Instead of thinking of everything he'd be missing, all he'd done was think about how good it would be to only have to worry about himself for a change. He wished he hadn't been so single-minded and selfish.

"I'm sorry I left you."

"Kyle, stop. All of this would've happened even if you had been here."

"Maybe not."

"It would." There was a pause, then she typed, "I'm going to ask Mamm if I can stay at home for my last year."

He used to tell Sarah that that was a bad idea. That she needed to be around other kids and get used to living in the world with her hearing loss. But now he was feeling as if that had been wrong.

"I don't think she's going to let you." Or that she should.

"I know, but she doesn't have to deal with what I do, Kyle."

He felt so helpless. Part of him wanted to get on the next Pioneer Trails bus heading south and see his sister. He was pretty sure if he started walking her to school every day that the *kinner* would stop making his sister miserable. He'd also tell Addie to do her job and get some control of her classroom.

Then, he could attempt to supervise his father's diet and the family's bank account.

Of course, he couldn't help their bank account if he quit. Then there was the fact that their father would ignore all his advice even if Kyle was standing right in front of him.

"Kyle?"

He groaned. "Sorry, I was just thinking about something."

"You can't come back here. You promised Aaron Miller that you'd help out his parents for a year."

"I know . . . Hey, why don't you come out here, instead?"

"Really?"

"You can ride the bus as easily as anyone else."

"You'd let me travel by myself?"

He could practically hear her squeal of excitement. "Let me ask Aaron if he can get you here halfway. If he can get you to Cincinnati, it's a straight shot to Berlin. I'll be in the parking lot when you get out."

"What about school? I should just ask Addie if I can have work to go?"

"I'm not sure. Let me talk to Ruthie. And, there's someone else I know who has some extra time on her hands. I think she would be able to help you, too."

"Do you promise that you mean this? You're not going to forget about me, are you?"

"I'm not going to forget, but give me a minute to talk to everyone." And to think things through.

"I'm not going to tell Mamm or Daed about this, Kyle."

"*Gut*. I want to tell them. We'll worry about them getting involved when everything is organized."

"*Danke*."

"Anything for you, Sarah. Chin up, now. I love you."

"I love you too. You're the best brother."

"I know. Ha, ha," he added, just in case Sarah didn't realize that he was teasing.

After he hung up, he looked at the worn down *dawdi haus* he was living in. It needed a fresh coat of paint and some fresh area rugs and maybe some curtains. Something to brighten up the place for his sister.

Sure, he was acting like it was a done deal, but he was finally feeling like he was doing something right. Now all he had to do was talk to the Millers about Sarah visiting. Maybe he could ask Daisy if she would consider helping Sarah with her schoolwork and with her confidence.

That was a lot of asks, but he was going to pray, too. He knew the Lord was on Sarah's side and as far as he was concerned, having her here would be the answer to a lot of prayers.

He just hoped he was right.

CHAPTER 20

"Daisy, you busy?" Kyle called out as he walked up their driveway.

"Not really." The truth was that he couldn't have shown up at a better time. She was sitting on the front porch and suffering through her second hour of hemming a dress. Not only had she stuck herself with the needle two times, she knew that her mother was going to have a lot to say about her uneven stitches. "What brings you over?" she asked as he walked up the steps. "You aren't going to try to court me again, are you?" she teased.

He chuckled. "Sorry, but I don't think I can put either of us through that again anytime soon." He sat down on the chair next to her. "What are you doing?"

"Hemming a dress."

"That looks relaxing."

"We both know that it's anything but that." Feeling guilty because all she seemed to do was complain, she added, "Forgive me, it's not a bad task. I just get frustrated with myself because my stitches aren't as even as they should be."

"Ah. Sorry I can't help you with that."

"I don't need help." Glad for the break, she gathered the dress, folded it a couple of times, and set it on the table next to her. "Are you out for a walk?"

"*Nee*. I came over to ask you about my sister."

"Your sister?"

"*Jah*. You see, she's fourteen and going through a hard time. She has a hearing difficulty and some of the kids in her school give her a hard time."

"That's awful." Unfortunately, she knew all about being teased.

"I agree."

"Is she in an Amish school?"

"She is." Looking away, he added, "Honestly, I think if she was at the public school, she might be having an easier time. They have services and teachers for *kinner* with special needs."

"I'm sorry you are so far away from her."

"I had an idea. I invited her to come up here. And . . . I thought that maybe you could help her."

That took her off guard. "Me?"

"*Jah*. You have some extra time." Before Daisy could interrupt, Kyle added in a rush, "You see, Sarah doesn't really like school because she can't understand the teacher very well. She wants to do the work on her own. Plus, she's good with animals. I thought she might be good company for Velvet."

That sounded like a lot of responsibility she wasn't qualified for. "I'm not sure if I would be the best help for your sister."

"Oh. All right."

It was obvious that he thought she was refusing for no reason. "I mean, I did okay with school, but I wasn't the best student. She might be better at her assignments than me."

"Don't worry about it. I'll think of something." Looking at the crumpled fabric on her lap, he said, "Though, I will tell you that she's great at sewing."

"Really? Do you think if I help her with her schooling she might want to help me with some chores?"

"If it's sewing, I do."

"Hmm. Listen, I don't want to refuse, it's just that I'm not sure. I don't want you to be disappointed. I'm happy to give your help a try. I'm surprised Ruthie and Mervin are okay with her visiting."

"I haven't talked to them about it yet. I wanted to have some things in place before I said anything to them." Looking pained, he said, "Now that I'm sharing everything with you, I am realizing that maybe I shouldn't have suggested she go to public school for a bit. Sometimes people are mean." He sighed. "I just feel like I need to help her though, you know?"

"I have two big brothers. I know all about brothers feeling the need to help their younger sisters." Her expression full of understanding, she added, "If Ben or Lukas was here, they'd offer a lot more suggestions."

He chuckled. "I'll keep that in mind."

"*Gut.*"

"How are you, otherwise?"

"You mean, when I'm not worrying about my future and complaining about sewing a hem?"

He smiled. "Yes."

"I don't know." The problem was that her mind felt as if it was continually flashing both options for her future and glimpses of the things she'd done wrong in the past. Sitting still no longer gave her any sense of peace.

But she didn't want to tell him that. It felt too much like whining. Most likely because it probably was.

So she settled for the most mature thing she'd been thinking of. "I'm coming to terms with the fact that I'll never have my own farm. I'm at peace with it."

"You've decided to settle."

His expression was filled with understanding, but the

comment still pinched. "I don't know if you'd call it 'settling' as much as facing facts. My reality is that I will never have enough money to run a farm by myself and even if I could, I would likely be doomed to fail because I wouldn't have enough money to afford livestock and their feed."

"I'm sorry."

"I am, too. Mostly because I shouldn't have ever gone down this path in the first place. I've wasted a lot of my life working toward a goal that wasn't sustainable."

"You are twenty-four. You haven't wasted anything."

"I would agree, except that I'm the one who is sitting on my parents' front porch attempting to hem a dress. I don't have a job, a boyfriend, or any man who is interested in me. Probably because I have too few feminine skills." She sighed. "I'd rather take care of horses and talk to cows than hem another dress ever again."

Kyle stared at her for a long moment. "There's nothing wrong with having dreams, Daisy. Just because the Lord isn't answering your prayers immediately doesn't mean He don't hear them."

"I agree. I think the Lord is listening to me." Taking a deep breath, she admitted the awful truth. "But here's the thing. He might hear what I'm asking for, but He might be thinking that I'm already wrong."

"Don't give up, okay?"

"I'll try not to."

He smiled as he stood up. "I'm going to let you go now. I've got to do some thinking about Sarah."

"She's blessed to have you."

His brown eyes seemed to warm. "Wait until you meet her. You'll understand why I think she's so special."

"I'll look forward to that happening very soon."

CHAPTER 21

Two weeks later, instead of just Sarah, Kyle's family came into town. His daed had arranged for a driver and said there was room for Aaron to tag along. Aaron hadn't needed to be asked twice.

All the company was a blessing, but it had thrown Ruthie into a tizzy. When Kyle started to feel guilty about it, Mervin confided that his wife enjoyed hosting company.

He'd been counting down the days, too. He missed his sister and it would be good to spend some time with his parents. He was also hoping that Aaron might give him some advice about how to deal with Ruthie and Mervin. Every once in a while Kyle felt as if he was overstepping himself with Mervin. He hoped Aaron could alleviate his worries.

But maybe he should've been more worried about all the trouble Ruthie had gone to for his family's visit.

"This is lovely, Ruthie. *Danke*."

Kyle thought that the Millers' dining room table looked like something out of a magazine. The plates, silverware, and glasses were arranged in perfect precision. Three small bouquets of flowers and two sets of candles ran along the center. It was all very pretty, but paled against the numerous serving dishes scattered all around.

Ruthie was standing in front of it all with a worried expression. "What do you think, Kyle? Does this look like enough food?"

"I think so."

"Are you sure?"

It took just about everything Kyle had to keep a straight face, because Ruthie had made enough food for at least double the amount of people they would be serving. Certainly more than enough for four additional people.

"*Mei* parents and Sarah don't eat any more than most folks, Ruthie."

"I didn't mean to insinuate that they did. But there's Aaron, too."

"If he needs more than chicken, meatballs, noodles, potatoes, coleslaw, Watergate salad, and beans for lunch, then your son might have a tapeworm or something," he teased. "Aaron will be fine."

She didn't crack a smile. "Kyle, dear, that's an old wives' tale."

"Forgive my joke. All I'm saying is that there is plenty. It looks amazing, too."

"I appreciate your help."

"You are welcome. I enjoyed it." He had, too. His mother had never wanted him in the kitchen, saying that it was women's work. Plus Sarah liked cooking.

But now Kyle was starting to think that he'd been missing out. There was something rather relaxing about peeling ten potatoes, slicing cabbage, and chopping apples. "Next time you need an assistant, I hope you'll ask me to help."

"I just might. You're a hard worker."

"*Danke*."

"Kyle, I know you told me that your sister doesn't need any special attention, but I'm still worried that she'll be struggling here because of her hearing loss."

"Sarah can hear out of one of her ears. Plus, she is pretty good at reading lips. She'll be fine. If she isn't, she'll tell one of my parents or me."

"All right. I mean, if you are sure."

"I'm sure. One day she might get a cochlear implant but until then, she's going to do the best she can."

"I suppose that's all any of us can do, ain't so?"

"*Jah*, Ruthie. That's all the Lord asks of us. And if that's all we can give, then it's enough."

"I'm sorry that Winter couldn't come over."

"It's kind of you to want to invite her, but I'm a little relieved that she had other plans," he admitted.

"Why is that?"

"I want to have a chance to talk to my parents and sister about her first."

"You haven't mentioned Winter to them?" When he shook his head, she asked, "Why not?"

"I'm not sure. It feels too fresh to share."

"I see." She opened her mouth to speak, but closed it abruptly when the front door opened.

"Mamm? You here?" Aaron called out.

Ruthie beamed at Kyle. "He's here!" She turned and hurried across the house.

Kyle waited a moment, wanting to give Ruthie time with her son before he joined the fray.

And sure enough, when he entered the living room, his parents beamed at him.

"There you are, son," his *mamm* said. "We missed you."

"I missed you, too." He hugged her tightly, before walking into his father's open arms. "All of you."

When his father released him from a bear hug, he stepped back but held him by his arms. "You're looking *gut*. Healthy."

"Ruthie takes care of me like her own," he teased as he scanned the room for Sarah. His insides warmed when he spied her standing off to the side.

He strode over to her. "You are a sight for sore eyes."

"Same," she said with a smile.

"Hi, silly," he said, taking care to face her so she could read his lips. "I've missed you something fierce."

She giggled. "Hey, that's my line!"

"I couldn't resist," he teased as he picked her up and twirled her around.

As he'd hoped, she squealed in delight. Just like she had when she'd been five years old.

After he put her down, Aaron was waiting to greet him. "It's been too long," he said.

"I agree. How's Hanna?"

"Uncomfortable, but the doctor says she is doing well."

"Only two months until her due date?"

"*Jah*. Eight weeks. We discuss the babe's arrival in weeks instead of months now," he explained with a smile. "That's when I'm not painting the nursery or helping Hanna get everything she needs."

"We have a lot to catch up on."

"I agree. But before I do anything, let me tell you that your sister is a sweetheart. Hanna is going to love her."

Looking at his sister, who was now trying to converse with a very excited Ruthie, Kyle smiled. "I think so too. Sarah is special."

Ten more minutes passed as everyone hugged and greeted each other.

Then Ruthie squeezed his arm. "Kyle, let's get everyone settled and then it's time to eat. I hope you're hungry."

"I hope you didn't go to a lot of trouble for us, Ruthie," his mother said.

"Of course she did," Aaron said with a laugh. "*Mei* mother loves having people over."

"Still. It's a lot of work."

"Not so much. Plus, Kyle helped."

His father raised his eyebrows. "You've been working in the kitchen, son?"

"*Jah*. I've enjoyed it." Wrapping his arm around Sarah, he guided her through a hallway. "Come on. I know a shortcut to the *dawdi haus*." He looked around. "Where's all your stuff?"

"Aaron told us to put our suitcases on that front porch."

"Ah. Good idea. Come on then."

They walked down a narrow hallway that Ruthie had painted a pale, buttery yellow. At the opposite side of it was the door that led to the living room of the *dawdi haus*.

Samuel Burkholder had explained to Mervin and Ruthie that the two houses had been connected that way because it had originally been built to house all of Samuel's aunts and uncles. His father had been one of eight children and by the time the twins had been born, the house had been near to bursting at the seams.

The addition had been built to first be an apartment of sorts for the eldest children, with the expectation that by the time Henry, Samuel's father, was ready to marry, the rest of the "main" house would be less full.

All that meant that the *dawdi haus* wasn't merely a bedroom, bathroom, kitchenette, and living area. There were three small bedrooms, a full bath, a smallish kitchen, and a very large living area.

Though Mervin and Aaron had had many a conversation about remodeling it into something more traditional, Kyle had told them that it wasn't necessary.

Kyle, for one, was very glad about the floor plan because it allowed his parents to have one room, his sister her own, and he was able to stay in his own bed during their visit.

It also gave them a small bit of privacy, which was going to be a good thing for Sarah. She could get overwhelmed if there was a lot of talking around her, and Ruthie was the type to chat nonstop.

"This is mighty nice, Kyle," his father said. "When you described your home, I kept imagining something like a rat's maze."

"It does have that feel about it when you're walking down the yellow hall, but it's mighty comfortable."

"I reckon so."

After they chose their rooms, Kyle helped Sarah put her things down and then led her into the kitchenette for a glass of water.

"Was the trip all right?"

"Oh, *jah*. I enjoy being on the bus. Much better than sitting in the back seat with just an English driver to talk to for eight hours."

"I feel the same way. Is there anything special you want to do? While you're here?"

Sarah shrugged. "I'm not sure. I want to meet all the animals, of course. Especially Velvet and Lizzie."

"We can do that." He winked. "Velvet is good company and Ruthie's silly hound will enjoy your company."

"I want to meet your new friend, too."

"Winter?"

She frowned. "Sure I want to meet her, but I was thinking of someone else. Daisy, right?" She spelled Daisy's name with her fingers. "Isn't she the woman who wanted to be a farmer here?"

"Oh. Sure. You're right. Yes, you'll have to meet her." He

hadn't told her yet that he'd talked to Daisy about possibly tutoring her.

"Meet who?" his mother said as she joined them.

"Daisy."

"Ah, yes. The bicycle girl. How is her leg healing?"

"It's doing better. To be honest, I haven't been spending too much time with her of late."

"Why not? Because you've been so busy here?"

"To be sure, but also I've been busy with other things."

Sarah frowned. "Like what?"

Like calling on Winter. He winked at her. "Like it is none of your business."

She glanced at their parents. Who, to his surprise, didn't look all that supportive of his sudden desire to keep his personal life private.

Feeling like he'd just made a mistake, Kyle tried to smooth things over. "Listen, it's not as if I'm doing anything all that special, it's just . . . well, maybe we can wait another hour before I am questioned any more."

"I understand," Sarah said. "I think I'll go get my things organized now." She turned and walked into her room and closed the door.

Things had just gone from bad to worse. "Sorry. I wasn't meaning to be short with her."

"She'll be all right," Daed said. "Sarah's just a bit touchy these days." He lowered his voice. "First was all the teasing at school. Then, the doctor said that it was time to either get the cochlear implant or accept that she will be deaf within the next year."

"It's a lot for a fourteen-year-old to handle," Mamm added.

"What is she going to do?"

"I'm not sure," Mamm said. "But she needs to make some choices soon."

"Aren't you going to make her get them?" His mind spinning, he added, "Hey, is it the money? If so, I can start sending you even more of my paycheck. I don't need much."

"*Halt*," Daed whispered. "It ain't the money. It's that we can't make Sarah do something about her ears. Whatever she decides is going to affect her for the rest of her life. She needs to make the decision."

"That seems like too much for her to handle."

"We're going to help her, Kyle. Of course we will," his mother said. "But getting the implant might not make her hearing perfect." After a pause, she added, "People will notice the implants, too. It will be another way that she is different, and she's already having a difficult time at school."

"That's because her teacher is Addie."

"*Nee*. It's because Sarah needs to learn to handle her disability." His mother lowered her voice. "Addie is not doing a bad job, Kyle."

It took a moment to understand what she was getting at. "So, you're saying it's everything else."

"*Jah*. She's got some growing pains, and they're tough ones. Not everyone is kind to someone who is different."

That killed him. He'd wanted to believe that her sheltered life in the Amish school would make everything easier, but he supposed teenagers were teenagers. Just because they were raised Amish didn't make them suddenly more thoughtful or kind. "I've talked to her about this some already. But maybe I should do something more. Do you need me to move back?"

"To do what? You canna go back to the eighth grade, son," Daed joked.

"If I walk her to school and pick her up, I'm sure everyone will think twice before being mean to her."

"It will also show everyone that she canna help herself. That she can't even get back and forth from school without help."

"I didn't think of it that way."

His mother patted his hand. "I think Sarah had a good idea about getting settled. Give us thirty minutes or so, Kyle. We'll meet you back in the big house."

He stood, feeling helpless as he watched his parents walk into the other room and close the door.

He suddenly felt like he was doing everything wrong and he had no idea how to make it better.

CHAPTER 22

Sarah looked so different than Daisy had imagined. She'd assumed the girl would've been awkward and shy. Maybe withdrawn. Instead, she appeared to be outgoing and confident. For a moment, Daisy wondered if Kyle saw the "real" Sarah when he was with his sister, or if she was destined to be permanently young and helpless in his eyes.

Sarah looked up when Daisy started forward on her crutches.

"Hi. I'm Daisy," she said as she approached Kyle's younger sister on the bench outside the Millers' barn. "I hope you are having a good visit."

Sarah looked up at her and smiled. "*Danke*. I am. I mean, I am, so far. We only got here yesterday."

Sitting down next to her, Daisy said, "Kyle told me that you read lips and know some sign language. Please let me know if you need me to move so you can understand what I'm saying." She paused then added, "Uh-oh? Am I being awkward? Should I not have mentioned your hearing?"

"You can mention it all you want. It's not a secret," she said. "I do have problems, but Kyle sometimes worries too much about everyone talking to me. I can hear pretty good when there's just one or two people to talk to in the room. Or outside, like we are now. I only have a lot of trouble when there's a crowd."

"Like at a party."

Sarah nodded. "Or at school. Or when a bunch of people are talking at once. That's when it's all kind of a jumbled mess in my head."

"All of that makes sense. I won't worry about you hearing me then." Remembering the supper that the Millers hosted for their arrival, Daisy said, "So how did last night go?"

"Not great." Sarah sighed in a way that made her look far beyond her fourteen years. "Last night was kind of how everything goes with my disability. My parents grow concerned, they speak to my teacher, and then they get Kyle involved and start to make plans without consulting me. And then . . ."

Daisy knew what was coming. "And then they decide to bring you here and throw a party where you can't really hear anything."

"*Jah*. Nothing like being in a houseful of noisy strangers to prove their points."

"He mentioned that you were getting teased at school. He's been worried about you."

She nodded. "I have been getting teased a lot." Looking embarrassed, she kicked out her bare feet on the dirt. "I was having a bad day and I got all upset. Which made Kyle want to fix everything for me." She wrinkled her nose. "Sorry. I bet you've never been in a situation like that."

"I don't know of anyone who hasn't," Daisy admitted. "It's part of growing up."

"I guess that's true."

"Sarah, one of the reasons I was looking forward to getting to know you is that I had a hard time in school when I was a teenager, too."

"What happened?"

"I became me, I think." Looking straight ahead, she added, "I've always loved working on the farm. I enjoy taking care of the horses, milking cows, fussing over the hens in the henhouse, that sort of thing. I like being outside with my hands in the dirt. I'd much rather be outside gardening or taking care of the animals than sewing or cooking or quilting or what have you."

"And let me guess, some of the other kids made fun of you because you were different."

Daisy nodded. "*Jah*. That is exactly what happened." Turning to face Sarah more directly, she added, "I'm not going to lie to you, Sarah. I had some really bad days. Some of the things the other kids said about me really hurt."

"What did you do?"

Sarah was staring at her intently. "I just put up with it."

"Oh."

The girl looked disappointed, and Daisy didn't blame her. She would've done anything to get Winter to stop teasing her years ago. "Obviously my way didn't stop the teasing. What have you been doing when kids have made fun of your hearing?"

"Truth?"

Daisy nodded.

"The same thing as you," she said sheepishly. "It's easier to ignore the comments and move on."

Daisy chuckled. "Good advice is easy to give but hard to take."

"*Jah*."

"Do you really want to quit school and move here, Sarah?"

"I thought I did, but no. I need to stay home and talk to the doctors about that cochlear implant."

"Maybe the doctor or a nurse could let you visit with someone who has had that operation. Then they can tell you what they think."

"I'll do that." Sarah smiled. "*Danke.*"

"Of course . . . and just for the record, please don't be too hard on your brother. He really is just trying to make you happy."

"*Mei bruder* worries too much about me, I fear. I'm afraid he is so intent on making sure I'm safe that he's forgotten that I'm usually pretty happy. I even kind of think that if I never get my hearing fixed, I'll still be pretty happy."

"I have two older brothers, so I know what you mean. They like to tell me what to do, even when it's something they aren't even sure how to do in the first place."

"That sounds familiar." Shifting again, Sarah added, "My parents have told me that I'm blessed to have someone care so much about me. I know I am. But that don't mean that I should always have to be grateful for his interference, right?"

"Right. Being thankful for kindness and grateful for 'fixing' a problem are two different things, I think."

"*Jah.*"

Looking at her cast, Sarah said, "Kyle told me that you broke your leg riding an electric bike. Is that true?"

"It is." She smiled. "I wasn't a very alert bicycle rider, I'm afraid."

"How come?"

"I kept looking at all the farm animals," she said with a laugh.

"Even though you were teased for being different, you are still the same person, aren't you?"

"*Jah*. And you know what? This conversation with you has done me a lot of good. I'm realizing that even though getting teased was no fun, it made me stronger." Reaching out she squeezed Sarah's hand. "I hope one day you will find the same thing to be true."

"*Jah*," she said softly. "I hope so too."

CHAPTER 23

Preacher Eli had been wonderful-*gut*. He'd had a lot to say about a great many things and his soothing voice had calmed all her nerves. For the first time since her accident, Daisy had found herself to be perfectly happy to sit still, pray, and feel the Lord's blessings in her life.

Never had three hours passed so quickly.

"Daisy, I'm so proud of you," Mamm said as they walked out of the barn.

"For what?"

"You seem at peace at last."

She was glad that her mother was pleased with her, but it was embarrassing if it was because she was finally sitting still and not fidgeting. "I do feel rather content," she replied. "But Preacher Eli had a lot of good things for us to focus on as well."

"You know what I mean, dear. You seem more at ease and positive. In spite of the fact that your leg is in a cast and you're a bit at loose ends."

"I think I've finally realized that so much that has happened was out of my hands. All this time, I've been upset that I had that accident in the first place. Now I realize that was a waste of time. I can't go back and change the past."

"That's right. You can only go forward."

Mamm patted her hand. "Do you want to sit with me and Daed at lunch?"

"*Danke*, but Lila and I were going to sit together."

"Okay. I'll see you after then."

When they separated, Daisy scanned the area for Lila. She was sitting next to her husband, Brandt, but there was plenty to room for Daisy there, too. She hurried over.

"Hi!" she called out. "I can't believe you already got your food."

"Hiya, Daisy," Brandt said. "This is my fault. I told Lila I was starving. I got in line before she did."

"Do you still not have your food yet?" Lila asked.

She shook her head. "*Mei muder* wanted to speak to me about something. I'll get it right now. Save me a spot?"

"Of course."

By the time she got in line, she noticed that Kyle was walking with his full plate to Brandt's and Lila's table. She hadn't realized that Kyle had gotten to know Lila's husband, but that was going to be perfect. The four of them would have lots to talk about. Maybe they could even plan to get together again, just the four of them.

Perhaps even at Lila and Brandt's house. It would be just like a date, and she'd finally feel grown up and independent. And boy did she need to feel that way. She'd had to rely on her mother for help during the last few weeks and hadn't been able to do her part of the chores. Or do much of anything.

Lukas and Ben were starting to act like she was a teenager again. She needed to remind her family that she was still capable and productive.

Feeling even more hopeful than she had during the service, Daisy reached for a plate.

"Oh! Daisy, wait a moment, would you please?" Winter asked as she hurried to her side.

"Oh. Uh, sure. Did you forget a fork?"

"*Nee*. I was inside helping Rachel with her toddler while she changed her baby and I'm only just now getting out here. I hate to ask, but would you mind if I got in line in front of you?"

There were only about ten people behind Daisy, so it seemed rather rude of Winter to ask. "Well . . ."

Winter glanced at Martha behind her. "You don't mind, do you, Martha? *Mei* friends are waiting on me and I sure don't want to make them wait any longer to start."

"I don't mind."

Winter smiled at Daisy. "See? It's not a problem."

No, she kind of thought it was a problem, but by now it felt wrong to say that. "Come on in, then."

Winter carefully stepped in front of her and picked up her plate, silverware, and napkin. "This food looks so good. Is the pasta salad as wonderful as it looks?"

"I don't know. I haven't gotten through the line yet."

Winter's eyes widened. "Oh! I had no idea. I thought this was your second time through."

"Why would you think that?"

"Only because you've done that before." She smiled at Daisy, but there was a bit of triumph in her eyes.

She couldn't believe it, but she supposed she shouldn't have been surprised. Winter's jab wasn't anything new. Five or six years ago, when the Beachys had hosted church, they'd needed extra help. She'd gotten up at dawn, helped Ellie Beachy with everything, from setting up tables to making punch for children, to cutting up vegetables. She'd skipped breakfast and had only half of a sandwich when she went through the line the first time.

After everyone went through the line, she and Ben had gotten back in line to get more to eat. Unfortunately, Lukas had teased them.

Even more unfortunately, no one seemed to pay any mind at all to Ben's second helpings. But several classmates noticed that she'd gotten more food and teased her about it for weeks.

"That was a long time ago, Winter," she said at last.

"Of course it was. All I was doing was making conversation." Winter put her plate down and carefully poured herself a glass of lemonade. "Oh dear. I always wish I had more hands," she joked. Loud enough for several men to look her way.

"I'll help you, Winter," Kyle called out as he strode forward.

"*Danke*, Kyle," she said in a soft voice. "I don't know what I would've done without your help."

He smiled at Winter as he carried both her plate and her glass across the grass.

Behind her, Martha grunted.

Well, at least Daisy wasn't the only person who tired of Winter's dramatics!

"I'll come back for my glass in a minute, Martha," Daisy said.

"Ain't no problem. You've got a good excuse. It's hard to carry much when one's hand is holding a crutch."

Daisy smiled at her before carefully navigating her way through the tables to Lila's.

And then, she couldn't believe it, but Winter was sitting in her spot. Right next to Kyle.

"What's going on?"

Looking embarrassed, Lila said, "Winter needed a place to sit and Kyle thought she could join us."

"Oh."

"Come sit over here at the end of the table," Brandt said. "James just stood up behind us. I'll bring his chair over."

"*Danke.*"

"Are you sure you don't want to just sit in James's empty seat?" Winter asked. "I mean, if you did that, Brandt wouldn't have to go to so much trouble for you."

"It's fine," Lila said quickly. "Brandt doesn't mind helping Daisy."

"Okay. If you say so."

Realizing that she'd forgotten to get her drink, Daisy stood up again. "I'll be right back. I need to get my drink."

"Hey, I can get it for you, if you'd like," Kyle said.

"She can get it," Winter blurted. "I mean, she ought to be able to do something on her own, right?"

Looking confused about what to do, Kyle turned back to her. "Daisy—"

"It's fine," she said before he could finish. "I'll be right back." Of course, it wasn't all that easy to move around the tables on one crutch, pick up a plastic cup, and then maneuver through the space without spilling her drink on anyone. She did it, though. Of course she did. She was even a little proud of herself for being so self-sufficient, too.

But every bit of those feelings of self-worth evaporated when she returned to the table. Brandt and Lila were already finished. On the other side of the table, Winter was smiling at something Kyle was saying. No one looked her way when she sat down.

While Kyle continued to tell a story about something that he and his friend Aaron had done long ago, Daisy bowed her head in prayer.

When she lifted her head, Winter was leaning close to Kyle

and gazing up at him with adoring eyes. Kyle appeared like he was very pleased.

She took a bite of her turkey sandwich.

"How is your sandwich, Daisy?" Winter asked.

"It is good," she replied as soon as she was able to swallow. "It's the same as everyone else's I imagine."

"Oh! Yes, of course. I suppose that was a silly question to ask." She fluttered her eyelashes. "I was just trying to think of something to say."

"It was a perfectly fine question, Winter," Kyle said. "You shouldn't be so hard on yourself."

"*Danke*. I mean, I do try to include everyone in a conversation. I don't want Daisy to feel like she is the odd one out."

Daisy exchanged a look with Lila.

"You are so sweet," he said. "I wish my sister, Sarah, had a woman like you nearby."

Kyle had told Winter about Sarah. Even though it felt wrong, Daisy still felt crushed. When Kyle had confided about his sister's hearing loss, Daisy had felt as if he was sharing something with her that he didn't often voice. She'd felt as if they were getting close.

But maybe it was just her who'd thought that.

"How old is your sister, Kyle?" Lila asked.

"She's fourteen. There's just the two of us, so we're close."

"That's a big age gap."

"It is, but I've enjoyed having a little sister. She was adorable when she was little."

"She's blessed to have you."

"She's a wonderful girl. The Millers enjoyed getting to know her when she and my parents visited a few weeks ago."

"They are kind people," Winter said. "I mean, it must have been hard to communicate with your sister since she can barely hear."

"They are kind, but Sarah did all right."

"Sarah was a lot of fun," Daisy said.

"Oh yes. You got to see her, too. I forgot you don't have a lot to do right now," Winter murmured. "Or have your circumstances changed?"

"Hmm," Daisy replied, which was the best she could do since she'd just taken another bite.

Lila giggled. "Winter, you have a knack for asking Daisy questions when her mouth is full."

"Do I? Gosh, I didn't notice. I'm so sorry, Daisy." Before Daisy could respond, Winter said, "So, are you two looking forward to hosting the gathering tonight?"

"We're not sure yet," Brandt joked.

"I don't blame ya," Kyle said.

"What gathering?" Daisy asked.

Lila flushed. "It's nothing. Just, ah, Brandt and I are hosting a party for some unmarried couples in the area."

"You know how it is," Brandt said. "All the parents want their kids to have a good time, but it's awkward because none of the teenagers relax because they're being watched by all the parents."

"This is news to me. I didn't know you two were hosting singings."

"This is the first one that we have hosted," Brandt said. He grinned. "It might very well be our last, too. Lila thought we should have hot dogs and s'mores. And watermelon. And lots of chips. She's been worrying about it for two weeks."

Lila had been planning it for two weeks and had never said a word to her.

You're still wearing a cast, she reminded herself. Of course Lila wouldn't mention a party that she couldn't attend.

Not wanting Lila to worry that she felt left out—even though she kind of did—she said, "You must be expecting a large group. I hope everyone has a good time and behaves themselves." Daisy grinned. She'd heard more than one story about teenagers sneaking off for a few unsupervised moments together. If she and Lila had been alone, they would've probably started giggling.

Back when they'd been in eighth grade, half their conversations had revolved around those parties and all the things they couldn't wait to do.

"Oh, it's not that kind of party, Daisy," Winter said. Lifting her chin, she said, "I think it's going to be a great group. We're all older, too," Winter said. "I don't think anyone attending the get-together is only fifteen or sixteen."

We. Winter had said *we*. "Oh. You're going?"

"I am." Resting her fingertips on Kyle's arm, Winter lowered her eyelashes. "We can't wait."

Kyle nodded, though he didn't look nearly as excited as Winter did. But it was probably because Daisy was feeling very awkward.

"Oh. Now I understand." She attempted to smile, but no doubt she looked as sick to her stomach as she felt. "I'll, um, have to hear about it when it's all over."

Winter clapped her hands together. "Yes! That will give us something to talk to you about when we see each other at church again in two weeks." She winked. "It will give you something to look forward to, Daisy."

Lila looked down at her plate.

"I can hardly wait," she said. And yes, there was a good amount of sarcasm in her voice.

But who could blame her?

She didn't care what anyone said. Winter Walker was not a nice woman.

She wasn't even close to being nice.

She could not even believe that Kyle was dating her. She couldn't believe that Lila had become such good friends with her either. When had that happened? When had everyone around her changed so much while she'd stayed the same?

But maybe everyone else wasn't the problem. Maybe everyone else had done what everyone had always planned to do, but she was the one who'd done everything wrong. She'd been the one who'd had the outlandish dream to own her own farm. Why had that been what she wanted instead of being a farmer's wife?

And just like that, every little bit of optimism and happiness evaporated. In its place was the same feeling that she continued to be unable to shake.

The feeling that she was never going to fit in and never going to be able to move on.

Holding her hands in her lap, she pinched the skin in between her thumb and forefinger. She needed to concentrate on that pain instead of what was going on inside her heart.

But maybe she should be used to it by now. After all, it was starting to feel true.

"Daisy?"

She turned to Kyle. Met his gaze. "*Jah*?"

"Um, are you all right?" He gestured to her plate. There was still half a sandwich, some fruit, a few chips, and a cookie on it. "You've hardly eaten."

"Don't worry about me. I'm fine. I always am." She smiled, though she was sure it was tight and awkward.

Luckily, the conversation moved on. Before too long, everyone stood up, cleaned their plates, and then helped clean up.

Eventually, she joined her parents and they helped her

climb into the buggy. The three of them sat on the bench, her mother for some reason discussing tomatoes.

Later, she'd lain on a lounge chair off the back patio, presumably to read. A barn cat joined her, choosing to doze under the shade of a sycamore tree.

Everything felt the same but so much different. Daisy wasn't sure if there was anything she could do about it or not.

CHAPTER 24

Lunch after church had been a disaster. Kyle couldn't remember feeling that uncomfortable since he'd briefly contemplated jumping the fence and had announced it the day before the entire extended family was due to arrive for Thanksgiving.

To this day, he wasn't sure if his mother had been more upset about him announcing that he wanted to be an Englischer or that he'd chosen to announce it when she was baking four pies.

Ironically, it had turned out that the timing of his announcement couldn't be better. Gathering around a table with his extended family and walking the fields of the farm with two of his uncles had changed his mind. Instead of pressuring him about getting baptized, his family had shown him so much love and support that he'd felt foolish for even contemplating an Englisch way of life.

This situation he was in, however, felt far different.

He'd become good friends with Daisy. In some ways, she was the best friend he'd had in Walden. She was smart, didn't complain about silly stuff, and knew almost as much about farming as he did.

The other day, when he'd stopped by to say hello, he'd found himself telling her about his ideas for the Millers' back pasture. He was thinking it would be a good spot to plant pumpkins. Someone in town had said that there had been a lot of tourists clamoring for pumpkin patches to visit.

Daisy had listened intently to everything he'd said. Then, she'd even asked him questions about irrigation and timing. Eventually, she'd brought up logistics, wondering where he'd want the tourists to park, and what path they would need to take.

Kyle hadn't even thought of those points. But when he'd admitted that to her, instead of acting like he should've thought about such things in the first place, Daisy had only said that she was glad to help.

He was coming to learn that that was Daisy. Helpful, strong, smart, and modest.

He liked her. He was glad he'd gone to her house and they'd become friends. He wanted to keep her in his life.

But Daisy wasn't the type of woman he'd always thought he'd marry. He liked a more feminine type of woman. Someone who needed him.

Someone like Winter.

But he didn't like the way Winter had talked to Daisy. It was almost as if she'd been trying to make fun of Daisy, but he had to be wrong about that. Not only had Daisy done nothing to encourage such ire . . . but it was obvious that she was going through a difficult time.

Surely a gentle woman like Winter wouldn't be oblivious to that?

Feeling both restless and tired, Kyle sat down on Velvet's milking stool. Velvet, who'd been napping, popped her head up in alarm.

He gently rubbed her side. "No worries, Velvet. I know I already milked ya today. I'm just taking a breather."

He could almost feel the energy in the barn shift. Velvet's

stance eased, and she stared at him intently. Almost like she was waiting for him to start a conversation with her.

"I sure wish you could talk. I could use some sound advice."

Velvet moved toward him. Not much, maybe just a few inches? But it was enough for him to run his hand along her nape. "*Danke*," he whispered. "I appreciate your support."

"Kyle? Is that you?"

"*Jah*."

As Mervin walked through the open barn doors, Velvet once again stepped backward into the shadows. Feeling slightly protective over her—though he wasn't exactly sure what she needed to be protected from—Kyle stood up.

"Did you need anything, Mervin?"

"Hmm? Oh, *nee*." The older man stuffed his hands in his pockets when he stopped in front of him. "I was, ah, just going for a walk when I spied you in here through a gap in the doors. You aren't working, are you?"

"*Nee*. I, ah, was just checking on Velvet here before I wrote my sister a letter."

"I thought you called her once a week."

"I do. But she likes receiving letters, too."

"You're a *gut* brother." He frowned. "Aaron cares for Bethany as much as any brother does for his sister, but he's never looked after her the way you do Sarah."

"Sarah's only fourteen." Plus, she had her hearing disability. "It's a habit, I guess."

"Of course. Sorry if I was sounding critical. I was just making a comment." He smiled. "Did I hear that you are going to a singing tonight?"

"*Jah*. I'm taking Winter Walker. Lila and Brandt Weaver, are hosting."

"Well, I hope you enjoy yourself."

"*Danke*." Right before the older man turned away, Kyle

called out, "Hey, Mervin, why do you think Daisy Lapp hasn't married?"

He raised his eyebrows. "Well, that ain't for me to say. I reckon she would have an idea more than me."

"I suppose that's true."

"But, I do remember when both Aaron and Bethany were courting. I could be wrong, but neither of my *kinner* had been looking for a match when they fell in love. Bethany was enjoying her first year of college when she met Phillip." He smiled. "As for Aaron, well, Ruthie and I were with him the first time he met Hanna. It was as if she had a bright light shining down on her just for him." Mervin's eyes lit up. "Aaron couldn't look away."

"He never told me that."

"I'm sure he wouldn't!" Mervin cackled. "Ruthie used to whisper that the boy was obsessed with that girl. I don't know if Aaron was obsessed, but he couldn't see her enough." Smiling softly, he added, "One evening, when I was up waiting for him to come home, he told me that his only goal was to get her to want to marry him."

"He got his wish, huh?"

"Indeed." Mervin shrugged. "All that means I'm not sure why Daisy hasn't fallen in love yet. I reckon it hasn't been her time, maybe because she was so focused on buying this piece of land. Or, perhaps it's Gott's plan, *jah*. Just like maybe there's a reason the Lord hasn't brought you the right woman yet."

"You're right."

Mervin folded his arms across his chest. "What has surprised me the most is that Winter Walker hasn't been claimed yet. Now, there's a girl who seems like she wants nothing more than to be married and to start a family." He shrugged as he stepped away. "But maybe none of the men in the area were the right ones for her, either."

"Thanks for listening. I'm going to go for a walk, then write that letter to Sarah."

"You do whatever you'd like." He snapped his fingers. "Oh! I almost forgot. Ruthie told me to tell you that she made some chicken salad. You're to help yourself before you leave for the Weavers' *haus*."

"Ruthie is the best."

Mervin's smile was so bright, it made him look ten years younger. "She is, Kyle. For sure and for certain."

Later that evening, after being at Lila and Brandt's for two hours, Kyle was ready to leave. The Weavers' house was lovely and their backyard had multiple sitting areas and a wide space in the back with a firepit and still more chairs surrounding that.

But even though the couple had gone to a lot of trouble to make the evening comfortable, he still felt like a fish out of water. Maybe it was because most everyone else had either grown up together or had known Brandt and Lila for quite some time.

Or, it could be that he was beginning to wonder if he'd been hasty with his infatuation for Winter.

She'd wanted to meet him there, which had first confused him, because he'd been ready to say hello to her parents before properly escorting Winter to the gathering. But after she arrived, Kyle began to understand why she hadn't wanted him to go to her house. She was a flighty thing, seeming to cling to everyone. And needing everyone's attention, too.

To his surprise, her distance suited him fine. He was even more confused about his feelings for Winter. She was so different than Mary. Mary had always been straightforward and vocal about her feelings.

Winter, on the other hand, appeared to be far more vague. He couldn't figure it out.

And . . . maybe she'd been feeling the same way, because after staying by his side for the first thirty minutes, she'd spent a lot of time with all the other single men.

He'd been cordial to the other single women he'd met, but for some reason taking the time to know them better didn't sound appealing. Most were far too young.

In the end, he'd manned the grill so Brandt could man the bonfire, going with another one of his buddies.

When Lila approached, he picked up a plate. "How many hot dogs would you like?"

"One, please."

After he placed the hot dog on a lightly toasted bun, he handed it to her. "Here you go."

"*Danke*." She stepped to his right and slathered a bunch of ketchup and mustard on hers and then took a bite. "Oh, yum. I haven't had a hot dog in almost a year. This tastes good."

He agreed completely. "I like them on the grill the best. *Mei mamm* likes boiling hers, but I don't care for that much. It ain't the same."

"I agree." After swallowing a second bite, Lila said, "I'm sorry you are stuck manning the grill tonight. If you'd like to go mingle, I'd be happy to finish up here."

"Thanks, but I'm okay."

"Are you sure?"

"*Jah*. I, uh, am not much of a mingler." Looking across the way, where Winter was talking to a group of five men and women, he added, "I guess I never picked up the knack for it. I'd much prefer to have something to do."

Looking reflective, Lila said, "Daisy is the same way. She gets bored at things like this. She always has."

"Is that why you didn't ask her to come over?"

Even in the dim light, Kyle could see her frown. "That didn't have anything to do with it at all." Looking even more uncomfortable, Lila tossed her empty paper plate in the nearby garbage can. "Lunch sure took a wrong turn, didn't it?"

"I'm not sure," he said diplomatically. "I did think that Daisy seemed uncomfortable though."

"It was worse than that. The whole thing was a mess. Every time I looked at Daisy, I felt guilty. I didn't know how to make things better, though."

Kyle was pretty sure that Lila could have done something. He'd thought Lila was a good friend of Daisy's. "Daisy did look upset about not being invited." He held up a hand. "I know I sound judgy and I'm sorry. I don't know the whole story."

"I don't blame you for pointing out the obvious. I knew she was upset, too. I honestly didn't mean to *not* invite her. I . . . well, it didn't feel like the right time. Not only does Daisy not enjoy gatherings like this, I also didn't think it would be comfortable for her."

"Because of her cast."

Lila nodded. "Brandt and I talked about it. We both agreed that walking around on crutches in the dark didn't sound safe. But, if she came and sat down the entire time, people might ignore her."

"You're right on both counts." Even though there were lots of sitting areas, so far the only people who had been sitting down were the couples next to the firepit.

"I didn't expect Winter to make her feel so bad, though," Lila muttered.

"Maybe Winter didn't realize how she sounded? I mean, sometimes people say things without realizing that they could be taken the wrong way."

Lila pursed her lips. "Kyle, I'm not sure how to respond to that."

"I don't understand."

Lila looked out into the distance, seemed to come to a decision, and then said, "Here's the deal with Winter. She's lovely and can be a lot of fun to be around."

"But?"

"But, Winter doesn't like Daisy. She never has. Honestly, it's like she decided to pick on her years ago and never grew out of the habit. And because of that? Well, it's made me realize that she is a person to watch carefully."

He was sorry to hear that. Not just for Daisy's sake, but for his own. He'd hoped that all the things that were starting to make him feel uneasy about Winter had been his perception. Of him being too critical.

But if that was the way she treated people, he would want to give her a wide berth in the future. "Is that why she hasn't already gotten married?"

"I don't know. It could be that she just hasn't found her match."

"Come on, Lila. Sorry, but you've known her all your life. Brandt has too, right?"

She nodded. "I know how Brandt has always felt about her, but it's not my place to share."

"I see." It was obvious that Brandt didn't like Winter very much. If he'd liked her, Lila would have said so.

"You know, the truth is that while Brandt and I were happy to host this gathering, we're not matchmakers. Also, everyone else's relationships aren't our business. I mean, things happen at different times for different people." Folding her arms across her chest, Lila added, "After all, you don't have a girlfriend, which is a surprise."

"I did. I courted Mary in Kentucky. We broke up shortly before I moved down here. It's one of the reasons I was willing to move so far away."

"You see, I had no idea about that. I'm sorry about the breakup."

"Me too. But Mary taught me a lot about myself, and for

that I can't complain." He was about to add something more, but Winter was walking toward them.

"Kyle, I've been waiting for you to leave that grill all night. When will you get a break?"

"Right now," Lila said. She grinned as she shooed Kyle away.

Winter wrapped a hand around his elbow. "Oh good. Now we can finally spend some time together. Where would you like to go?"

She was looking up at him with such a sweet expression, all his reservations about her faded away. Perhaps Winter, too, had something in her past that had made her the way she was.

He gestured toward a pair of chairs situated a little away from the rest of the group. "Would you mind if we sat down and talked, just the two of us?"

Her pale blue eyes appeared luminous. "I wouldn't mind that at all," she whispered.

"Have fun," Lila called out.

Kyle winked at her but Winter didn't seem to notice anything but him. She clung to him as they crossed the yard. She was pretty and made him feel needed.

Maybe things between the two of them were going to work out after all.

CHAPTER 25

"You have been a very good patient, Daisy," Dr. Alvarez said as they stared at her X-rays together in the examining room. "Look how much your bone has mended."

The crack in the bone did look much better. Even her inexperienced eyes could see the difference between today's picture and the one that had been taken on the day of her accident. "It looks much better."

"How is it feeling? Have you been able to put much weight on it?"

"Some. Before you cut off the cast, I was able to get around pretty well with just one crutch now."

"Yes, that's good progress." He continued to study the X-ray films on the screen.

As always, her impatience got the best of her. "What do you think? Do all your questions mean that I won't have to wear a cast anymore?"

"I'm afraid it doesn't."

"Oh."

"Now, there is some good news. We aren't going to put

back on a plaster cast. We're going to switch to a removable brace instead." Holding the contraption up, he smiled. "This one should give you a bit more mobility. Plus, there's the added bonus of you being able to remove it when you shower."

"That does seem better." Not having a smelly cast on her leg would be a big improvement.

Turning to the nurse who was standing near the computer, the doctor called out some numbers and dates.

She nodded as she typed in his orders. "I'll take care of it."

"Thanks." Smiling at Daisy, he said, "I'll see you in six weeks."

Six? And he was leaving? Just like that? "*Nee!*" she called out. "I mean, wait, please."

He turned back around to face her. "Yes?"

"Are you sure I have to have this new cast on for that long?"

"I'm afraid so." His voice was crisp but sympathetic. "The bone is mending, but it's not near strong enough for you to not take its healing very seriously." He drew a breath. "Also, you live on a farm, yes?"

When she nodded, he added, "I grew up on a farm, Daisy. It's a demanding life. I'm afraid if your tibia doesn't have the support it needs, the fracture will worsen. You might even need to get a pin put in. We don't want that, right?"

"Right. I don't want that at all."

"You take care now." He smiled as he walked out.

Distressed, Daisy watched him go. It was obvious that his mind was already on his next patient.

"This is terrible," she muttered.

Cheryl, the nurse, chuckled. "Sorry for laughing, but you have just blurted what almost every other patient has said."

"I understand his concerns, but I need to get a new job," she admitted. "My old boss fired me when she realized that I couldn't work for a month."

"That's terrible. I'm sorry, too. But I'm afraid that Dr. Alvarez is right. Impatient patients don't speed up their healing. Most of the time they make things worse."

"Am I being impatient if all I'm doing is trying to get my life back on track?"

"If I was your girlfriend and sitting across from you at a cute coffee shop, I would say not at all. I'd say that you have every right to get this cast off and find a new job. Everyone has bills to pay."

She took a deep breath. "Unfortunately, I'm your nurse and I must tell you the honest truth, which is that you have every right to refuse to wear the new cast. But if you do that, you'll be in pain and there's a very good chance that the bone will break again, this time worse."

"I understand."

"Are you ready to get this taken care of then?"

"*Jah*. Sure."

Cheryl's expression brightened. "Very good. Now, let's get this on and make sure it fits well."

"Okay."

She winked. "Good choice," she said as she strode toward the door. "I'll be back with the tech and we'll get your cast taken care of in no time."

"Thanks."

When Daisy entered the waiting room thirty minutes later, Ben was frowning at his cell phone's screen.

"Here I am," she said. "Sorry it took so long."

His smile faltered as he took in her new brace. "This journey isn't over yet, is it?"

"Nope."

As they walked out the door, he said, "How long does this one need to stay on?"

"Six weeks." As she crutched down the hall, she said, "I'm so tired of this, Ben."

"I know."

"I need to get a job."

"No you don't. Not really. You know Mamm and Daed and Lucas don't care if you help out around the house."

"But I care. I feel like I'm in limbo."

"That's not a surprise. You are in limbo."

"Ben!"

He held the door to the front of the building for her. "Hey, settle down," he said as they walked to the parking lot. "You need to look on the bright side. You won't have a cast on forever, and having a few months to rest and evaluate your life ain't that bad."

"It is."

"Something else is going on. What is it?"

"I don't know." Of course, that wasn't true, but how could she tell him what was going on inside her head? Both he and Lukas always did the right thing without complaint.

After Ben helped her get inside his SUV and he paid for parking, he turned to her. "Come on, D. Don't be shy. Tell me what you've been stewing about."

"I'm starting to think I don't fit in anywhere, Ben."

"You will. Like I said, just give everything some time. Your leg will heal and you'll get a new job. It's all going to work out. It always does." Lowering his voice, he added, "You need to be patient."

"This isn't about patience. What I'm trying to tell you is that I think I'm a misfit."

"Come on. You are not a misfit, Daisy."

"Don't laugh. I'm being serious."

"I am, too. You're fine. I promise."

"You don't know what happened last weekend. I found out that Lila and Brandt hosted a gathering on Sunday night, but I wasn't invited."

Pulling out of the parking lot, Ben frowned. "Are you sure?"

"I'm positive. I was sitting with them, then Kyle, and then Winter showed up and I discovered that Kyle has been *courting* her."

Ben wrinkled his nose. "Wow. Well, I hope Kyle had a good time with her. If he did, he's a better man than me."

"Ben, I'm really upset. I canna believe that you are joking."

"I'm sorry, but let's be real. Winter Walker is a spoiled girl who's never been nice to a lot of people. She treated you terribly. If Kyle enjoyed her company, then he deserves all the pain she'll eventually put him through."

There was a part of Daisy that kind of hoped that Ben's dark prediction would be true. She doubted it, though. "I think he likes her a lot."

"That's his choice." Softening his voice, he added, "Daisy, listen. I know you kind of like this guy, and I kind of like him, too. He seems decent and kind. But he's not the only available bachelor you're going to meet. Plus, you have time. You're still young."

"All my other friends have already found their matches."

"Well, neither of your brothers have. And, for the record, neither of us have been fretting about it too much. Sooner or later, the Lord will bring the right matches for us. I truly believe that."

Oh, but she hated when Ben and Lukas tried to compare her situation to theirs. "That is completely different."

"Because we're men?"

"Obviously. You have a career, and Lukas has a future on our family's farm. I don't have either. I'm supposed to find a husband and have *kinner*."

"You are also supposed to be happy. Marrying the wrong man will not make you happy. Having children with him isn't going to make things a lot better either."

Ben sounded bitter, which reminded her that he had seriously courted a girl when he was a teenager. When she'd moved away, it broke his heart. Though he'd never admitted it, Daisy thought that breakup was one of the reasons he'd decided to become English.

"You are right," she said at last. "I'll do my best to be patient."

"That's good. Keep your chin up, sister. I think you are in good company. It could be that we Lapps are late bloomers in love and marriage." He pulled into a fast-food restaurant parking lot. "Now, let's eat. I'm starving."

"Okay, but you're buying," she teased.

"Fine, but when you can walk again and start working . . ."

She smiled. "I'll buy. I'll buy you a wonderful-*gut* lunch wherever you want."

Resting his hand on the steering wheel, Ben chuckled. "I don't doubt that for a minute, little sister."

CHAPTER 26

The day was so sunny and beautiful, Ruthie had felt she had no choice but to take Velvet out to the pen next to the barn. It was Kyle's day off. If he'd been around, she would've asked him to take their dairy cow to the field on the hill. There was a nice thicket of trees on one side, which all the animals seemed to enjoy. Velvet, especially. Whenever Kyle walked her to the field, she could be found contentedly either standing next to the trees or lying on the grass, in the shade.

That meant that she knew the exercise pen wasn't Velvet's favorite place to spend an afternoon, but she figured it was better than nothing. Ruthie imagined that even a cow in a blue mood would appreciate a burst of fresh air.

"I know you'd rather be out in the grass, but the arthritis in my knee is acting up a bit today. I'm afraid the walk is more than I'm willing to do right now," Ruthie explained as she clipped the lead to Velvet's bridle and slowly led her to the pen.

To her delight, Velvet didn't seem to mind the pen at all.

After Ruthie released the bridle, the cow gave a little shake. It looked a bit like something Lizzie had done when she was a playful pup. Sometimes, she'd get so excited for a walk in the woods, her whole body would wiggle in excitement.

Of course, Velvet was no basset hound puppy. The cow could very well just be shaking off a pesky fly.

"You've still got a lot to learn about farm life, Ruth Anne," she muttered to herself.

After she closed the gate, Ruthie leaned on the top of the wooden fence. Mervin had painted it a fresh white the day after they'd moved in. To her, it was a symbol that dreams often did come true, thanks to hard work and the Lord's help. Ruthie never got tired of admiring it.

Deciding that the morning sun wasn't too hot, she rested her elbows on the top of the fence and watched Velvet wander around a bit.

"How are you doing, Velvet?" she called out. "Are you finding this to be to your liking?"

Velvet didn't respond with a moo, but she did turn her head to gaze at her with those big brown eyes of hers. After a few seconds passed, she blinked.

Well, she didn't exactly look happy, but the heifer did seem to have a bit of a pep to her step.

That had to be a good thing.

"I found that a good dose of sunlight works wonders for my disposition," she admitted. "You know, doctors say that one can get some vitamin D from the sun, and that helps bones. It's never too early to think about osteoporosis, right?"

Velvet yawned.

"*Jah*, to be sure. Discussing bone health ain't the most exciting of conversations, but what can you do? Not everything that's on one's mind is exciting, right? I mean, sometimes it's just life. What do you think? Do you agree?"

Velvet seemed to nod. Or maybe she was simply chewing her cud.

Ruthie was beginning to feel sillier by the minute, but for some reason that wasn't enough to propel her to go inside. All that was there for her were a dozen small chores to do. Besides, wasn't this what retirement was all about? She'd spent many a moment at Sew and So listening to customers talk about their lives. Sometimes the stories were amusing and the ladies felt like friends. Other times? It was nothing like that at all. Sometimes their stories were ones she'd already heard a dozen times and it took everything she had to appear interested.

And that was when they weren't so busy cutting fabric, answering phones, unpacking boxes, cleaning, and vacuuming after a busy day.

"Well, I, for one, have found comfort in boring days. Excitement is overrated. Not that I think your company is boring."

After gazing at her for a moment, Velvet approached. Ruthie stood still as the cow walked right over to the other side of the fence. She was now close enough for Ruthie to reach out a hand and pet her sweet face.

Which she did. Gratefully.

Lowering her voice, Ruthie said, "Well, you showed me. I know, I said I wanted to give you some sunlight, but you are giving me what I needed to get today. A bit of an ear." Just like those ladies at the shop she'd just been thinking about.

"I guess that saying is true, huh? What goes around, comes around." She rubbed the soft area just above Velvet's nose. "Here's my confession. I think I'm standing out here in the sun talking to you for a far different reason than to absorb some vitamin D."

She took a deep breath. "I'm here because I want to know what you thought I should do about this farm."

Velvet yawned. Obviously, it was time to get to the point.

"Okay, brace yourself, because my secret is a doozy." She lowered her voice. "Believe it or not, Mervin and I have had more than one conversation about maybe selling this farm."

Velvet tilted her head to one side. Kind of like how Lizzie did when Ruthie tried to take her out for a walk in the pouring rain.

The cow didn't think she was making a bit of sense, which made her feel even more embarrassed than she already did.

"I know, standing here with you here, beside this old red barn is everything I dreamed of. For years! But the other parts of farming? I'm not enjoying it." Lowering her voice to a near whisper, she continued. "Velvet, the truth of the matter is that Mervin and me aren't quite the farmers that we thought we'd be.

"What do you think? Has there been a big difference between the way Mervin and me do things and the way that the Burkholders ran things?"

When Velvet looked down at her front hooves and sighed, Ruthie knew she needed to be a bit more clear. "What I'm trying to ask is do you think we're missing that perfect 'farmer' spark?"

"Moo," Velvet said. Er . . . mooed.

"What does that mean?"

"Moo!"

"I'm sorry, but I have no idea what you are trying to tell me."

After giving Ruthie what appeared to be a spiteful glare, Velvet turned around. Why, it was almost as if she was presenting Ruthie with her backside! Which was ridiculous. Cows didn't do such things.

Did they?

"Velvet, I'm real sorry if I'd offended you, but I have no idea how to make things right in my life."

The cow didn't respond.

"Ah, Ruthie, is everything all right?"

She turned to find Daisy approaching. Today, the girl had on a bright orange dress, a smaller blue cast, and just one crutch. But the prettiest part about her was her smile. It was genuine and warm. Like her.

"Daisy, what a surprise! How in the world did you get over here?" she asked.

"Um, I drove the courting buggy."

"You were able to drive the buggy with a cast on your foot?"

"To be sure." She crutched over to her side. "I don't know if you've noticed, but the horse does all the work."

Ruthie chuckled. "Forgive me. I'm, uh, afraid I'm not at my brightest right now."

"What's wrong?"

"I'm afraid I've offended Velvet."

Daisy made her way to Ruthie's side, then rested her arms on the top of the white railing next to her. "Why do you think that?" she asked.

There wasn't a bit of sarcasm in her voice.

"You really aren't going to make fun of me for imagining that a milk cow is in a snit?"

"Uh, do you want me to?"

"*Nee*. Of course not." She pressed a hand to her face as she attempted to pull herself together. "Forgive me. I . . . I just don't know what to do." Of course, she was talking about her life, not just Velvet. But Daisy didn't need to know that.

Daisy's expression grew more concerned, but to Ruthie's relief, instead of pressing her for more information, she whistled at Velvet.

Velvet turned around and looked directly at Daisy.

She held out a hand. "Hiya, Velvet. I came over here to

visit with Ruthie for a spell, but I'm happy to see you, too. You're looking well."

Velvet approached her, just like an eager pet would.

Ignoring Ruthie's gasp, Daisy started talking. "What do you think of my new cast? It's called a removable brace. But at least it's blue, right?" She looked down at it. "What do you think? Should I have gone white? I don't know why I chose a color, but the truth is that I was real disappointed to be receiving a new one at all." Leaning down on the rail, she added, "You see, I'd been hoping that the doctor would take the old one off, declare me good as new, and then send me on my way."

"I'm sorry about that," Ruthie said.

Daisy darted a glance her way. "Me too. But my *bruder* was quick to remind me that healing takes time, and if I ignored the doctor's advice, then I might be able to walk around all right, but I could easily do some damage and make things worse."

"That is *gut* advice. Bethany broke her arm when she was playing softball and slid into third base. She fell, got tangled up with the player on third, and broke her arm."

"Wow. That's a story."

Remembering how incredulous some of the hospital staff had been when Bethany had described what had happened, Ruthie chuckled. "It sure is. Bethany was rather slight and tiny. No one ever imagined that *mei* petite daughter would have a competitive streak a mile wide." She took a breath. "Anyway, my point is that Bethany hated that cast and hated the second one she received—after playing on the playground at recess—even more. My point is that it didn't matter if she liked wearing a cast or not. Some things in life just have to be done. Like healing. Or working. Or waking up in the morning. Gott needs us to be patient."

"*Jah*. Everything worthwhile takes time, ain't so?"

Thinking of how hotheaded she'd been in her own situation, Ruthie nodded. "I fear I've been struggling a bit with impatience myself."

"I guess I'm in good company."

"Would you like to come in for a coffee and some zucchini bread? I know everyone is making it right now, but this was from a new recipe, and it turned out pretty *gut*."

"I happen to love zucchini bread. *Danke*." Glancing at Velvet, Daisy added, "Would you mind if I stayed here for a moment and talked to your cow? I'd feel terrible if I walked away without giving Velvet a bit more attention."

"Not at all. I'll go make a fresh pot and slice up some bread for us both. Take your time."

"Thanks."

As Ruthie walked back to the house, she heard Daisy speaking in soft, sweet tones to Velvet. Just as she opened the front door, Ruthie heard Velvet moo again. But this one sounded far less argumentative and more like a happy reply.

Realizing what she'd just thought, Ruthie chuckled to herself. A happy reply? What in the world! Cows didn't have different tones of "moos." Did they?

She hoped Daisy would let her know.

CHAPTER 27

This hadn't been how Daisy had thought her visit to the Millers would go. She'd been sitting around the house all morning, half feeling sorry for herself, half attempting to make a shirt for Lukas for his birthday, when she couldn't take herself anymore.

She was too blue, too confused, and sure, too inept to be making clothes for anything other than a doll. And so, on the spur of the moment, she'd told Lukas that she was going to take the courting buggy next door.

She'd been so sure that Lukas would either offer to take her or that he'd attempt to convince her that she should stay home. Instead, he'd attached Blackie's reins to the courting buggy and waved goodbye.

Blackie was so pleased to be out for a drive that she'd first turned right instead of left and took her down a series of country roads that were essentially empty. The few vehicles on them were farmers in less of a hurry than she was. Within a few minutes, Daisy's mind had eased and her spirits had lifted. She'd become less irritated with herself and a bit more calm.

With only the buggy horse for company, she allowed herself to face facts. Winter Walker was a lovely woman and there were surely many qualities about her that Kyle would like.

Okay, that was a lie. She didn't actually think there were many things about Winter that were good. However, that was a Daisy problem, not Kyle's. She needed to remind herself that she could only be in charge of her feelings. She couldn't take responsibility for Kyle's.

The realization helped. Which made her feel as if she was in a much better frame of mind than when she'd been attempting to stitch small, even stitches on a shirt that Lukas would likely never be able to fit his broad shoulders in.

Now, here she was, doing sneaky things again. She'd just coaxed Ruthie away on the premise that she and a dairy cow needed privacy.

Which was baloney.

Or, perhaps not.

Because Velvet was currently looking at her intently and she was pretty sure that this cow had something important to get off her chest.

"Velvet, now that Ruthie's gone, I think you need to be honest with me. Why are you still feeling blue? Are you still missing Samuel and Rachel? If you are, then I think you might have mad cow disease or some such. No offense."

She lowered her voice. "Samuel was a *gut* farmer and could grow an impressive field of corn, but he was sorry company, and you know this."

When the cow blew out air, just as if she did not want to hear any words of wisdom, Daisy clucked her tongue. "That attitude isn't going to get you anywhere, miss."

Velvet snorted.

"*Jah*, I know. You think you know everything, but I think you could maybe learn some new things, too. For example, just the other day you were happy with Ruthie, but now you've been obstinate with her yet again. I think you should start counting your blessings. After all, you are here in this pen instead of standing alone all day in a dusty barn, ain't so? Things could be worse."

Velvet shifted as she faced Daisy.

"There you go, Velvet. I'm glad you're beginning to understand the facts. Now, here's some advice. And, *jah*, I know that you are a cow and you will do what you want, for better or worse."

She lowered her voice, "Velvet, I really do think that you need to open your heart a bit and listen, okay? And the fact of the matter is that the Burkholders left. But listen, they were going to leave no matter what. And if the Millers didn't buy the farm, it would've been a stranger."

Velvet huffed.

"*Jah*, I know. You and me thought I'd be here with you. I tried to do that, too. I tried, but the honest truth is that I wasn't going to be able to save enough money for this place for at least another two years. I just wasn't making enough."

Reaching out, she ran a finger along a tuft of fur sticking out in between Velvet's ears. "That means that things could've been a lot worse."

After making sure that Mervin wasn't nearby, Daisy added, "While I agree that Mervin and Ruthie still have a lot to learn about farming, they have good hearts. And they're smart, too, because they hired Kyle, and he definitely knows his way around a farm. And we like Kyle, right? He's not only capable and strong, but he's handsome. Not every farmer is blessed with blond hair, warm brown eyes the color of molasses, and good biceps." She waved a hand. "I mean, that right there is a plus. Don't you agree?"

Velvet mooed. Her eyes lit up a bit, too.

So much so, that it was obvious that she had been listening intently. Daisy grinned. "I'm glad we're on the same page, cow."

"Sorry, but I'm pretty sure that Velvet was greeting me, Daisy," Kyle said.

Daisy raised her eyebrows at Velvet. When the cow looked down at her front hooves, Daisy knew exactly what that cow should've done. That cow should have stomped a hoof or something.

"Blackie would've helped me out, Velvet," she whispered. "A warning about Kyle approaching would've been nice."

"Sorry, you might have all the advice, but I'm the one who milks her every morning. In the dairy cow's world, I win," Kyle teased.

Right before he started laughing.

Turning to face him as best she could, since she had a crutch and a blue cast, Daisy tried to look mad.

But how could she fault him for laughing? She'd just been telling a neighbor's cow that the farmhand was cute.

"Please don't ever tell anyone what I just said."

Walking to her side, he reached out, played with the end of one of her *kapp*'s tails. "Daisy, I like you a lot, but there's no way on earth I'm not going to tell someone about this. Sorry."

She couldn't deny it. She was completely embarrassed. "I need to go. Ruthie is waiting on me."

"What for?"

"Not that it's any of your business, but we're going to sit and chat and have coffee and zucchini bread."

"I'm sorry I'll miss it, but I'll do my best to be useful. Maybe I'll talk to the cow about the world's events."

"Moo," Velvet called out. The sound was peppy, as if she was looking forward to the conversation.

"Velvet, you traitor," Daisy teased.

Kyle started laughing again.

And because it took her a bit to crutch her way to the Millers' front door, Daisy allowed herself to giggle a bit, too.

After all, there was no one around to see.

CHAPTER 28

It didn't seem to matter that this was Kyle's third visit to the Walkers' house. He still felt nervous and more than a little bit unsure if he was doing the right thing.

"Nothing you can do now," he reminded himself. "You're here and they saw you park your buggy."

Realizing that Winter was probably wondering what he was doing, standing in her front yard like a scarecrow, Kyle shook himself off, trotted up their front steps, and knocked on the door.

It opened immediately.

"Kyle, it is *gut* to see you again. *Wilcom* back," Jediah Walker said as he gestured for him to go in. "Winter will be downstairs in a moment, but I'll take your jacket from ya."

"*Danke.*" Kyle passed Jediah his jacket. It was slightly damp. They'd been experiencing an unusually wet summer, which was good for the land but annoying for travel. He looked down at his boots. They were free of mud but damp as well. "Would you like me to take off my boots?"

Jediah glanced down at Kyle's Red Wings. "No need for that, son. A little bit of water never hurt a floor."

"I guess not."

Jediah once again looked completely at ease and relaxed. Since Winter seemed so high-strung, that surprised him, but he probably should've known better. The Lord knew that he and his parents took much in stride after Sarah's hearing worsened. One couldn't worry about everything.

Also, since the Millers and the Walkers belonged to different church districts, he hadn't had too many occasions to speak to Jediah. They'd met once at an auction in Mount Hope, but that had only been in passing.

"How were the roads on your way over?" Jediah asked as they entered the living room.

"Muddy but decent." He smiled. "As good as they can be in the rain."

"Hopefully most of the vehicles were giving you a wide berth?"

"Wide enough." He shrugged. "I'm grateful it's summer. Driving a buggy home in the dark can be a challenge."

"*Jah*. And the rain makes it worse." He smiled. "Well, Winter will be glad you've come calling again. I'll go see what's keeping my daughter."

"Yes, sir."

When he was alone, Kyle looked down at his shoes and pants, hoping that neither had gotten too wet from when he'd tied the horse's leads to the hitching pole and then walked the few yards to the front door.

As the minutes passed, he started thinking about how wet Angel was going to be by the time they got home.

Every time he'd taken the buggy out during the last few days, coming home had involved another hour's worth of work. The horse needed to be dried, her hooves cleaned of mud, and then, of course, the buggy needed to be wiped down.

He knew not everyone took such care with their horses and buggy, but he wasn't the type of person to neglect either the horses' health or the Millers' property.

But that didn't mean that he didn't wish he could simply release Angel, put her in her stall, and close the barn door.

"Hello, Kyle," Winter said as she came downstairs.

"Hi, Winter." He stood up, as stunned by her beauty as he was the first time they'd talked. Tonight, she had on another violet dress, this one leaning toward a grayish lavender. It made her pale skin seem even more luminescent and her pale blue eyes even more striking. "You look pretty."

She smiled softly. "*Danke*." Her smile deepened as she took him in. "You look a bit wet. Are you cold?"

"*Nee*. I asked your father if he'd like me to take off my boots. He said not to worry about it."

"I'm only teasing you."

Maude appeared in the doorway. "Hello, Kyle. Would you like water or *kaffi*?"

"*Kaffi*, please."

"Very well."

He glanced expectantly at Winter. Whenever he had called on Mary, she'd be the one to bring them refreshments, not her mother. "Do you need to help her?"

"*Nee*. Why?"

"Oh, no reason."

Winter smoothed the skirt of her dress. "Does this look wrinkled to you?"

He glanced at the fabric that she was pointing to. "It looks fine to me."

"Hmm. I don't know if I'll want another dress made out of this fabric again. Every time I wear it, I feel frumpy." She lifted her head, gazed at him with wide eyes.

And he was at a complete loss of what to say.

Mary had been modest about her looks, though her golden hair had been especially beautiful. Then, too, he and Sarah had been raised to not dwell too much on appearances. It was a person's character that mattered.

Realizing that he was finding fault with Winter's worry, he cleared his throat. "I don't think you look frumpy, Winter. I don't know if you could ever look that way."

"*Danke.*" She relaxed a bit.

"Here we are. Coffee and cookies," Maude said as she brought in a tray and set it in front of Kyle. "Winter, I'll bring you a glass of water in a moment."

"Okay." She crossed her legs. "Please, help yourself to the cookies. I think they're rather good."

"Did you bake them recently?"

"Oh, *nee. Mei mamm* did. I don't enjoy baking all that much."

Remembering just how awful the lemon bars she'd served him last time were, he murmured. "I see."

"Here's your water, Winter."

Winter took the glass and set it down in front of her.

"Would you like anything else, Kyle?"

"*Nee*, Maude. Everything is wonderful. *Danke.*"

"You are welcome." She smiled pleasantly before turning back to the kitchen.

Kyle felt antsy, though he wasn't exactly sure why. Winter's parents were gracious and the coffee was good.

Plus, Winter was gazing at him in a pleasing way. No, that wasn't describing it. She was staring at him as if he was something special. As if she was truly happy that he'd driven over in the rain to see her.

Conversations with her were so different than with Daisy Lapp. Whenever he was around Daisy, the two of them could hardly stop talking. She needled him about this and that and he teased her about things that didn't matter. They laughed together.

Even when they were standing in a field and talking to a milk cow.

Immediately, he was ashamed of himself. Here he was, sipping coffee in the Walkers' living room but he was thinking about another woman. That was rude.

After all, it wasn't Winter's fault that he couldn't think of anything to say to her.

He cleared his throat. "You know, it just occurred to me that I don't know much about you."

She frowned. "What do you want to know?"

"Oh, I don't know. What do you like to do? Do you have any dreams?"

"Dreams?"

"Sorry. I sound foolish. I guess I was wondering if there was a place you'd like to see one day. A trip you might like to take. Or . . . a hobby you'd enjoy learning."

"A hobby?" She wrinkled her nose. "No, not really."

"I see."

She looked down at her lap before glancing up at him with a distressed expression. "I'm sorry if you find me boring."

"*Nee*. I didn't say that—"

"It's just, well, my needs and dreams are simple. I've always just wanted to be a good man's wife, keep his house in order, and raise a houseful of children."

"Ah." Kyle struggled to keep his expression neutral. Nothing about her goals was unexpected, so why was he feeling let down about Winter's confession?

Her cheeks pinkened becomingly. "Since I'm an only child, me and my parents have prayed that I'll find a man who would want to live here with me and run this farm. That's all I want. Someone to share my life with here." She tucked her bottom lip against her teeth. Seemed to bite down.

Kyle couldn't help but watch. Mesmerized.

"Do you think that's a terrible dream, Kyle? Do you wish I wanted to do something else? Something more selfish?"

"*Nee*. No, of course not."

She folded her hands on her lap. "My parents said when I get married, they'd build a *dawdi haus* and then my husband and I could have this house as our own. That's what I think about when I go to sleep. I dream of one day sitting in here in the evening with my husband." Her voice turned deeper. Smooth. "We could talk about our children or maybe what our plans are for the farm . . ." She gazed at him again. "Would you hate that?"

Would he hate living in this pretty house gazing at his beautiful wife after working on a farm that was as successful and large as this one? "*Nee*," he said honestly. "I would not hate that life at all."

Winter exhaled as her body seemed to relax. "I'm so glad about that."

"Winter, forgive me if I made you uncomfortable. I . . . well, I just wanted to know you better."

"I want the same things that you do."

"I'm stunned you haven't already been snapped up."

"Thank you for saying that." She lifted a shoulder. "But a lot of the men around here seem to want different things. I knew if I prayed hard enough He would answer my prayers." She smiled shyly. "Perhaps He has."

"Perhaps," he said. Well, croaked.

Thirty minutes later, he was driving the Millers' buggy home in the pouring rain. It was slow going. He took care to keep their buggy horse on as many back roads as possible. When the downpour slowed to a faint drizzle, Kyle finally allowed his head to accept what his ears had heard. If he married Winter, he could finally have a farm of his own. And children. He could live in that sprawling, well-built farmhouse and wake up every morning next to a beautiful wife.

It was obvious that that was what Winter wanted. And though he'd barely talked to her parents, they'd certainly been welcoming, too.

Within a year it could all be his.

He just didn't understand why his heart wasn't all in.

He didn't understand that at all.

CHAPTER 29

"Here for another stack of books, Daisy?" Lucinda asked when she spied Daisy walk through the doorway.

"I guess I am." She smiled at the attractive librarian. "I can't seem to stay away."

"That's a good thing for us. You always bring a smile. How were the books? Did you enjoy that new author?"

"Kind of," she said honestly. "I liked her characters but the mystery seemed a little too easy to figure out."

"That happens sometimes, doesn't it?"

"*Jah*, but thank you for the recommendation."

"I'll be happy to give you some other cozy mystery authors' names to try. Or, are you feeling like you won't have as much time to read anymore?"

"I'm afraid I'm going to have too much time," she said as she lifted the canvas bag off her shoulder and plopped the four books on the countertop.

"How come?"

After checking behind her to make sure that there was no one else in line, Daisy said, "I still have a cast on my foot.

Obviously." She took a deep breath and then decided to confess everything. "Then there's the fact that I lost my job."

"Where were you again?"

"At the bulk food store." Not wanting to make it sound as if Melissa had been completely unreasonable, she tried to explain. "The job there involved a lot of heavy lifting. We got in big boxes of food and other items and they all had to be unpacked and put on shelves. I can't do a lot of that with a bad leg."

"I'm sorry." Her expression full of sympathy, she said, "What about when your cast is off? I bet then they'll let you reapply."

"To be honest, I think I want to find something else. I didn't enjoy my job there all that much."

Lucinda leaned forward. "Want to know a secret?"

"Sure."

"I've never really enjoyed going in that store," she whispered.

"Well, bulk food ain't for everyone."

"It wasn't that. I found a lot of items there that I wanted. It was the manager. She never smiled and no one working there did either."

Daisy figured the reason for that was because no one enjoyed working for Melissa. But that seemed rather mean to say. "I'm sorry about that."

"Well, if you ever want to think of a career change, come see me."

"What do you mean?"

"I'm in need of a personable librarian assistant and I think you would be great."

"Truly?"

"Of course. You like to read, you usually have a smile on your face, and you can chat with most everyone. Plus, if you are used to working at the bulk food store, that means that you're used to working hard. That Melissa might be a lot of things, but a slacker isn't one of them, is it?"

Daisy chuckled. "It certainly ain't." Still thinking about the job, she said, "Lucinda, were you being serious about me being able to apply?"

"I was being very serious. Ryan was terrific but he moved to Florida now that his wife has retired from her job. This just happened about a week ago, but I haven't posted the job because I've been dreading the interview process."

"Does the job pay anything?"

Lucinda blinked, as if the question surprised her. "Yes. Of course. Now, you won't make a fortune here, but I'm pretty sure it's about the same amount of money per hour as the grocery store or a couple of other small retailers in the area pay." She smiled slowly. "Daisy, are you seriously thinking about it?"

"I am. I mean, I want to think about it, and I'd need to know more about what you expect. You do realize that I never went to school past the eighth grade?"

"Like I said, I know what I'm looking for, and it isn't necessarily a person with a degree." She smiled at an older man who just stepped into line. "How about you think about it for a day or two? I'll hold the position for two more days."

"You'd be willing to do that?" That was hard to believe, especially since it was on a hunch. It felt like a lot of pressure, too.

As if Lucinda was reading her mind, she reached out and clasped Daisy's hand. "Daisy, all I'm presenting is an opportunity. And not all opportunities are meant to be taken. Go home, talk about it with your friends and family. Pray about it. If you decide that this isn't a good fit, I'll understand."

"But what if I do want to pursue this opportunity? What then?"

"If that is what you decide, then we'll start discussing pay and schedules and the number of hours you want to work."

"Thank you for telling me about this. It might just be what I need to do, but I'm going to need to go home and discuss the details with my family."

"Yep." Lucinda's smile was brilliant. "Do what you need to do, Daisy. But, at the very least, don't forget to look at those cozies in the mystery section before you leave." She named three authors. "I promise, those women's novels are delightful. I feel certain that you're going to love one of their series."

This was why Lucinda was such a good librarian. She talked to the patrons and made them feel seen. If she ended up working there, she wanted to be the same way. "*Danke*. I'll go look at them right now."

Feeling as if she was in a daze, Daisy walked down the mystery aisle and perused the titles, and the authors Lucinda had mentioned. She did what she had come in to do, which was scan the backs and inside covers of several of the books and picked out four to try.

But as she did so, Daisy found herself thinking about shelving books and maybe even eventually helping someone else. She liked that idea. She wasn't sure if she was willing to give up all her dreams about being a farmer and spending her days working on the land, but Lucinda's offer certainly did make her feel as if there were other choices in her life that she'd never contemplated before.

Daisy was still thinking about becoming a librarian's assistant when she ran into Winter and her mother on the sidewalk near the fabric store.

As much as she wanted to dart into the hardware store in order to avoid them, that wasn't an option. They'd already seen her. Plus, she needed to stop letting Winter get under her skin.

"Hi, Maude and Winter. I hope you both are well. It's a lovely day, isn't it?"

"Hello, Daisy," Maude replied with a warm smile. "It is indeed a lovely day. How are you feeling?"

"I'm doing better, *danke*."

"How much longer will you have to wear that cast?" Winter asked.

"A few more weeks, at least." Tapping one of the Velcro fasteners, she added, "At least I can take this one off to shower. That's a blessing."

"I bet," Winter said. "And then what happens?"

"Then, I will be, hopefully, as good as new."

"But what if you aren't?"

Daisy was taken aback by Winter's slightly condescending tone. Then she reminded herself who she was talking to. Winter had always acted as if she was a little bit better than everyone else. "If I'm not, then I might have to have another surgery. The doctor says that ain't likely, though."

"I hope that isn't the case, dear," Maude said. Giving Winter a meaningful look, she added, "It's always better to look on the bright side of things."

"I feel the same way. It's in the Lord's hands, though."

"The Lord's and your own," Winter corrected. "Should you even be out walking with just one crutch? It looks foolish. If you could easily fall."

Mrs. Walker frowned at her daughter. "Winter, what in the world?"

"Oh, I'm sorry. I didn't mean how that sounded. I mean, if I sounded confused," she continued in a slow, sweet tone. "I was just worried about you."

It was so tempting to finally tell Winter just how tired she was of her mean comments. But it wasn't worth it. Winter wasn't going to change. Not any more than Daisy was. They were who they were. "I appreciate your concern, but I am not doing anything I shouldn't. I hope you both have a nice afternoon."

"Oh, we will. We're going to shop for fabric for a new dress," Winter said. "Now that Kyle Hostetler has been calling on me so much, I've realized that some of my older dresses are too bedraggled for company." She laughed, though it sounded very fake. "I'm sure you understand."

"I do."

"Please tell your *mamm* hello, Daisy," Maude added. "It's been too long since I've spent time with her."

"I'll be sure to tell her that you asked about her," she said before she was finally able to escape the conversation and head home again.

But as she heard the fabric store's door open and shut behind her, Daisy realized that her mood had plummeted again.

Sure, she and Kyle had gotten off to a bad start, but they'd become friends.

Good friends.

And while she'd occasionally imagined that their friendship could eventually grow into something deeper, she'd also accepted the fact that he might never see her in a romantic sense.

But why did he have to see Winter that way? Daisy would be so disappointed if he took Winter as his wife. Winter was so mean and petty. Kyle could do a lot better.

Feeling tired all of a sudden, Daisy sat down on a bench near Walden's town square. There was a park right in front of her and several children were squealing and playing, just like she, Ben, and Lukas used to do.

The group in front of her was a little different. Some were Amish and some were English. Most of their parents were off to the side, half watching them, half talking to each other and glancing at their phones. But that moment in time was as familiar as it was a common sight.

It was also a welcome reminder about the way one's life

moved on. No one stayed in one place for very long. Babies became toddlers who became busy, exuberant kids like the ones currently in the park.

Eventually, they grew up and got married or had jobs. And then one day, they'd take their children to the same park where they used to play.

It was how everything was supposed to be.

One couldn't wish that everything stayed the same, because it wasn't possible.

"You need to accept your reality, Daisy," she whispered to herself. "You need to stop having childish dreams and accept your adult responsibilities." And those responsibilities included the knowledge that she was never going to be able to buy a farm and run it all by herself. It was too much work and too much money.

She was never going to enjoy sewing.

An electric bicycle was never going to solve her problems or make her feel better.

And Kyle Hostetler might enjoy her company and like being her friend, but he was never going to see her the way he viewed Winter Walker.

Those were the facts that she needed to face.

As she walked the rest of the way home, Daisy reminded herself that accepting the truth was a good thing.

Even if it hurt a bit.

Looking down at her cast, she said, "You're living with a bit of pain right now and you're surviving just fine. You'll be able to do it again."

CHAPTER 30

"Kyle, would you please run this basket over to the Lapps' for me?" Ruthie asked when he was walking down the short path to the *dawdi haus*.

He was a sweaty, exhausted mess. He'd been working in the fields all day. He wanted a shower, about a gallon of water, and to collapse, and not even in that order.

Delivering a basket to the neighbors' farm felt like climbing Mt. Everest. No, it felt like climbing a flight of stairs. Even something as small as that felt like too much. "Can it wait until tomorrow, Ruthie?"

"Tomorrow? No, it cannot. It's a cake."

Hadn't they just given the Lapps a pie? "Why did you bake them a cake?"

"Pardon me?"

She looked completely taken aback by his tone, and who could blame her? He was being surly and rude. "Sorry, but I am awfully tired right now."

"That's why I'm asking you to go over there now. Before you get comfortable and relaxed."

Her reasoning made no sense to him, but he was beginning to come to terms with the fact that a lot of times it didn't. Ruthie and Mervin were used to doing things like they wanted. Whether or not their choices were good or bad never entered their minds. "All right. Fine."

"*Danke*. When you get back, I'll have your supper ready for you. We're having cheeseburgers, freezer pickles, baked beans, corn on the cob, and tots." She beamed.

And before he realized what he was doing, Kyle was smiling, too. Sure, a lot of Amish men might yearn for fried chicken or a succulent meal of roast beef and mashed potatoes. He loved burgers. And tater tots? Well, they were his guilty pleasure. He loved them. And somehow Ruthie, for all her quirks, she was a whiz at cooking Tater Tots. He had no idea what she did, but the tots coming out of her kitchen were amazing.

So amazing that he might even deliver a cake to the neighbors.

"You wouldn't lie to me about supper, would you?"

"I certainly would not. We're having everything I said. And I made us a dessert, too. We're having peach cobbler."

"That's my favorite dessert."

Ruthie's gaze softened. "I know, son. So, will you please deliver the cake for me?"

"Sure." Looking down at his grubby hands, he said, "I need a minute to get the worst of the dirt off, and then I'll walk over there."

"Thank you. It's much appreciated." She set the cake holder next to the steps leading into the *dawdi haus*'s entrance. "It will be here when you are ready." Then, she turned around and headed back to the front of the house with a certain pep to her step.

Kyle watched her for a second. It sure seemed like she had

a lot more energy than he did. He had no idea why she couldn't have made the walk to the Lapps'.

But as he got inside his own home and strode barefoot into the bathroom, he smirked at his reflection in the mirror. "She didn't want to make the walk because you work for her, you idiot. It's your job to make her life easier, not the other way around."

Plus, he couldn't deny that she looked fresh and clean while he looked . . . anything but that.

Lifting the front of his shirt, he groaned. "You not only look dirty, you smell, too."

He turned on the shower and stepped in the enclosure while the water was still running cold. The spray felt like needles against his skin, waking him up and reminding him to be thankful for his blessings.

By the time he had walked over to the Lapps', he was almost feeling like himself. He had a plan, too. He would say hello to the family, check in with Daisy for a minute or two, then take the fifteen-minute walk back, with hamburgers and tots in his future.

Before he reached their front steps, Daisy's father, Jed, walked out to greet him. "Hiya, Kyle. This is a nice surprise. What brings you here this evening?"

He held up the cake carrier. "I'm making a delivery for the Millers. Ruthie made you all a cake."

He took the carrier, but frowned. "How come?"

"I'm not sure, but Ruthie was intent on me bringing it to you tonight."

"Hmm. Well, thank you. I'll let *mei frau* know. Would you like to come in for a spell?"

"Thanks, but Ruthie's holding supper until I get back."

"I get that. I bet you're starving. And, maybe tired?"

"I can't deny either," Kyle joked.

"I spied you out working in the fields today."

He nodded. "*Jah*. I was there all day."

"Lukas was, too. It's a hot'un."

"*Jah*." Just as he was about to head home, Kyle realized there was someone there that he wanted to see. "Hey, is Daisy around? I'd say hello to her before I walk back."

"She is. She's over near the coop."

Jed looked like he was amused by something. "Is she feeding the hens?"

"*Jah*. But . . . it's more than that. Both Lukas and Ben are out there with her." He grinned. "Our Daisy came up with something that I still can't wrap my head around."

Kyle was still confused about why Jed sounded so mysterious. "What did she do? Is it bad?"

"Oh, *nee*. Not at all." Grinning, he stuffed his hands in his pockets. "It's . . . well, you've got to see it to believe it," he added with a chuckle.

"Now you've really got my interest piqued."

"It should be," he said with a laugh. "Go on over there and say hello." He raised an eyebrow. "If you have time, that is."

"I'm going to make time now. She's in the barn, you said?"

"*Nee*. The pen near the henhouse." He frowned. "Don't worry. You won't miss everything that's going on."

"*Danke*." Feeling even more curious, he strode down the flagstone path that led from the front door to the barn. Over the years someone had taken care to line it with flowers and shrubs. It was as lovely as it was practical.

When he realized that the stones must have been recently power-washed or scrubbed, he knelt down on one knee to inspect it more carefully. His parents' walkway could use something like this, he decided. He didn't think anyone had made any improvements to it in decades.

Unfortunately, it looked like it, too. He made a mental

note to try to remember to tell his *daed* about it. Maybe he'd want to power-wash it in the fall.

Then he heard the laughter.

"Daisy, look at Gladys! She doesn't want to get off."

"I know," Daisy said in a merry tone. "Have you noticed how Darren and Phil are standing in line? This is gonna be a problem."

"I'm going to take a picture of this and send it out. Daisy, you're going to make a fortune."

"I don't think so, Ben. I mean, maybe it's just our chickens who enjoy swinging."

Swinging? Every bit of his exhaustion long gone, Kyle picked up his pace.

And then gaped at the sight before him.

There was a hen swinging on a little perch. No, it really was a little, chicken-sized swing. Right smack in the middle of the hen's pen outside.

"How many of these do you think you could make in a—oh, hiya, Kyle," Ben said.

"Hey. Uh, what's going on?" Which sounded like a pretty silly question, he realized. Because it was very obvious what was going on, and that was that Daisy's chickens had decided that they enjoyed swinging in their spare time.

Never in his life could he have imagined such a sight.

Lukas raised his eyebrows. "Well, as you can see, we're all watching the hens wait in line for their turn to swing."

"Uh, why?"

"Why what? Why are they waiting in line? Why won't Gladys get off?"

It was obvious that Lukas was attempting to hold back his laughter. Kyle would be laughing too . . . if he wasn't so shocked. "Why do your chickens have a swing in their coop?"

"Daisy made it."

"I overheard that." He could still hardly look away from

the sight before him. "When did you decide to make . . . chicken swings, Daisy?"

"Today."

She sounded so perplexed, he walked closer. "Why?"

"I read about it and thought, why not? I've had a lot of time on my hands." She shrugged.

"I'm sorry . . . but I still don't understand."

"I'll give you the short version," Ben said as he stepped forward. "*Mei* little sister here went to the library, got offered a job, checked out some books to look at while she considered it, read a mention of a chicken swing, and then decided to make one for the girls."

He took a breath. "Within ten minutes, Betsy hopped on. Then, since she's a diva, everyone else followed suit. But now there's a problem because Gladys likes to think of herself as a queen bee and now won't get off. Is that about right, Daisy?"

"Pretty much." She was gazing at the group. "There's a lot of drama going on. Honestly, I thought things were bad when I was a teenager, but these hens are being just as catty."

"Poor choice of words, D," Ben said.

She rolled her eyes. "Whatever. You know what I mean."

Lukas shook his head. "Sorry, brother, but you've completely left out the part where we both think that this chicken swing thing is ingenious. Ben is going to put his Englischer schooling and classmates to good use and start marketing it."

Kyle's head was spinning. Chickens. Divas. Swings. "I see . . ." he said slowly.

"Oh!" Ben added as he wrapped his hand around Daisy's shoulders. "We're all pretty sure that our little sister is about to become rich."

Kyle wasn't sure if he was going to be able to smile any bigger than he already was. "Daisy, you've had a much more entertaining day than me."

She grinned. "I can't deny that I have. It's . . . well, it's been a great day." She drew in a breath. "Oh! Look! Cupcake has made a move."

Lukas laughed. "That goofy hen just side-checked Gladys."

"No, wait . . . look, they're sitting together," Kyle said.

Ben's eyes lit up as he lifted his cell phone and took another half dozen pictures. "Daisy, this is awesome! It's going to be another selling point. Hens can swing in pairs."

She snorted. "What kind of selling point would that be? Why would they ever want to do that?"

Kyle jumped into the conversation. "Sorry, but who cares? I never would've believed that a chicken would want to get on a swing."

"I'm sure it's a selling point," Ben added. "I mean, just think about all those gentlemen farmer Englischers who buy fancy chickens without knowing how to clean a coop."

Lukas frowned. "What does that have to do with hens on swings?"

"Everything. Those folks are the ones who buy magazines that feature articles about hen psychology."

"Are there really such things, Ben?" Daisy asked.

Kyle smirked as he moved to stand closer to Daisy. "I don't think that's a thing."

"No, it is," Ben protested. "It's all a thing, and Daisy is going to make all those quaint Englischer farmers up in New England so happy with their Christmas presents for their flock."

"No one thinks of their chickens at Christmas, Ben," she said.

"No, they do," Lukas said. "But it's more that they're wondering which one to have for supper."

Daisy giggled. She looked so cute, Kyle couldn't help but join in. Lukas did, too.

Ben folded his arms across his chest. "Guys and Daisy, laugh all you want, but I'm telling you the truth. This is great. Daisy's going to have tons of orders and we'll all help get her business off the ground."

"Sorry you came over in the middle of this wacky discussion," Daisy whispered to him.

"There's nothing to apologize for, though . . . and no offense . . ."

"But what?" Lukas asked.

"I mean, come on. All anyone would have to do is drill holes in a proper tree branch, thread it with rope, and secure the ends of each."

Ben shook his head. "No offense, Kyle, but you have no idea how many folks will have no idea how to do such a thing. What do you think, Daisy? Are you willing to give this a try?"

"Um, I'm not sure. I mean, just yesterday I had kind of made my mind up to be a librarian's assistant."

This was new to Kyle. "Why do you want to do that?"

"I like to read."

"And?"

"And the librarian asked her," Lukas said.

Daisy lifted her chin. "It would be a *gut* job and I could start working there even with a cast on."

"You could also make chicken swings with your time, too," Ben said. "Though I think making these swings sounds like more fun than shelving books."

Daisy turned to him, her blue eyes bright with curiosity. "What do you think, Kyle?"

"Have you given up farming?"

"I think so," she said, all traces of mirth gone from her expression. "Lukas, of course, said I could help him, but the longer it's been since I didn't get my wish, the more I'm starting to believe that this is a case of it being a blessing that the Lord didn't answer my prayer."

"I'm so proud of you, Daisy."

"For what?"

"Every time I see you, you're thinking of something new. You haven't given up. You just keep working."

"Well, it's not like I have a choice. The alternative isn't *gut*, Kyle."

"I can't disagree." He had a sudden urge to pull her into his arms and hold her close. Daisy had so much to offer other people, but he wondered if she actually believed that.

"Supper!" Mrs. Lapp called out.

"Are you staying for supper, Kyle? Is that why you came over here?" Lukas asked.

"*Nee*. Ruthie asked me to drop off a cake for all of you. And now I'm sure she's wondering where I am, because she made supper at her *haus*, too."

"Do you want to stay here?" Ben asked. "You can use my cell phone. They have a kitchen phone, right?"

"Thanks for the offer, but Ruthie made burgers, beans, corn, and tots."

"I love tots," Daisy said.

"I don't know anyone who doesn't," he teased. "Now, I better go, and you three better get on in. I don't want your mother blaming me for your supper getting cold."

"Yeah, see ya around, Kyle," Lukas said.

Though Ben and Lukas had turned around and were walking toward the house, Daisy stayed where she was.

The pull to stay by her side was strong. Was it friendship? Or was it that he saw something inside her that he recognized in himself? "Daisy," he said gently, "I really should be going. We both should."

"I know. But, ah . . . would you answer something for me?"

"I'll try."

"What do you think about this hen swing?" She lowered her voice, as if she was afraid someone else in the world would overhear her and laugh. "I mean, honestly." Looking frustrated, she blurted, "I mean, do you think Ben is right? Do you think that I could sell some of these?"

He did. He thought it was an ingenious idea. A lot of people—Amish or English—loved the idea of getting something interesting and fun that they didn't know they needed.

Plus, watching those hens wait in line was the most amusing thing he'd witnessed in years. Who wouldn't want to see that?

But, on the flipside, he was worried about encouraging Daisy. She'd already had a number of disappointments of late. What if she invested money into this scheme and it failed?

He wasn't sure that he could live with that.

"Daisy, the truth is that it doesn't matter what I think. This needs to be your decision."

"But if it was? Come on," she added when he hesitated. "I wouldn't ask you if I didn't want to know. At the very least, please tell me what you would do."

She was standing so close to him. He wasn't sure how, but even after being out in the barn and around a flock of chickens, she still managed to smell like vanilla and orange. He wondered where the scent came from. Her shampoo? Lotion? He took a step back, realizing he was in danger of leaning closer and sniffing her neck.

Her eyes filled with emotion. Then doubt.

Daisy thought he was retreating from her. Pulling away. But the opposite was true. She was making him feel things that he couldn't unfeel. "If it was up to me . . . I'd do it, Daisy."

"Really?"

He nodded. Afraid she would think that he was just giving her words, he forced himself to attempt to sound matter-of-fact. Not caring and tender.

"It sounds like a no-brainer to me. I mean, why wouldn't

you want to give this idea a try? Your brothers could help you, you could make them at home, and it's a cute thing for chickens."

He cleared his throat as he warmed to the idea. "In addition, you wouldn't have to spend a lot of your savings, just to get a look-see. The materials aren't expensive. The most expensive part might be the shipping and packaging. But even that wouldn't be too horrible, because you could make those fees known when they buy the product, and everyone is used to paying for shipping and handling anyway."

"You're right. There's nothing wrong with that, is there?"

"I don't think there's ever anything wrong with giving something a try, Daisy." Pretending he was offering advice to Sarah, he added, "Why, the worst thing that happens is you make ten or fifteen swings that don't sell. They can be spares!"

She chuckled. "That's true. I don't think these hens are ever going to want to not have their new toy."

"There you go. See? You've got this." Unable to help himself, he wrapped his arms around her. Gave her a hug.

Daisy's body stiffened for a few seconds before she wrapped her arms around his waist. Relaxed against him.

He leaned closer. Ran a hand down her spine. Pressed his lips to her temple.

"Daisy! Come eat!"

Kyle pulled away. "You better go eat."

"*Jah*." She was wide-eyed.

What had he done? Becoming more flustered, he blurted, "I'll ah, see you soon. I can't wait to hear about how many orders you get the first week."

"It would be something if I got some that quickly."

"It will happen, Daisy. There's no doubt in my mind that you'll do great."

Her answering smile almost took his breath away.

Kyle forced himself to turn around and walk away. Daisy needed to go eat, he needed to get back home, and whatever had just happened between the two of them needed to pause.

Because he was pretty sure that it had been something big and he wasn't going to be able to walk away from it a second time.

CHAPTER 31

Kyle had hugged her. He'd wrapped his arms around her, held her close, and against her better judgment she'd relaxed against him. It had been nothing like the hugs she'd received from her two older brothers. The way he'd held her had felt more personal for some reason. No, it had felt like he'd thought she was special. Cherished, maybe.

And then there was the kiss. He'd kissed her temple. Sure, it was chaste. And quick. It was very much like the kisses Ben and Lukas gave her from time to time. Nothing memorable.

Except that it was.

Quickly, Daisy washed her hands. Pressed them to her cheeks while they were still damp. Attempted to stop being so moony.

She was loved by her family but she was certainly not cherished by Kyle.

Even the thought of him feeling that way about her was ridiculous. He liked Winter. No, he was courting Winter.

Plus, she'd never been the type of woman who men sought

to cherish. The cold, awful truth was that this was her first hug from a man who she liked.

So it meant something to her, but had likely not meant anything to Kyle. She needed to remember that, or her heart was going to feel bruised.

Maybe even broken.

"Finally!" her father gruffed. "We're so pleased you decided to join us, daughter."

"I'm sorry you had to wait for me," she mumbled as she moved to her seat. She gave Lukas a grateful smile when he held her chair out for her and pushed her in, then set her crutch against the wall.

"Let us bow our heads and give thanks," Daed said.

Daisy felt her insides tighten. Her father seemed really mad at her. Was it just because he was hungry and she'd made him wait for his supper?

Forcing herself to clear her head, she quickly gave thanks for the food and her family. When she raised her head, her mother picked up a bowl of noodles and passed them to one of her brothers. She picked up the roasted zucchini, took a portion, and then passed it on.

And so it continued as everyone's plates were full of hamburger patties, noodles, zucchini, corn and pepper casserole, and hot rolls. "This looks wonderful, Mamm. *Danke*."

"I hope you will enjoy it, dear."

Daisy darted another look at her father. He still seemed out of sorts. Several years ago he'd had a bit of gout flare up in his toe. Maybe that was happening again?

After several minutes of silence, her father spoke. "I saw you outside hugging Kyle Hostetler, daughter."

"Oh?" It was more like "oh, no." Obviously, her father's toe was just fine. She was the one who'd sparked his temper to flare up.

Across the table, Ben was visibly fighting a smile.

"Oh? That is all you have to say?"

"Is 'I'm sorry' any better?"

Beside her, Lukas shook his head.

"I want to know why he was hugging you, Daisy."

"I don't know. I was asking him about what he really thought about my chicken swings and he told me that he thought I should do it. He made it sound like it was a good idea and wouldn't cost too much to try." She took a breath, hoping to convey how good it felt to hear that he believed in her. "I was really grateful. I might even have been on the verge of tears. I think that's why he decided to give me a hug." Starting to get a little irritated that her father was making such a big deal out of such a small act of kindness, Daisy added, "It didn't last long and then he went home."

Her father didn't look appeased.

"Daisy, why were you about to cry?" Mamm asked.

She put her fork down. "You know why. It's been a hard couple of weeks." She waved a hand, correcting herself. "*Nee*, it's been a difficult several months. I've felt like a failure because not only was I not able to buy the Burkholders' farm, I haven't ever been courted, and I got fired from my job."

"And broke her leg," Ben added under his breath.

"Still, you should have been more circumspect."

"Mother, look at me. I'm twenty-four years old. I've never had a caller. Some of the girls I grew up with are not only married, but they have children at home. Who cares if the neighbor boy gives me a hug? What does it even matter?"

Her mother flushed. "Daisy."

Feeling those stupid tears threaten yet again, Daisy shook her head. "Mamm, Daed, I'm trying to be the best version of me I can be, but I'm far from perfect and I deserve happiness, even if it's just a reassuring hug. Please, don't twist it. Don't turn it into something bad, because it's not."

Her mother looked pained, but persevered. "Daisy, I am sorry that you've been having such a hard time. I know it's been difficult for you." Glancing at her father, she continued. "We both know." She took a deep breath. "However, I fear you are getting your head wrapped around things that aren't real."

"I don't understand."

"Everyone in the community seems to think that Kyle has set his sights on Winter. There are even rumors that if they marry, her parents are going to give him the farm. It's a *gut* opportunity for him. A once in a lifetime opportunity."

"*Jah*. I would imagine it is."

"And, as far as this henhouse swing goes . . . well, child, we've let you make things like this because we knew you were bored. But it would be a mistake to imagine that such a business, if it could ever be called a business, could be a success."

"You don't think so?" She was crushed.

"It's just another dream that you shouldn't waste your time on, child." Her father looked regretful but firm. "Take that library assistant job and start staying away from Kyle. It will be better in the long run for you."

He'd been so intent on crushing her dreams, Daisy was surprised she could still sit upright. Bitterness flowed through her, both because of his words and the worry that her parents were right.

Added to this was having to listen to it all while sitting at the dinner table with both of her brothers looking on. "Is there anything else you feel compelled to tell me?" she whispered.

"Yes," Lukas blurted. When all four of them stared at him in surprise, he added, "Mamm, Daed, I love you both, but I think what you two just said is horrible. I'm ashamed of you both."

Ben tossed his napkin on the table and stood up. "I am, as well. Don't ever tell my little sister again that she doesn't stand a chance against a piece of land." Turning to her, he said, "I know what I saw an hour ago, and the way Kyle looked at you had nothing to do with mere friendship. It's obvious that he likes you, Daisy."

"I agree," Lukas said as he also got to his feet. "Not only was Kyle staring at you like you were the world, but I know he wouldn't marry anyone just to get his hands on some land."

"You don't know—"

"He's a capable sort, Daed. He cares for his sister. He stopped on the side of the road to make sure Daisy received help. He's brought her flowers and he's checked on her time and again. He likes her. They're friends."

He took a breath. "And if, for some reason, Kyle decides that it's Winter that he wants to marry, it's going to be because he loves her. But last I heard, it was possible to be friends with one woman and in love with another."

Lukas reached down for Daisy's hand. "Come on, D. You don't need to sit here any longer tonight."

"Children, you can't just get up and leave," Mamm said.

Ben shook his head. "That's the thing, Mamm. None of us have been children for years. And I can promise you this, Daisy is going to make a success of her hen swing. I know it. And I hope she will still be talking to you when you decide to apologize."

"Daisy, are you coming?"

She looked from her mother's stricken expression to their father's irate one. As shocked as she was, she was positive that staying put after her brothers left was a bad idea.

"*Jah*," she said as she took his hand.

Ben wrapped his arm around her shoulders while Lukas picked up her crutch and helped her put it under her opposite arm. And then the three of them walked out of the dining room and into the entryway.

"Where are we going?" she whispered.

"We're going for a drive," he said. "I've got my wallet and my keys in my pocket. Let's get out of here."

It wasn't until the three of them were in Ben's vehicle and onto the main road, that everything that her brothers said sunk in. "I can't believe you two defended me like that."

"If you're surprised, then I guess I need to tell you those things more often. You are going to be just fine, Daisy."

"Ben's right," Lukas said. "One day you're going to fall in love with a good man, you're going to live the life you want, and everything that's just happened is going to make sense."

"You sound so sure."

"I am. No matter what, I'm going to make sure of it."

CHAPTER 32

Though the sun was still hanging low in the sky, it was too late to be receiving a caller. Kyle wondered if something had happened with either Aaron or Bethany.

When he realized that it was Ben Lapp in the vehicle and that he was looking straight at him, Kyle wondered if that impulsive hug had been taken wrong and that Daisy's brother was about to give him an earful.

Did he deserve it? Maybe.

"You here to see me?" he asked after Ben got out of his SUV and started walking toward him.

"I am."

"Would you care to sit outside or in?"

"In, if you don't mind. I'm pretty sure I spied Mervin watching me from his window. If he sees us out here together, he might decide to mosey over for some conversation."

"Good point. Well, come on, then." He looked over his shoulder as he walked inside. "It's warm, though."

And it was. Unlike the main house, the former owners

hadn't built a basement for the *dawdi haus*. At the end of summer, the heat seemed to have given up the fight and warmed up the house. Luckily, he had a propane-powered air conditioning unit that he plugged in for a few hours every night. Otherwise, Kyle didn't think he'd ever be able to handle the warmth.

"It's a warm one, for sure."

"I'm surprised that you don't have an apartment in town. You could be living with all the advantages."

Ben shrugged. "I'd be cooler, that's true. But air conditioning and television ain't the only advantages in life. I tried it for a spell, but I ended up moving home. The bills were expensive and, well, I got lonely for my family."

"I can see that. I miss my sister and parents something awful."

"I like that we have that in common."

"Parents or a sister that we feel protective over?" he joshed.

His words seemed to relax Ben a bit. "So you know why I'm here."

"I'm guessing that it involves Daisy, but no. I don't know why you're here."

"After Daisy got to the table, my parents had a lot to say about your relationship with her."

"Listen, I'll agree that I maybe shouldn't have given her a hug, but that's all it was."

"Daisy knew that. Lukas and I did, too." He rolled his eyes. "Honestly, I think my parents knew it, too."

"Then . . . what's the problem?"

"They cautioned Daisy against you because they're certain you're about to propose to Winter."

"Winter Walker?"

"I think we both could agree that we only know of one woman named after a season."

"True."

"Is it also true that you're in love with the woman?"

"No."

"Are you sure?"

"Not that it's any of your business, but *jah*. I am very sure."

Ben propped one foot on the opposite knee. "I also happened to learn that her parents are willing to include farmland with her hand."

Kyle almost choked. "Nothing has been said about that."

"Are you sure?"

"Winter said something, but I'm learning that she says a lot of things that she might not mean."

"You know that she didn't treat Daisy well in school. She turned a lot of the kids away from her. I'd like to say she's gotten better with age, but that would be a lie."

"Ben, I don't know what that has to do with Daisy."

"Well, Kyle, my father knows you would love a farm of your own, and so he told my sister that she could never compete with that."

"What?"

"Worse, she believed him," he added as he stood up and began to pace. "You know, I always wondered why my sister has always carried a bit of insecurity about her when she's with her peers. But now I know the reason." Turning back to face Kyle, he continued. "It's now obvious that that is the kind of nonsense our father has been telling her." His voice turned strained. "That . . . that she would never be more special to a man than a piece of farmland."

He was shocked. "That was cruel of him to say."

"Is it wrong, though?"

"Of course it is. What kind of man do you think I am?"

"I'm not sure."

"Well, I may not be perfect, but I can tell you that I'm not the kind of man to use a woman in order to grab a piece of land."

"I didn't think you were."

"Really?" Kyle wasn't sure if he believed him. Otherwise, why would he have shown up and asked him such things?

"Listen, no matter how much Daisy might have denied it, I know she's sweet on you. I can see it in her eyes. In the way she watches you whenever you are near. Plus, I've watched the two of you together. There's something between you two."

"I've never taken advantage of her."

"No, you might not have kissed her and told her a mess of sweet things, but it's obvious that she means something to you."

"She does." But he'd never come out and said that.

Ben's expression became even more strained. "Kyle, I realize that I'm not going about this the right way. If there ever was a right way. But, I just wanted to tell you that if you are falling in love with Winter . . . or, if you aren't falling in love with her, but are enjoying the idea of one day running the Walkers' farm . . . then you need to step away from Daisy. Don't let her get her hopes up anymore than they already are."

He took a breath. "But, if you do feel something for Daisy, please let her know. And make sure you use the sweet words she needs."

Kyle raised his eyebrows. "Sweet words?"

"Yeah, obviously it's good that I'm not dating anyone right now. I don't know how to be a good boyfriend." He lowered his voice. "I do know how to be a good brother to my sister, though. I'll say whatever I need to. No, I'll do whatever I need to do in order to protect her. Do you understand?"

Ben's expression was hard. Kyle reckoned he was attempting to scare some sense into him—or maybe he simply wanted him to step up. But whatever the reason, the guy had done a good job, and he respected that.

"*Jah*. Sure. I understand."

"Good." He turned around and walked out the door. Kyle watched him stride to his vehicle, get in, and drive away.

Then, as he sat in the old *dawdi haus*, he watched the sun fade into the night and he thought about his future. It was time. He knew who he needed in it. Someone bright and vibrant . . . but who also was a little bit unsure.

The rest of the world might think of Daisy Lapp as tough and independent. He knew better. She had a tender heart that needed protecting and he was the man for that.

CHAPTER 33

"Hey," Kyle said as he sat down on the milking stool next to Velvet. "Ah, how are you?"

The cow turned her head and snorted.

He could practically read her mind, it was so clear what she was thinking. "*Jah*, I know this isn't our usual routine. But I'm not here to milk you. I came in here for a chat."

Velvet's dark brown eyes stared at him for a long moment before she turned her head. Her tail swished a few times. Maybe she was attempting to swat at a fly. Or maybe it was a symbol of how low he'd sunk in her estimation.

A year ago. No, even two months ago, he would've rolled his eyes at such a thought.

But that was back when he'd thought he'd known everything about life. Now he realized that he hadn't known anything. Worse, he had realized that he was perfectly capable of ruining most everything in his sight.

At least what was important.

He cleared his throat. "So, ah . . . obviously, I'm pretty bad at this. I mean, talking to cows. But I figure that everything else I've been doing hasn't made me feel better, so I thought I might as well try this." He frowned, realizing how he sounded. He was being rude, which wasn't very nice.

"Not that I don't appreciate you or anything." He leaned back. Shrugged. "I mean, I like your milk just fine."

Velvet blew out a wet burst of air and groaned.

"Plus, the other day, Ruthie made butter, and it was amazing. I hadn't had fresh churned butter on warm bread in ages." He closed his eyes, trying to remember when he had it. But couldn't. "Maybe it was the only time. So it was great."

Velvet mooed under her breath.

If Kyle didn't know better, he'd swear that she was making fun of him. Then he remembered that he was sitting next to her for that very reason.

He was learning that he didn't always know better. As a matter of fact, there were a lot of things he didn't know much about at all.

"Don't take offense, now. I mean, you are a milk cow. It's your thing, right?"

Kyle froze, then ran a hand along her side. Wanting to be sure she was feeling all right. "You good, Velvet?" He swallowed. "I mean, you aren't cramping again, are ya?"

The heifer didn't react. No impatient groan, no sideways eye. Worse, no leaning.

But of course, she only leaned on Daisy.

"All right. I get what you're saying. I need to be more honest, don't I? I mean, it's not enough to just show up and sit with you. I need to do more."

He ran his hand along her side again. To his relief, she didn't flinch. She didn't do much at all. Just stood there.

He decided to take that as a win.

"You know, I have to admit that I didn't get it. I didn't understand why Daisy liked to talk to you so much." He rubbed her side again. "I'm ashamed to admit that part of me thought that the reason Daisy enjoyed spending time with you so much was because she didn't have a lot of other people in her life to confide in."

He dropped his hand. "That's on me, ain't so? I was so full of myself, so pleased with my relationship with my family, with Aaron, with the Millers. Yeah, even with Winter, I didn't even think that sitting with you had value."

Velvet's tail twitched again.

"Okay, you're right. I didn't realize just how special and unique Daisy is. I didn't appreciate her enough. I should have told her how I felt."

Thinking about how Daisy would probably not give him the time of day if they were the only two people on a street, he sighed. "Velvet, the truth is that I've been a fool. A stupid, prideful fool, and I don't know how to make things better between us."

She said nothing.

He sighed as he stood up. "I'd pay a month's paycheck if I could understand what you're thinking. That is, if you are thinking about anything besides eating or taking a nap."

He wasn't sure, but he thought she seemed to be taking pity on him just then. Her stance relaxed and when her eyes met his again, Kyle was sure that they seemed a lot more sympathetic.

Pleased that she was relaxing, he ran a finger along her forehead. "You know, I never considered cows to be all that pretty. Not like horses. I had a pony when I was a boy called Tangerine. Yeah, yeah, I thought it was a strange name for a horse, but she was a reddish-orange color with a black mane and tail. And you should've seen her prance." He chuckled. "The thing about Tangerine was that she didn't care that she was an older pony that most people thought was only good for an eight-year-old.

"As far as Tangerine was concerned, she pranced like she

was an Appaloosa or Arabian show horse. Once, the vet's assistant came about another horse, but when she was done helping out, she went into Tangie's stall, pulled out some rubber bands, and made the most gorgeous braid out of her mane that I'd sure ever seen. That pony stood still as a board while she did it, too."

Remembering the moment like it was yesterday, Kyle whispered, "When I put a bridle on her and took her out to the pen, she pranced." He chuckled. "No lie, Velvet! She was practically high-stepping. Everyone stopped to watch her go. Even *mei daed* stopped and stared at her. She was the prettiest thing that I'd ever seen," he whispered.

Remembering.

"So, um, that is why I'm saying that I have a fondness for pretty horses. But until you, I had never given a cow much thought."

He ran his finger along her forehead again.

"But I was wrong, wasn't I? You have a white mark on your head that looks a lot like a heart. And your eyes are perceptive. Why, I'd even go as far as to suggest that maybe there's more to you than most people realized."

Kind of like Daisy.

Sure, he'd thought she was a good friend, and he'd admired how much she seemed to know about the Millers' farm. And of course he'd seen her dark hair and thought it was shiny and pretty.

But she was so much more than good looks and a pretty smile. He just hadn't wanted to see it.

"I should've recognized how special she was from the beginning, shouldn't I?" he whispered.

"I should've been encouraging her more." Complimenting her more, and not just on the stuff that didn't matter, like how easily she could look at the clouds and know when it was going to rain.

"I should've given her all the words. I should've told her

that I thought she was brilliant and beautiful. How much I liked her eyes and her smile." He lowered his voice. "How good she felt in my arms. So good that I never wanted to let her go."

A lump formed in his throat.

And even though he'd been taught that men don't cry, he felt tears threaten.

"Now I don't know what to do, Velvet. I'm pretty sure I lost her forever. What's worse is that I have no idea how to get her back." He laughed under his breath. A faint, sarcastic sound that sounded shrill and echoed in the empty space. "All my life I've been sure I've been the fix-it guy. The man who could do just about anything on a piece of land. But I sure have no idea how to make things better with Daisy."

Lowering his voice, he added, "I'm pretty sure that there is no way to make things better. Sometimes things are so broken that they can't be fixed. They're ruined forever."

CHAPTER 34

"Hey now," Mervin said from their spot just outside the barn door. "He—"

Ruthie slapped a hand over his mouth. "Shh."

When his blue eyes widened, she hastily lowered her hand. "Sorry, but Kyle can't know that we're here."

"How come?"

Ruthie groaned as she reached for his hand and tugged him out of the way. To her relief, Mervin allowed her to lead him back down the path to the house.

"*Nee*," he said when she attempted to lead him into the house. "It's too warm in there. We can sit here on the front porch."

Their favorite rockers were at least two feet apart. Added to that was the fact that sometimes Mervin's hearing wasn't quite what it used to be. Bethany and Aaron had each told them that more than once they'd overheard their private conversations. "We need to talk quietly. He mustn't overhear us."

"Woman, you are sometimes too bossy for your own

good. Come here." This time it was he who did the hand-reaching.

She was so stunned by him calling her "woman," she didn't protest. Instead, she sat down where he directed, which was on the front steps. "Since when did you start calling me *woman*?"

"Since we moved here and you've gotten so bossy."

His eyes had a twinkle in them. That same kind of twinkle they used to have when he'd taken her courting. When they were fifteen and sixteen, Mervin's favorite form of courting was to meet her at singings and then stealthily maneuver them out in the woods. Sometimes they'd walk, sometimes he'd guide her to a clearing and they'd share all their dreams for the future.

And later on, the moment they'd been out of sight from everyone except for the fireflies, he'd pull her close to his chest and kiss her until she could barely stand without holding on to his shoulders.

It would take her so many precious moments to right her clothes and fan her face, but even when they returned to the group and stood under the glow of tiki torches, Ruthie would know that she'd looked thoroughly kissed.

And Mervin would be wearing that same, mischievous glint in his eye. Letting her know that he had a pretty good feeling that her attempts to look prim and proper weren't fooling anyone.

Perhaps that was why her parents didn't try to convince her to wait several more years to marry. Mervin had asked her when she was seventeen and he was eighteen. Instead, her parents had nodded and said they were pleased.

"You are sure quiet all of a sudden."

"I was thinking about how my parents never tried to make us wait to get married."

"Of course they didn't." He winked. "My father warned

me at least a dozen times about how wrong it would be to ah, rush things." Reaching for her hand, he whispered, "Daed was mighty afraid that you might have a shotgun wedding."

"Certainly not! I was a good girl."

"Sorry, but I was smitten with you, Ruthie."

She leaned closer. "I was the same."

"Why were you thinking of that?"

"I overheard Kyle talking about Daisy and it made me think about how hard it is to look back on decisions after they're made."

"I still don't know what you're talking about."

She placed a hand on his arm. "Do you remember how nervous we were to talk to our parents about getting married?"

"I remember how nervous I was. Your father was practically shooting daggers at me. I was fairly certain that he could read my mind when it came to you."

"You were in love with me! There was nothing to be ashamed about that."

"*Jah*. For sure, I was. But that wasn't the only thing I thought about when it came to you, Ruthie." Mervin lowered his voice, as if the conversation had happened just yesterday instead of many, many years before. "I'm still surprised he said yes."

"He didn't have a choice. I was so in love with you. But what I'm getting at is that we didn't know what the future would bring."

"That is true. My parents kept reminding me about how wives were expensive and children even more so."

She chuckled. "I reckon they weren't wrong about that." Bethany had had an infected tooth when she was nine and because she'd had to get two teeth pulled, she'd had to get braces. Back then, she'd never heard of any Amish getting braces, but Bethany hadn't had a choice. She'd been teased, and Ruthie and Mervin had both worked extra hours to pay for the unexpected expense.

Now, Bethany had the brightest smile out of all of them, thanks to those braces. But even more importantly, she'd learned to not let gentle and not-so-gentle teasing affect her too much. It had been an important lesson for their sensitive daughter. And likely a lesson that wouldn't have been ever learned if she hadn't gotten a sick tooth and a set of metal in her mouth for two years.

"People always say that one mustn't look at the past with twenty-twenty vision," Mervin said. "I know you want to help Kyle and Daisy, but we don't know what the Lord has in mind for them."

"That's true, but don't you think He could use a little bit of help?"

"*Nee.*"

"But maybe he put us in Kyle and Daisy's path in order to help them."

"He might have, but then again . . . we might have nothing to do with their story. You could step into something that isn't any of your business and make things worse."

Ruthie thought about that and shuddered. "You might have a point."

"I know I do. Plus, Kyle has a good head on his shoulders and knows his own mind. Just like our Aaron. Can you imagine what our son would've had to say about us getting involved with his romance with Hanna?"

"He would've had a lot to say." Their son had never learned the fine art of holding one's tongue.

"All that is why I think it's best that we just watch and wait for a spell. If one of them needs us, they'll let us know. And if they don't, then we can enjoy the show."

"I reckon you're right. One of them might have a set of braces in their future."

Mervin frowned. "*Nee*, I think their teeth are just fine, Ruth."

She patted his arm again. There was no need for her to explain what she'd just been thinking. "I dare say you're right, dear."

"Come on then. Let's go sit down with Lizzie and relax a spell. We've earned it."

Figuring he had a point, she followed him into the house.

CHAPTER 35

It had been an odd week, that was for sure and for certain. After spending a rough twenty-four hours feeling sorry for herself after her father's rather rough lecture about Kyle, Winter, and her lack of prospects, she'd spent many long hours in the barn making hen swings. Ben and Lukas had been amazing. They'd helped her gather suitable branches and spare pieces of wood together and bought her lots of rope, and even a good pair of gloves so the rough rope wouldn't give her splinters as she worked with it.

In addition, a cute woman friend of Ben's named Sydney came over with her computer. She spent two hours helping Daisy name her swings. They now had a name, Bird Benches, which Daisy thought was rather silly. Sydney also took tons of pictures of all the hens resting on their swings, wrote up lots of cute notes about the fun the hens were having, and then discussed how much to charge for the items, both for the item and then shipping and handling.

Daisy felt a bit like a child playing dress-up. No matter what Lukas, Ben, and now Sydney had to say, she still didn't believe that anyone would want to spend so much money on such a silly item.

However, if she'd learned anything over the last few months, it was that even the best-laid plans could fall apart. She continued to tell herself that the worst thing that could happen with her Bird Benches was that no one would want to buy one.

Plus, at the very least, the whole enterprise was helping to keep her mind off of Kyle and Winter. That counted for a lot.

All that was why she'd been cautious but agreeable when Ben suggested she, he, and Lukas all spend the night in Sydney's parents' vacation home in Millersburg. Her parents had a lake house on Buckhorn Lake and there were tons of bedrooms. The most important part, was that the house had excellent internet and a large desktop computer.

Her swings were going to go on sale on the websites of a number of very large online retail stores, and Ben wanted them all to see how they did.

Unfortunately, their parents weren't supportive at all. Daed even went so far as to try to tell Lukas that the farm wouldn't be all right if he wasn't going to be there at five the following morning. Lukas, to his credit, only said that he disagreed.

It was only when they were driving over to Sydney's house—after a really tasty stop for tacos in Sugarcreek—that Daisy's stomach began to churn. "Are you sure the perches have been for sale for six hours already?"

"Yep," Ben said.

"Do you think anyone will have bought one yet?"

"Yep," he said again.

"Ugh."

Lukas, who was riding in the passenger seat, turned around

to face her. "Daisy, remember what you told Sydney when she came over?"

She didn't have to guess what he was referring to. "I remember. That the worst thing that happens would be that I don't try."

"Exactly. That means that you already have something to celebrate. You tried something new."

"And, the three of us went out to eat and now we're going to spend the night in a fancy lake house," Ben pointed out. "I, for one, am going to sit on the back deck of the house and look at the lake all evening."

"That will be nice, but I wish we would've brought some ice cream or something. Do you think we can stop, Ben?"

"We can, but I think Sydney is pretty anxious for us to get there. Let's get settled in, and then if we need something at the store, we'll go. Sydney might want something special for breakfast."

"I could make biscuits for everyone in the morning. If she has baking powder . . ."

"See, that's just what we were talking about. We've got time."

"All right." She leaned back and tried to relax. Looked out the window. Tried to concentrate on the moment and not let all her doubts begin to get the best of her. Getting herself in a dither about the possibility of living at home as an old maid with nothing to do but talk to cows and sew uneven hems wasn't going to help anything.

"Okay, here we are," Ben said after another fifteen minutes.

Lukas whistled low. "These houses are nicer than I thought they were going to be."

"What did you know about this area?" she asked.

"I've got a couple of buddies who do remodeling work.

They'd had some jobs here. To be honest, I thought they were exaggerating about how big some of these places were. I reckon I owe them an apology."

"Help me look for the address, Daisy," Ben called out. "12257."

She noticed that none of the addresses were on the same place in every house. Ben drove slowly as they all called out the numbers as they saw them.

"12253!" she called out.

"And, here is 12255," Lukas added, just as Ben rolled to a stop in front of a light gray, three-story house that looked vaguely like it belonged on a Swiss mountaintop instead of next to a lake in the middle of Ohio.

"Ah, finally," Ben said. "12257. This is the place. I wonder where . . . Oh, I guess we just park on the side of the road." He parked, set the parking brake, and they all got out.

Daisy was so glad that she had a doctor's appointment scheduled in just one week. She couldn't wait to get her dirty brace off once and for all and stop hobbling around. At least she wasn't using the crutch much anymore. If she just had to cross the room or walk down the hall she was able to do it fairly easily now.

She sure needed help today, though. There were several steps to climb up until they reached the front door. Inside was cool, slick tile, which took her a moment to get her balance on. When she realized that she was going to need to climb a staircase to put her tote bag in the guest room, she groaned to herself.

Sydney noticed. "Please sit down, Daisy. Or, if you need to freshen up, the bathroom is right through there," she explained as she pointed to a door on the left down the hall.

"*Danke*. You're right. I'll just get cleaned up and then sit in one place. I sure don't want to slip and break something else."

"You sure don't, especially since I do believe we're going to have a busy night."

Daisy noticed that Sydney exchanged a grin with Ben. She wondered what that was all about. After heading down the hallway, Ben called out to her. "Meet us at the kitchen table, Daisy. Sydney put the computer on it so we could all gather around and see the screen."

As she hobbled over to join them, she felt butterflies flutter in her stomach yet again. *Don't worry about sales*, she kept telling herself. *If you don't sell any of your swings, then you aren't any worse off than you were this morning.*

"Daisy, come take this chair," Ben said. "We want you to have the best seat."

"That ain't necessary," she protested, but she sat down anyway.

When they were all settled, Lukas said, "Sydney, the suspense is killing me. Stop beating around the bush and tell us what you've found out. Has anyone bought one of Daisy's swings?"

"Let's see." Her smile grew as she leaned forward and clicked the mouse a couple of times. "Here's the first site. It's the biggest and I had high hopes for your launch day."

Daisy looked at the ad that Sydney had made. There were the pictures of Henrietta on the swing, looking happy as a clam.

When Sydney pressed on an icon, more graphics came up, showing measurements, and the swing with and without a chicken on it.

"Obviously, here is your ad, and you can see that it turned out really well."

"It does look nice." Daisy smiled at her.

Sydney paused, "To be honest, Daisy, I had low expectations for your launch day. We didn't pay much for any ads, and your item probably won't be of interest to most visitors to this site."

"I understand." She smiled. "Well, I guess we did all we could do, right? I mean, I was just reminding myself that I should focus on the fact that I hadn't sold any swings this morning but I was still having a good day."

Sydney treated her to an encouraging smile. "I think that's a great way of looking at things, Daisy, but you actually have sold some swings." She clicked the mouse again.

"I have? Well, isn't that something. How many?" She secretly hoped for five. That was a handful.

"Ben, you want to do the honors?"

He swallowed. "Well, now." He took a deep breath. "I . . . well, yeah. I guess I could."

Daisy turned to him in confusion. What was going on? Ben looked amused and . . . maybe flabbergasted? "Ben, tell me how many swings people ordered!"

"So far today, you've sold five hundred eighty-three."

"Eighty-four," Lukas corrected. "There goes another one."

"What?"

He reached for her hand. "You heard right, little sister. "You've sold almost six hundred swings on this site alone."

"Are you serious?" Her hands started shaking.

"Oh, yeah." Ben wrapped his arms around her. "Daisy, your Bird Benches are selling like hotcakes! You've sold hundreds."

She had hundreds of orders. Hundreds. "But . . . but I've only made twelve."

Sydney frowned. "You're going to need to make a whole lot more."

"I sure am. I don't know how, though."

"You're going to need some help."

Daisy nodded. "It would seem so."

All business, Sydney clicked on the mouse again. Another

retail site appeared on the screen. "Let's look at the other two places where I put your item up for sale. These aren't as big, but sometimes items have better sales here because more of the customers are actually looking to buy items for their chickens."

Perching on the edge of her seat, Daisy watched Sydney scroll through the screens, then finally get to the order information.

"Three hundred seventy here."

She was feeling weak. "That many?"

"Now for the final site . . . give me a second," she mumbled as she clicked and moved the mouse. "Ah, here we go. Two hundred ninety here."

"You've sold over a thousand Bird Benches!" Ben beamed as he gave her a hug. "What do you think of that?"

"I don't even know." Warily, she glanced at Lukas, who had been sitting relatively silent. "What do you think?"

When he turned to her, there were tears in his eyes. "I think that I've been proud of you all my life, but this? Well, this moment makes me exceptionally proud, D. This is wonderful. Better than wonderful. *Wunnerbaar*!"

She laughed before worry claimed her again. "What do you think Mamm and Daed are going to say?"

Lukas shrugged. "I know what they should say, and that is that they are very proud of you."

"But you aren't sure that they will be?"

"I know they love you and that might be enough for now, D. The truth is that you made a swing for our hens, a lot of people want to buy them, and I have a feeling that you'll have more orders tomorrow. We're going to be busy."

Panic was setting in. "What if I can't make all of them?"

"You will," Ben said. "How long did it take you to make those twelve swings?"

"I don't know. Maybe an hour?"

"I'll help you, and I know Ben will, too. And maybe Kyle will as well. We'll all work together."

"But if there are more and more orders . . ."

"We'll see if more friends could help. Or even hire someone to give us a hand."

"I don't know how many people can work in the barn, though," Daisy said.

"Then we'll have to make sure you have a workspace in the center of Walden," Sydney replied. "That way the UPS driver can stop by there all the time."

Office space? Pickups and deliveries. "This is all way beyond my expectations."

Ben got to his feet, pulled her into his arms, and spun her in a circle. "The best things are, D. We need to celebrate."

"We should go get an ice cream cone."

"I hope you don't mind, but the three of us decided to order you a cake." With a flourish, Sydney opened up the box that Daisy hadn't noticed until that minute.

Inside was a beautiful white cake with yellow daisies all over it. In the center, written in green icing were the words, CONGRATULATIONS DAISY!

"When did you say you ordered this?" Daisy asked.

"A couple of days ago," Ben said.

"But that doesn't make sense. A couple of days ago, we had no idea if we would sell a single swing."

"That is true," Lukas said. "But we still had something to celebrate."

Daisy shook her head. "I don't understand."

"We got you a cake because you tried something new, D," Ben said. "You took a chance and looked forward instead of back. That's worth celebrating, don't you think?"

Feeling speechless, Daisy nodded. And stared at the cake some more.

It was beautiful. And special.

It was everything. Oh, not because she'd finally done something that could become a career. Though that was gratifying, it was that she was surrounded by love and support. She had a feeling that her brothers would have taken her to this lake house for the evening even if Sydney had hinted that not a single Bird Bench had been sold.

This moment reminded her about what was important, and about what she could control. In fact, there was very little that seemed to be in her hands. Not her leg, not her relationship with Kyle, not even with the way her parents seemed to view her. The only thing that she could completely control was the way she viewed herself, and she was pleased with herself.

No, she wasn't perfect, but she didn't need to be. All she needed to be was Daisy Lapp. That was enough.

She burst into tears.

CHAPTER 36

It had to be done. Kyle kept repeating that phrase to himself even though parts of him were cringing about what was about to happen.

He now knew Winter well enough to realize that she didn't do anything by half measure. She wasn't going to take his decision lightly. Her parents probably wouldn't either.

This was when he wished his sweet sister, Sarah, was beside him. If she was there, she'd be giving him a pep talk. Most likely, she'd be detailing all the reasons he needed to break things off with Winter. She wouldn't spare her words, either.

Instead, he was on his own.

The Walkers' driveway came into sight far too soon. Since no one was around, he slowed Angel to a walk. He not only wanted to eke out every single second he could before facing the Walkers, he couldn't help but admire their beautiful property. It was everything he used to dream about having. Several dozen acres of prime farmland. A solid, large home. Nice enough to make his wife happy and for their children to have plenty of room to grow.

He had a feeling that Jediah Walker would've been supportive, too. The man obviously knew a lot about keeping a successful farm and Kyle would've been happy to actively listen to everything he had to say.

He could've been happy here.

But Winter wasn't Daisy and that made all the difference.

"Let's go, Angel," he said as he pulled on the lead.

The horse turned to the left and then picked up her pace. If he wasn't so stressed out about the upcoming conversation he would've chuckled. Angel seemed to be in complete agreement about the beauty of this farm. She was practically prancing on the smooth, black asphalt driveway.

When they arrived at the top of the drive, he set the brake and then went about tying Angel's lines to the hitching post.

Jediah came out from the barn to greet him. "Hello, Kyle."

"Hi. *Gut ohvet.*"

"Yes. Good evening." He smiled. "Do you want to unhitch your mare and put her in a stall? There's one empty for her. We won't mind if you use it."

This was killing him.

"*Danke*, but I'm afraid I won't be staying very long today."

Concern brushed Jediah's features as he approached. "I'm sorry to hear that. I thought perhaps you and I could sit out back and have a cup of coffee later." He smiled knowingly. "After you have your special time with Winter, of course."

So Kyle could formally ask for Winter's hand in marriage. He knew that was what Jediah was getting at.

And yes, it was rushed, which was part of the problem, he thought. The Walkers had their own goals and timelines and the man for Winter needed to be able to handle that. But even if he hadn't fallen in love with Daisy, Kyle knew that he wouldn't be able to have a father-in-law who was so pushy.

Maybe Mr. Walker saw something in Kyle's face, or

maybe he was realizing that he should've not made any assumptions about what Kyle had in mind. But whatever the reason, some of the teasing light in his eyes faded and his posture became far more formal.

"Here. I'll walk you in."

"*Danke*."

"Winter, Kyle is here to see you."

She turned to him. "Kyle? Hello! My, this is a surprise! A good one, of course," she added as she reached for his hand. "I didn't expect you to come over until tomorrow night."

"I'm afraid I can't stay long today. May we go somewhere and talk privately?"

Twin spots of color appeared on her cheeks. "Of course." She led him to the library in the back of the house. Two of the walls held books, the third was mostly windows that looked over the backyard, and the fourth contained the door on one side and a fireplace on the other.

He'd been in there once before and had fallen in love with the space. Her mother had confided that though they called it the library, it was their family's catch-all space. Winter's mother sewed and quilted in there, her father read the paper, and Winter both read books and did puzzles on the game table.

After hesitating at the sofa, Winter walked to the game table and sat down in one of the chairs. After he joined her, she neatly folded her hands in her lap and stared at him.

Waiting.

Much in her posture and in the slight wariness of her expression reminded Kyle of the first time he'd met Winter. He'd been struck by how tentative and shy such a beautiful woman was.

Now he realized that while she might be those things, she was also far more complex than that. Of course, everyone was usually more than their first impression.

"Winter, I came over to let you know that I think you're a nice woman and you have a lot to offer, but I don't think that I'm the man for you."

A small line formed in between her brows. "I don't understand."

Ack! This was excruciating. "What I'm trying to say is that I won't be calling on you anymore."

She stared. Said nothing.

When the silence felt oppressive, he added, "I am sorry if this hurts your feelings."

She inhaled sharply. "If this hurts my feelings? Kyle, you have led me to believe that you were going to propose."

"Winter, I'm sorry if you felt that way."

"You're sorry?" She shook her head. "*Nee*. That isn't good enough. You've been calling on me all the time."

"I've called on you a handful of times."

"We went to Lila and Brandt's party together."

"I met you there."

"You've had discussions about the farm with my father."

"Your father and I discussed the pros and cons of a hay supplier."

"That is practically the same thing."

"It is not." Stunned, and now more than a little bit aggravated by the way she'd twisted his actions into something that they weren't, Kyle cleared his throat. "Winter, I didn't make this decision lightly. I knew when I drove over here that you were going to be upset. I truly am sorry about my decision."

Two perfect tears slid down her cheeks. "You are breaking my heart. I thought you loved me as much as I love you."

The things she was saying! It was mind-boggling. He stood up. "Winter, surely you didn't think we were that serious. I've never told you that I loved you. I never even kissed you."

"I would never have kissed you unless we were engaged, Kyle."

Her tears continued, but they were no longer making him feel guilty. Instead, he was starting to feel as if he'd dodged a bullet. For a while there, he'd thought she was perfect for him.

Now it was more than apparent that she was anything but that.

"I'm going to leave. I hope one day you will agree that this was the right decision."

"I can't believe you. What are you going to do now? You don't have a farm at home. Plus, you have a sister to take care of. All you do is work for the Millers, who know next to nothing about farming. You don't even have a future."

He stared at her but said nothing. Her words hurt but he knew she was lashing out. He supposed he deserved it.

"Goodbye, Winter."

"I hope you aren't off to go see Daisy Lapp!" she hissed under her breath.

Unable to help himself, he turned to face her. "Do not bring Daisy into this."

"How can I not? She's obviously been flirting with you." Her tears fell harder. "I bet you've kissed her."

"What is happening between you and me has nothing to do with her. Don't start making up rumors."

She stood up. "I wouldn't have to make up anything about her. She's awkward and boyish and everything I never want to be."

Winter's words caught him off guard. Though they were thrown out and meant to hurt, he couldn't deny that there was more than a grain of truth to them. Daisy was awkward, endearingly so.

She was a bit tomboyish, and he loved that she knew so much about livestock and farming. He also admired that she wasn't afraid to lend a helping hand to any task or chore that came up.

And yes, it was the honest truth that Daisy Lapp was nothing like Winter Walker. Thank the good Lord.

"I know she's nothing like you, Winter. I couldn't be happier about that."

He heard Winter gasp behind him, but he didn't turn back around. Instead, he walked straight to the front door and opened it.

He gave thanks when neither of her parents hurried to his side to ask him questions. He couldn't wait to leave.

He untied Angel's lead from the hitching post, got in the buggy and clicked the lines so the mare would head back down the drive.

"We need to head back to the Millers' farm, Angel," he said. "It might be imperfect, and it certainly isn't as fancy as this place, but I reckon it will suit me just fine."

The horse blew out a snort of air and then picked up her pace. Kyle was grateful for that.

There was a different future waiting for him. He wasn't sure if it was the one he hoped it would be, but he knew that he wasn't going to miss what he'd just left. All he felt was relief.

CHAPTER 37

Two weeks after the impromptu party at Sydney's and the first burst of good news about her Bird Bench, Daisy was back at the doctor's office.

At long last, the brace was off. Her first steps had been tentative and nerve-racking. She'd been so worried that the bone was going to be frail and her muscles were going to be weak and that she would feel unsteady.

It hadn't felt that way, though. Sure, putting weight on it felt strange, but it was okay.

Now, though, as she sat on the examination room table and waited for the doctor, she couldn't help but frown at her calf. It was pasty white, rather spindly looking. It was in need of a good scrub. And goodness. It was hairy! Her leg looked hairy, skinny, and white. It was ugly.

"Daisy, what's wrong?" asked the doctor as he walked into the examining room. "Are you hurting?" he asked as he strode directly to her leg and studied it.

"*Nee*. I'm okay."

"Are you sure?"

"*Jah*. I um, was just fretting about how my leg looks. I didn't imagine that it would look like this."

The doctor grinned. "Everyone has that same response after we remove their casts. But don't worry. Once you're moving around a bit and get a little sun on your skin, your calf will look a lot better. Within a few weeks, if you do your physical therapy, you should feel almost like you did before the accident."

"I hope so."

"What matters the most is how it feels. Did it hurt to put weight on it?"

She tested it out. "It feels tender and maybe weak?"

"But pain? Are you feeling any sharp stings?"

"No. I didn't even feel that when Julie took it off."

He reached out a hand and helped her climb off the table. "Take some steps for me, please."

"All right." Dutifully, Daisy took a couple of steps. Once again, she felt a little unsteady, but she wasn't worrying about falling. Most importantly she didn't hurt. "It only feels sore, like my muscles haven't been used. But it's not painful."

"That's good news." He nodded to Julie, who'd just joined them. She was holding a set of X-rays and clipped them on a light panel. When he illuminated the board, Daisy could see two sets of X-rays. The first were the three from the day of her accident and the second was the set taken just an hour ago. It was easy to see where her bone had mended itself.

She thought her bone looked much better, but she wasn't the doctor. "What do you think?" she asked.

Dr. Alvarez asked Julie a couple of technical things, the nurse answered. Then, after studying the films for another minute or so, he smiled. "I think your bones did a good job, dear. They did what they were supposed to do. I'd say you're almost as good as new."

"I'll take that."

"Don't forget, it's going to take some time to build back the muscles, so there might be some aches and tenderness, so take it easy. But, all things considered, I think you should be riding your bicycle before you know it. But maybe with a little bit more care?"

"I don't think I'll be riding that bicycle ever again."

"Really?" Julie asked.

"Oh, *jah*. I think I'm done with my electric bike for now. I paid a call to Jonny Shrock at his bicycle shop. He was able to fix my bike. He got a nice price for it so I took the money instead."

"I don't blame you. But how will you get back and forth to work now?" the doctor asked as he was looking at his notes.

"I'm not going to go back to the bulk food store. I started my own business while I had this cast on."

"What business is that?"

"The Bird Bench business," she said with a smile. After describing the swings for the hens, she shared that they were now selling on the internet.

"I didn't know chickens liked to swing."

"I had heard that they might, which is why I made one out of a branch and some rope. Our hens seemed to like swinging a lot."

Julie grinned. "If we looked up Bird Bench on that retail site, we'd find it?"

"To be sure." Unable to hide the pride in her voice, she added, "We're selling them all over the country. I wouldn't have thought that so many people wanted their chickens to have a toy, but I guess our hens weren't the only ones."

"I'm going to order two for my brothers for Christmas."

"Thank you."

"Well, I can't say that I ever want to raise hens, but I do admire your gumption," Dr. Alvarez said as he handed the file back to the nurse. "As bad as the day of your accident was, it seemed like the Lord gave you a silver lining."

"We've said that very same thing."

"Yes, it sounds like everything is working out for the best after all."

"I hope so."

He held out a hand. "Daisy, it was a pleasure to meet you."

"*Danke*," she said as she shook his hand. "To you as well."

"I mean this in the best way. I hope we never have an occasion to see each other again."

She laughed. "I feel the same way." When she walked back to the waiting room, she felt much lighter. Both on her feet and in spirit.

Lukas, who'd been reading a magazine, looked up as she approached. "Hey, look at you!"

"I know. I'm almost back to my regular self."

"How does wearing your tennis shoe feel?"

"Strange but okay."

"Do you have to come back?"

"I don't think so. The doctor talked to me about taking things easy. But as long as I don't rush my progress, I'm good."

He gave her a hug. "Congratulations. You are now on the other side of it."

"*Danke*."

As they walked down the hallway, he said, "We have about an hour before the driver comes to pick us up. Want to get some lunch?"

"Sure."

The office was in the middle of a shopping area. There was a mall across the parking lot and several restaurants nearby. "What sounds good? Your choice."

"Can we go to the food court in the mall? If we finish early, I want to look at the stores." She knew this was Lukas's least favorite thing to do but she couldn't help herself. She wanted to celebrate.

"*Jah*, sure."

After they walked inside, and each decided to get pizza, Lukas told her to sit down while he paid and carried everything to her.

"This smells good," he said.

"I agree."

After they said grace and had a couple of bites, he said, "What do you want to do now?"

"You mean after we look at the stores?" she teased.

"*Jah*. Have you thought about looking at office space in Walden yet? Or hiring more help?"

"I'm not ready to leave the barn. I like working in there with all the animals. I do need to hire some help, though. I'm going to ask some women this Sunday at church."

"Let me know if you need me to help with the search. I'd be happy to ask around."

"*Danke*, but you've already done enough. Everyone in the family has."

After eating a few more bites of pizza, Lukas said, "It's been good to see Kyle so much in the barn. He's a hard worker."

The change in topics surprised her, but Daisy went with it. "He's been more than that. He's been so helpful and supportive about my little business."

"He's a *gut* man, Daisy. He would be great for you."

She thought he would be great, too. But he obviously didn't see her that way. "He's become a good friend."

"Friends can become something more than that, don't you think?"

"*Jah*, but not in this case. I . . . I don't think Kyle is ever going to see me in a romantic sense." She'd thought for a moment that she and Kyle had a future together, but his fascination with Winter had changed that. When she'd heard that they broke up, she had hoped he might begin to see her differently, but he hadn't.

"You might be wrong about him," Lukas said. "He might simply need a break before he starts courting again."

"I don't think so."

"You know, some people are talking about going up to Shipshewana. A whole group wants to travel together and go to the flea market. It could be fun. What do you think? Do you want to go?"

"Maybe. Do you?"

"I'm seriously considering it. I haven't met any women here. Maybe I will there. Plus, that flea market is supposed to be amazing."

"Going on a trip does sound fun. I'll think about that, too."

"Mamm and Daed seem like they're finally supporting you."

"I suppose." They'd helped her some. They'd even almost congratulated her on the Bird Bench's success.

However, she continued to feel as if they wished she'd never built that very first swing for their hens.

Which hurt.

Taking a chance, she said, "I feel like I've disappointed them. Like even though lots of people want Bird Benches, that's not the future they wanted for me."

"You think they wanted you to be married by now."

"*Jah*, or at least had a beau."

"That's not on you. I know you liked Kyle."

"I did. I wish I could've been different for him, but that wasn't possible."

Lukas wrapped an arm around her shoulders. "If Kyle can't see how special you are, then I'm sure some other man will."

"I hope so. We'll see." She smiled at him, not wanting to admit her most secret fear, that no one would ever consider her to be special—because she wasn't. Not wanting to burden him with such negative thoughts, she added, "Lukas, we're a handful, aren't we? You are thinking about finding a wife at a flea market, and I'm going to concentrate on Bird Benches instead of relationships."

"If it makes you feel any better, Ben isn't doing much better in that department either."

"He says not to worry about him," Daisy said. "Lukas, I think he might be dating someone and just not telling us about her."

"I've thought the same thing. If Ben is seeing someone, it doesn't make sense to me that he isn't telling us about it, though."

"I feel the same way. He knows we'd be nothing but supportive. He's done so much for me."

"I guess he has his reasons." He sipped his soda while she finished her slice of pizza. "So, were you serious about wanting to walk around this mall?"

"I was. And sorry, but I'm not going to let you change your mind."

"I wasn't going to," he grumbled. "But if you want to go, then come on. We don't have all day long to waste."

"If we were at Tractor Supply, you wouldn't be telling me to watch the clock."

"That's because Tractor Supply has good stuff," he teased. But after they threw out their trash, her brother seemed to have a good time. They looked at windows, people watched, and simply enjoyed the moment.

After all, it was a very good day.

CHAPTER 38

A lot had happened since Kyle had broken things off with Winter. The most important had been that he'd finally gotten his head back on straight.

First, he'd called home and talked to his parents and Sarah. His parents had been supportive of his decision, but Sarah had been delighted.

"Winter sounded so boring, Kyle," she said. "I didn't care for her one bit."

"I'm not sure if she was boring or not, but she wasn't the right woman for me." After a pause, he added, "It turns out that she wasn't a lot of people's favorite person."

"I like Daisy a lot."

Kyle had grinned when he read Sarah's response. He'd almost wished that he could see those words on his phone every day. It would make him happy to remember just what an impact Daisy had made on his sister after just one talk.

After he'd gotten his family's advice, he'd begun going over to the Lapps' barn whenever he had a spare moment. Daisy needed tons of help making Bird Benches, filling orders, and folding boxes. One hour there would fade into two and sometimes three hours.

Her mother would make snacks for everyone. At least once a week, Ruthie would come over with a pair of pies or a box of cookies for all of the workers.

But it was always the highlight of his day.

First, because there were always a lot of people there. Sometimes it was just Daisy and her brothers. Other times, Lila and Brandt were over. Or a couple of other folks from town. One time Jonny Schrock and his wife, Treva, came over with their entire family and helped make Bird Benches for four hours.

Jonny had said it was the least he could do since it was one of his bikes that had set off the Bird Bench chain of events for Daisy.

So, there was no better place for him than at the Lapps'. He enjoyed himself. He was making friends. He was making a difference for Daisy.

But even if he wasn't helping to get her new business off the ground, Kyle knew he'd be there for one very important reason, and that was because that was where Daisy was.

He belonged with her. He knew in his heart that she was the one for him.

That evening was no different.

"I'm so tired, I'm tempted to crawl into Velvet's stall and fall asleep," Daisy said after everyone finished for the day.

Sitting down in one of the many folding chairs that now decorated the barn floor, she smiled up at him. "Did I remember to thank you for coming over tonight?"

He pulled over a chair and sat down beside her. "Nope."

"I'm sorry. Thank you for helping tonight." She wrinkled her nose. "What did you work on? I forgot."

"I did your least favorite task. I drilled holes in benches."

"Oh yeah! Yay!"

He wrapped an arm around her shoulders. "Yep. Yay." He squeezed her shoulder. "And please stop thanking me. I wouldn't be over here if I didn't want to be."

"Okay." She leaned against him with a sigh. "I suppose I'll just have to show you my appreciation by falling asleep on your shoulder."

"I wouldn't mind if you did that," he whispered.

She pulled away to check his expression. "Hey," she said, all wide eyes and wonder. "You sound like you're serious."

"That's because I am. I like being with you, Daisy. I also like taking care of you."

"I guess you do," she said with a soft smile. "After all, you're the one who first helped when I had my accident."

"It's more than that. When we're not together, I can't seem to stop thinking of you. I've begun to realize that I need a daily dose of Daisy."

She pulled away. Bit her lip. Attempted to laugh. "Sorry, I'm uh . . ."

"Speechless?" he teased.

"I guess so. You've taken me by surprise. I don't know what to say."

"You don't have to say anything. I just thought . . . well, I thought it was about time I told you how I felt."

Those blue eyes he loved so much grew wide. "So, you're serious? I mean . . . you mean it?"

He nodded. "I mean it."

She blinked at him in wonder. Blinked again. And then. Just like that, she burst into tears.

Kyle turned, pulled her into his arms. "Shh. It's okay. If you don't feel the same way, I can back off."

"*Nee*! That's not it. I just can't believe it."

When the tears started up again, he handed her a soft red bandana that had been half sticking out of his pocket. "Here. Use this, at the very least. You're going to hurt yourself."

She dabbed her cheeks. Held up the cloth to look at it. "I didn't know you carried a handkerchief."

"I reckon that you don't know a lot of things about me. But you're learning, right?"

"*Jah*. We're both learning a lot about each other."

"Come on. Let's get out of this barn." He noticed that her family was inside but the gas-lit front porch lights were on. "Let's go sit on the front porch steps."

"Will you keep holding my hand?"

"*Jah*, Daisy. I won't let it go."

She held his hand. It was so much larger than hers. Rough and warm. So capable. She imagined she could put every dream, hope, and fear in his hands and he'd take care of them.

He was so good to her.

Kyle sat down next to her on the front steps. It was now almost September. Labor Day was coming up, and then fall would be here. All of the harvest preparations would be over. Kyle, Lukas, and most every other farmer in their community would be thinking about the upcoming winter.

It was the nature of a farmer's life. Cyclical. Steady.

Continuing. She wished she would've taken that into consideration when she'd pushed and schemed and planned for the future. For some reason she'd been so sure that if she hadn't been on top of everything, she would lose all her dreams.

But the harder she'd tried to control everything, from the Burkholders' sale, the Millers' purchase, her broken leg, Kyle's companionship—even Velvet's depression—she'd forgotten that the Lord had already planned for everything to happen in His perfect timing. When she'd finally stopped attempting to be in charge, everything in her life had seemed to come back into sync. Now, she had a thriving business, found her confidence, and had fallen in love with the best man she knew.

Everything was going to not only be okay, it was going to be wonderful.

"You know what?" Kyle asked, pulling her out of her reverie. "I just remembered that I learned something this summer that I kept meaning to talk to you about."

"What is that?"

A secret smile played on his lips. "It's something I learned about daisies."

"Are you making some joke at my expense?"

"*Nee*. Of course not. I'm talking about the flower. Mainly Shasta daisies, if you want me to be specific. But what I learned can be applied to most any type of daisy."

"You sound so proud of yourself, I suppose I should hear about this. What, exactly, did you learn?"

"That daisies need six to eight hours of sunlight a day." He kicked his legs out. "Isn't that something?"

Was it? She wasn't sure. "I suppose," she said diplomatically. "But all plants need sun, ain't so?"

"*Jah*. Sure. But some, like impatiens or, say, bleeding hearts. Those flowers don't hardly like pure, hot sun at all. If they get too hot or too whatever, they won't thrive. A farmer could kill them in a matter of weeks."

"That makes sense."

"Sure it does. But to my surprise, I never had thought that much about daisies. When you look at the front yard, with everything blooming like it is? Well, you think that they are near to being indestructible. As if they're so hardy and steadfast that nothing can wear them down."

Kyle lowered his voice. "But that's not true at all. They can get plagued by mites or pests, or suffer from lack of water."

He turned to her. "But the most important thing I learned is that a lot of people take them for granted. They forget that the delicate petals need just as much care and feeding as a fancy rose bush. And most of all, those need a warm, sunny environment to do their best."

"I . . . I didn't know any of that. It's, ah, interesting."

"Do you think so?" He leaned closer. "Because I do. Especially since I realized, just when I was discovering so much about those flowers, is that a certain beautiful daisy I know needs much of the same thing." He smiled.

"I suppose I do need a good amount of care and feeding," she joked.

He reached for her hand. Placed it in between the both of his. Then, to her surprise, he brought it up to his lips and he kissed it.

Right on her knuckles.

Then he turned her hands over. Found her palms. And kissed them, too.

"You need sunlight, Daisy. You need someone to notice you. To care for you, yes. But just as importantly, you need me to make sure that you get to shine."

Looking at her intently, he whispered, "I'll make sure you get that light. I'll make sure you're not forgotten. That you're never neglected. I will never put you in the dark. I'll make sure you are never taken for granted."

All his words! They were outlandish. Sweet. Surprising. Beautiful.

They made her giddy and hopeful.

And maybe wish that she could say some of those same things back to him. "I don't know what to say."

"Say that you'll let me take care of you, Daisy Lapp. Say that you'll let me love you."

Kyle loved her. He didn't want her to change. He loved the woman she was. Fighting off tears again, she nodded.

"Of course I will. I'll let you love me, Kyle, because I love you, too. You probably knew that, though."

As sudden worry crossed her mind. "But, Kyle, what if my love isn't enough for you?" She waved a hand. "I mean, did you happen to read anything about the proper care and feeding of Kyles?"

He laughed. "I already know what they need. All I need is you, Daisy. If I have you, you're going to make my life bright. It's going to smell good. It's going to look good."

"Kyle."

"No, listen. Daisy, with you by my side, my life is going to feel festive. Jaunty. Colorful. I'm going to have laughter. It's going to be perfect."

"You are making me sound like a miracle worker," she teased.

"Nope. We already have a miracle worker in our life. I'm making you sound like the person you are to me. Everything." He bent down. Kissed her softly. Then pulled her close and kissed her again.

All this time. All those faint touches, tiny looks. Secret hopes. None of it could compare to the reality of being in his arms, feeling his warmth, enjoying his kisses. Feeling desire and hope and love.

Feeling everything she was starting to think was going to pass her by . . . because she was just Daisy Lapp.

"Marry me?"

She looked into his eyes. Saw everything she needed to see. "Yes."

Kyle's brown eyes were soft. The arm that he wrapped around her shoulders felt secure and warm. She leaned closer. He kissed her again. And again. Those kisses were warm and passionate and vibrant. Wonderful.

Daisy held on to him so he wouldn't let her go.

And then she realized that he'd already been holding her tight without her even being aware.

He'd been taking care of her all along.

"We're going to have a good life together, Kyle. I can feel it," she said when she finally came up for air.

He gazed into her eyes. "Good," he said.

She smiled.

Because that was enough.

AUTHOR'S NOTE

Dear Reader,

For as long as I've been married to my husband, Tom has had a not-so-secret desire to own a big farmhouse in the middle of a couple of acres. He'd love to have a huge garden. A pond, too. Maybe a walking path, or a patch of woods. Tom says he would love to spend his retirement fussing with all of these things.

I don't disagree.

I, too, think living in such a place would be lovely. However, it all sounds like a lot of work to me. More work than I might want to do. Because of that—and the fact that we now have four adorable grandchildren—Tom's put aside his big dream of country living. At least for now.

I guess my husband's dream of being a gentleman farmer has been on my mind a lot of late . . . which is why I was so excited to write this next trilogy in my Amish Alphabet series. Letters D, E, and hopefully F will focus on Ruthie and Mervin Miller, city-living Amish who dream of spending their retirement years in the country. As one might expect, they are hopelessly unprepared for farm life and have to ask a lot of people for help. I can't help but think that Tom and I would have to do the same thing if we were them!

I hope you will enjoy this series about a good-hearted older couple who are determined to prove that it's never too late to have big dreams. More importantly, no matter what your age, I hope you have a dream or two that you're holding close to your heart. That's important, I think.

Wishing you many blessings,
Shelley

ACKNOWLEDGMENTS

Once again, there are a great many people who help make my books come to life. First and foremost, I'm indebted to the terrific team at Kensington for being so encouraging and supportive. A special shoutout goes to my editor Elizabeth Trout for championing this alphabet series. Elizabeth, thank you for your edits, your encouragement, and for being the type of editor who googles bird swings instead of writing me notes about why I shouldn't want a chicken in my book to have her own swinging perch.

I'm also so grateful for the lovely book cover, the continual promotion of these books and everyone's hard work to make these books so beautiful. Thank you, Kensington!

In addition, no acknowledgment note would be complete without mentioning my longtime agent, Nicole Resciniti; Lynne Stroup, my hardworking first reader; and Jean Volk, who manages my street teams and Facebook group. Thank you, ladies! I would also like to thank Kerri Carpenter, who somehow turns a couple of photos and a paragraph into a beautiful newsletter every month. I'm so grateful.

Finally, I owe a great deal of thanks to my husband, Tom, who took care of so much while I wrote this book. Tom, thanks for driving down to Amish country again and again with me. Thanks for pickling vegetables. Thanks for listening when all I want to talk about are cows and chickens. Thanks for being you.